Agent of Judgment

Agent of Judgment

Robert Rice

FORGE®

A TOM DOHERTY ASSOCIATES BOOK
NEW YORK

AGENT OF JUDGMENT

Copyright © 2000 by Robert Rice

This book is printed on acid-free paper.

Edited by James Frenkel

Book design by Virginia Norey

A Forge Book
Published by Tom Doherty Associates, LLC
175 Fifth Avenue
New York, NY 10010

www.tor.com

Forge® is a registered trademark of Tom Doherty Associates, LLC.

Library of Congress Cataloging-in-Publication Data

Rice, Robert.
    Agent of judgment / Robert Rice—1st ed.
        p. cm.
    "A Tom Doherty Associates book."
    ISBN 0–312–87050–7
    1. Kidnapping—Fiction. 2. Terrorism—Fiction. 3. Cults—
Fiction. I. Title.

PS3568.I294 A7 2000
813'.54—dc21

                                                    00–031791

First Edition: September 2000

Printed in the United States of America

0 9 8 7 6 5 4 3 2 1

For Linda, of course

The author gratefully acknowledges the help provided by many people in creating this story. Special thanks to Dr. Dell Fuller for insights into medical procedures, to Dr. Carl Johnson for information on the CDC, to Michael Wright for details about the structure and function of the FBI, and to Dr. Pat Jordan for information about veterinary procedures. Any factual errors are, of course, my own. Thanks as usual to Kitty Donich, Barb Heinlein, Mary Schultz, Stan West, LuAnne Rod, Scott Ellis, and Ray Ring for their helpful comments. And many thanks to my agent, Don Gastwirth, and to my editor, James Frenkel; and to Kathleen Fogarty and all the other people at Tor/Forge whose efforts make it possible.

Agent of Judgment

1

As she changed lanes on the Bayshore Freeway south of San
Francisco, Ursula Walker glanced in the rearview mirror. Two cars
behind her a white Buick matched her change, a move she scarcely
noticed. Ursula had more important things to think about than
traffic, such as the fact that she had won. Flat-out, in-your-face,
thank-you-judge, *yes*, victory! She smiled and rubbed her bulging
abdomen. "Mommy won, sweetheart. Summary judgment!"

Osborne had granted her motion, which she hadn't expected,
the old fart. The case should have gone to trial, and if she'd had
to defend in front of a jury and TV cameras, she knew she would
have lost. Mutual of California versus 112 people left homeless by
the earthquake. Nobody could have won that. Especially three days
before Christmas.

She remembered the photos of the apartments in flames, felt a
twinge of pity for the home owners, then, irritated, suppressed her
sympathy. She wasn't God; she didn't make the buildings burn.
She was just doing her job. They had no case anyway, no earthquake insurance. Trying to argue that their fire insurance covered
the loss, ridiculous. Of course they lost.

Her first solo insurance defense. She heard again the surprised
pleasure in Hoffman's voice when she called in to report. "Well
done," he'd said. *Damn right. And you haven't seen anything yet.*

An Eldorado Touring Coupe flowed by in the next lane, its lights on in the dusk, and she watched it. She could afford one, but she'd never buy an Eldo. Too old, although the dark green was nice. Maybe when she was fifty. The knowledge she was worth nearly a million net, and her thirty-fifth birthday still a month away, was a warm background to the bright glow of her victory. She moved her Saab 9-3 SE into the left lane and increased her speed.

Behind her the white Buick did the same.

The baby kicked and Ursula took one hand off the wheel to rub her belly. "Have a nice nap? Thanks for being a good girl during the hearing. How does Allison sound today?" Ursula had planned to start her maternity leave next week, after the trial. Hoffman had offered to let her begin it tomorrow, even though the baby wasn't due for two weeks. She'd turned him down, thinking to impress him with her dedication. Now, with the adrenaline of combat wearing off, she thought maybe she should have accepted. She was tired. She needed a rest. And right now she needed a bathroom.

Traffic had thinned. Off to her right Candlestick Park came in sight, the stadium darkened. She didn't like sports, but she enjoyed seeing the oval stadium lit up in the dusk, a bowl of light at the edge of the bay. The thought of lights made her realize the sun had set, and she turned on her headlights. Except for the Buick behind her, the other cars had already done the same. It was that fact that finally made her fully aware of the car, a late model, probably last year's. Boxy. Now that she thought about it, she remembered that it had followed her onto the freeway when she left San Mateo.

She slowed to fifty and looked to see if it would pass, telling herself she was being silly. A lot of cars were heading for San Francisco. But as she watched it, she grew certain she'd seen the car before. That round bumper sticker. It was too dark now to see the sticker clearly, but last week there'd been a car behind her on Geary that she'd noticed because of the yellow smiley face in the same spot on the bumper. A white Buick.

The Buick slowed, matching her speed.

Alarmed now, she increased her speed. The Buick kept pace, still without lights. She was being followed! But who? Why? An irate plaintiff? One of the home owners who had lost? She couldn't imagine that, but who else would do it?

Ursula moved into the left lane. The Buick stayed in the center lane and fell back a little. Maybe she was imagining things. She pressed the accelerator and the Saab jumped ahead, seventy-five, eighty. The distance between her and the Buick grew, the white car making no effort to keep up.

The Buick finally faded from sight, and with a sigh of relief she slowed to sixty-five, cruising into the city, across I-280, onto the Central Skyway. *Too many action movies,* she thought, *too much television news.* The skyway dumped her into Fell, and she drove toward Golden Gate Park, then turned left toward her house.

Wheeling down into her driveway, she pushed a button on the garage door opener. The door slid open, then shut behind her. For a moment she sat in the car, forcing herself to relax, to breathe.

When she was calmer she got out and climbed the stairs to her living room and, feeling sheepish, pulled the window curtain aside enough to peer out.

On the street below, the white Buick cruised slowly past her house.

•••

Friday, December 22, 10:20 P.M.

As the moon rose over the swamp behind it, the trawler *Leslie Ann* slipped out of a hidden cove near Cedar Key, Florida, and made its way quietly into the Gulf of Mexico. Its outriggers were raised like arms, and the throb of its diesel engine was muffled by insulation. From the pilothouse Arnold Cobbs watched his nine-year-old-son, Orley, the first mate, scamper over the deck, readying the nets Arnold hoped would haul in several hundred pounds of shrimp before dawn.

Orley had been shrimping since he was six, and Arnold had been doing it a long time before Orley was born, long enough to remember when there were liberal seasons and few restrictions, back in the seventies and eighties, when everyone who wanted to could make a good living at it. Now the shrimp were almost gone. The seasons had been shortened, but the number of shrimpers had quadrupled. The only way to make a living was to ignore the regulations, to shrimp outside the seasons. It was dangerous; the penalty for being caught was a fine Arnold could never pay and having his boat seized. But he had to live. People like him, he thought grimly, were more of an endangered species than shrimp.

Far out in the shipping lane a freighter's lights winked as it made its way north, probably toward Mobile. Arnold kept his own running lights dark. He had even turned off the lights on the little Christmas tree he'd put up for Orley in the pilothouse.

Half an hour later, Arnold throttled back and the trawler slowed, rising and falling on the gentle swells. He pulled a lever, watched the outriggers lower into place, and gave Orley a signal. The boy started the winches, shooting the nets from the outriggers into the warm Gulf water. There were no holes in these nets, no Turtle Exclusion Devices, no chutes to allow bycatch to escape. Of course he'd catch other species, too—these days maybe a hundred pounds of fish for each pound of shrimp. That was just the nature of the work, and if most of those fish died, so be it. He needed to make a living.

A few minutes later Arnold gave Orley another signal and the winches whined, hauling the full nets aboard. Fish spilled across the wet deck, small sharks, stingrays, tropical fish, and a few shrimp. But something was wrong.

Arnold went on deck and stooped to inspect them. The fish should have been flopping, struggling to escape, but they were barely moving, a sluggish mass of slime.

"Dad, look!" Orley pointed to the water off the bow. A handful of dead fish floated on the surface. In the moonlight the water looked cloudy, brown-colored. "What is it?"

Arnold sniffed the air, the warm breeze tainted with the faint smell of rotting fish. He looked again at his catch. The shrimp were now dead, and so were some of the fish. The rest were dying. "Some sort of fish kill," he said. "Let's dump this mess and try another spot."

They cleaned the decks of dead and dying fish, and Arnold gunned the engine, running west across Apalachee Bay, around the point. Finally he slowed, the lights of Panama City visible in the distance.

"Daddy?" The boy was staring into the water.

Arnold looked. The water was still brown. Dead fish were thick on the surface. "What the hell?"

Something else loomed ahead. He spun the wheel hard and narrowly missed plowing into a pod of dead bottle-nosed dolphins.

Concerned, he came about and headed out to sea. Concern changed to worry, then to panic as the stench of rotting fish chased him. As far as he could see in all directions, there was a dead ocean.

2

In Montana, Michael Walker leaned against his pickup truck and took a drink from a pint bottle of Early Times. On his radio the six o'clock news was saying something about forest fires raging in eight western states, how arson was suspected in many of them. *Forest fires in winter,* Michael thought. *Weird.* It was this damn weather. In Sweetwater, Montana, in December, it should be too cold to stand outside without a coat. He was in his shirtsleeves.

He stuck the bottle in his hip pocket and strolled across the Christmas tree lot to the darkened Conoco station next door, squinting at the big round thermometer on the wall while he took a leak. He could just make out the needle pegged at sixty degrees. No snow, even on the mountains south of town. No wonder people weren't buying Christmas trees. Yawning, he walked back to his truck.

He took another pull of whiskey and studied the burn. Troxel, his teetotaling boss, had warned him not to drink on the job. Normally Michael didn't drink at all, except when the nightmares got bad. Lately they had been, so tonight he'd brought the pint with him. He didn't much care about the job anyway. He didn't much care about anything anymore, except staying hidden someplace so far out of the way they could never find him. And he couldn't think of anyplace better than this, a treeless two-horse watering hole in the middle of nowhere.

Bored, he eyed the trees, wondering if he could find one worth stealing for his trailer. A Scotch pine caught his eye, and he walked over and brushed the branches. Needles flew. FRESH CUT MONTANA TREES, the sign on the fence said. He snorted. Grown in Arkansas, cut sometime around Halloween, machete-slashed to an imaginary tree shape, then painted green. Christmas in America in the twenty-first century. He took another drink.

On the interstate behind him a diesel sped past, tires whining. It sounded lonely, and it made him think of Darby, something he tried not to do. She'd be spending Christmas at Etta's farm. He wondered whether they'd invite him. No, he decided, they wouldn't. It would make his former lover too uncomfortable.

Christmas in the trailer, then. With Jack the Ripper, the tomcat who hated Michael as much as he hated the cat. Why Jack hung around his trailer was one of life's mysteries. He took another drink and watched a red Lincoln pull off the interstate, then slow and turn into the lot.

"Oh, great." He screwed on the cap and tossed the bottle in the open window of the pickup.

The Lincoln stopped, the door opened, and a short, bald man in boots and a tweed sport coat climbed out, holding his hand up to ward off a gust of wind and dirt. "How's business tonight, Walker?"

"Slow, Mr. Troxel." He walked toward the car.

"Well, we'll stay open a little longer. There's always a few late ones."

As Michael got near Troxel his boss sniffed the air, his nose wrinkling like a rabbit's. "Say, is that alcohol?"

"Nah," Michael said. "Diesel fumes from the highway, maybe."

The little man sniffed again. "No, sir. That's nothing like diesel fumes. It *is* alcohol. Say, you haven't been drinking?"

"Probably my cough medicine." He turned away.

Troxel scurried around and stuck his nose in Michael's face, sniffed, then hurried over to the pickup. Standing on tiptoe, he reached through the window. "I knew it!" He held up the Early Times. "This is no cough medicine."

"It is to me, sir."

"I told you no drinking. What will people think?"

"I don't see a lot of them around to think anything."

"I knew I should have hired someone local. I'm going to have to let you go." He dropped the bottle in disgust. It clanked on the gravel but didn't break, and Michael bent over with as much dignity as possible to pick it up.

"Get off my tree lot," the man said. "Right now."

Michael looked at him, thinking he probably should shoot him. But Michael had given up shooting people, a decision that, at the moment, he regretted. He sighed. The job wasn't worth it anyway, just another of a dozen like it he'd taken in the last few years to keep himself alive. "Can I have my check?"

"Nosirree. I don't owe you a thing. I gave you an advance, remember?"

Michael looked at him, then at the bottle. Enough left to get through the night; it wasn't so bad. He walked to his pickup, got in, and backed carefully out into the street.

The trouble with drinking, he thought as he steered the pickup slowly out of town toward his trailer, was that it didn't really work. There was always some small, watching part of his mind he couldn't numb. And as he drove, that part of his mind began taunting him again, telling him what a loser he was. He had to admit he'd come a long way down, so far down that right now he even wished he'd stayed in the army. If he'd reupped, he'd never have been arrested.

The memory of that night swam to the surface again. He'd been standing in line at Miami International, thinking about what he wanted to do with the rest of his life. He'd been thinking about that, as a matter of fact, for the last six months of his hitch in the army. The November day he got his discharge papers he'd boarded a plane for Montego Bay, Jamaica—no reason to suffer in the cold while he thought about it.

Problem was, surrounded by white sand and blue-green water and nearly naked women, he found it hard to think about anything at all. So two weeks later, when he found himself back on the plane and landing at Miami, he wasn't any closer to a decision.

The real trouble, he thought as he retrieved his duffel from the baggage claim area and carried it to the customs line, was that the army had lied about teaching him a skill. Unless you counted shooting people from a long way off as a skill, which Michael didn't. In basic training they'd discovered he had a talent for marksmanship, and once they discovered that, there went the electronics they'd promised him when he enlisted. Instead, they assigned him to Fort Benning and more weapons training. He spent all day, every day, shooting weapons, guns he'd never known existed. Shooting lying on the ground, shooting sitting, snap shooting, wind doping. "Your country needs you, son," he was told. "There's still a lot of enemies out there."

Then the Gulf War came and they sent him to Iraq as a sniper. Michael didn't pay much attention to politics. His targets were his country's enemies; so he was told, and so he believed. One shot, one kill. He was one of the best. He tried not to think much about what he was doing.

But he knew he didn't want to re-enlist, even though they tried to persuade him to, first with flattery and promises, then with guilt. "You owe us, son; we got a lot of training in you." Enough of paranoia and killing; he was ready to go back to the real world. Except there weren't many jobs in the real world that had rifle shooting as part of their description. So now he had to start over.

When he reached the airport customs inspectors he was thinking he'd like a job where he wouldn't have to travel; he was tired of traveling. He didn't care about the money so much, as long as he liked what he was doing. Something outdoors, maybe.

The inspector, a short, stocky black guy, looked at him, glanced at a clipboard in his hand, and said, "Step over there, please."

When Michael stepped over to where he was pointing, another inspector, a lot bigger than the first and wearing a holstered pistol on a belt high up on his waist, said, "Empty your duffel, please, sir."

Michael reached in and pulled out his dirty clothes—shorts and T-shirts mostly, with a little sand stuck to them—and when his fingers touched a smooth plastic package, he knew he was in trouble.

He straightened, wondering what to do.

"Empty the rest of it, sir," the customs man said, his hand on his pistol butt.

Michael did.

He turned the duffel upside down and emptied the clothes onto the concrete floor and watched as two plastic baggies of white powder fell out among them.

"Lean against the wall and spread your legs," the inspector ordered, not saying "sir" anymore, and Michael, used to following orders, did it, wondering how the cocaine had gotten into his duffel and who had set him up. And why? That girl from San Antonio he'd slept with in Montego Bay? What reason would she have, just a secretary on vacation? The army? He didn't think they would do that, but he was at a loss to think of anyone else.

In jail, Michael discovered that what he'd saved on a corporal's pay wouldn't buy him much of a lawyer. That left him the choice of asking one of his relatives for help or using a public defender. His mother had died four years before, his father had disappeared a long time ago, and Michael was ashamed to call his sister, Ursula, because she already thought he was a screwup. Which left his older brother, James.

Michael had always idolized James, the closest thing to a father he had. Yet no matter what Michael did when they were growing up, James never seemed to approve. Once he had called Michael a loser, and the words still stung. Now he was beginning to think James was right.

Michael called him at his office in Washington, D.C., a real estate company. James listened, was sympathetic, but he'd just taken a new job and money was tight—he was sorry; he knew it was a tough break. But then Michael shouldn't have been smuggling dope.

Michael's public defender told him he could maybe get the charge reduced to possession, instead of possession with intent to sell. He'd get ten years, or out in five or six.

"But it wasn't my dope," Michael said. "I don't know how it got in my duffel."

"Of course not," the lawyer said sympathetically. "None of my clients are guilty."

If it hadn't been for Cedric, the old black man Michael shared a cell with in the Gun Club, Miami's jail, while he was waiting for trial, he knew he wouldn't have survived a week in prison. Cedric taught him how to do time. Said, "Man, you got six hundred forty and some losers livin' in metal cages under them fluorescent lights. And most of 'em don't give a shit about life. Not yours, not theirs. You know what I'm sayin'? Man standin' in the yard mess you around, you back him off or just as well pull your pants down and bend over. Believe it."

So when a skinhead with a swastika tattooed on his forehead started giving the new guy the con stare his first day at Oakdale, then walked up to him, breathing through his mouth, and told Michael to hand over his jacket, he hit him as hard as he could and broke his nose. In the fight that followed Michael got his own nose broken, too, and he would spend three weeks in solitary. But he also got a little respect.

There were worse men in Oakdale than the skinhead, though, and punching them would only get you shanked, or worse. Men like Lorenzo Rey, a huge black con who had killed three white inmates already and had his way with most of the rest. Michael knew his chances of surviving five or six years in that place without becoming somebody's old lady were nonexistent.

Four weeks and three days after Michael's arrival, Lorenzo Rey blew him a kiss in the yard.

That same morning, Michael had a visitor, his first. As he walked into the visitation room, he was surprised to see his brother, James, on the other side of the Plexiglas. A visit from anyone would have been appreciated. A visit from James was more than he'd hoped for.

James looked great, wearing a silvery gray Italian suit that made him appear even taller than his six-three. His blond hair was styled, and his hands were manicured. Michael was embarrassed by his own prison blues.

His brother smiled and said into the phone, "I feel bad about letting you down. I came to see if there's anything I can do."

"Thanks," Michael said.

"How are you getting along?"

"OK." He wanted to tell James about the kind of men who inhabited this place, about Lorenzo Rey. But Michael had already learned in prison you keep your mouth shut.

"I don't see how you can stand it, Michael."

He shrugged. "You survive." Sounding tougher than he felt.

"Maybe you can do better than survive." James leaned forward, lowered his voice. "Since you called, my position has changed. Maybe I can help you a little."

"Yeah?" he said. "That'd be great." Hoping for an offer of money. Cash could do a lot of things in Oakdale.

"Maybe I can get you out."

Michael stared at him to see if he was joking. He didn't seem to be. "How could you get me out?"

"Well, it's complicated, but I work for the government, an agency you've never heard of."

"I thought you were in real estate."

"A cover, Michael. Look; I've spoken to some people and they might be willing to let you serve your sentence working for us."

"Yeah? What would I have to do?"

"The same thing you did in the army."

"How do you know what I did in the army?"

James smiled. "Are you willing to work for us?"

"Did the army set me up?"

"If you were set up, which I doubt, I'm sure the army didn't do it."

"Are you connected with them?"

"No. Now, are you interested or not?"

He hesitated. The thought of becoming a sniper again was repellent. "Do I have a choice?"

"Of course. You can serve your time. Look; I have another appointment in a few minutes. I need to know if you're interested."

"Let me think about it."

James looked surprised. "You need to think about whether you'd rather serve your country than spend ten years in prison? You disappoint me, Michael." He checked his watch. "OK, sure. Sleep on it. I'll check back with you tomorrow. I've got to go."

That night in his cell, Michael thought about Lorenzo Rey and about spending five more years in Oakdale. To survive, Michael would probably have to kill Rey. If he had to kill someone anyway, it might as well be an enemy of the country and he might as well be outside.

When James came back the next morning, Michael asked, "Are you sure you can get me out?"

"Yes," James said.

"Then you've got a deal."

James looked pleased. "Great. Just keep your mouth shut and wait."

And two weeks later he was out. It was that simple. A sentence review, a realization that a mistake had been made. This young man with no prior trouble with the law, who'd served his country, deserved another chance. The new sentence ordered him to do community service for the remainder of his original ten years, he to be remanded to the personal custody of his brother, James Walker of Washington, D.C. Should he fail to carry out the conditions of the sentence, he would be sent back to prison for the full nine years, ten months, and twenty-seven days remaining on his term.

In his pickup Michael shuddered, remembering. He pulled into the campground where his RV trailer was parked, stopped, and glanced at the nearly empty pint of whiskey. He knew it would take more than what was left to get through the night.

3

In Oklahoma City, Nestor Pruitt absently smoothed his gray pompadour as he watched his secretary, Cyndee, walk across the thick plush carpet of his new office. She was young and pretty, especially that rounded bottom, the last thing he saw as she closed the door behind her. And she was attracted to him, he thought; she'd even told him he looked like Jimmy Sunday, the TV evangelist. That tickled him. He sighed. He was married, and the Devil lurked in the direction of that rounded bottom. But even born-again Baptists, unfortunately, were subject to temptations of the flesh. His phone beeped.

"Yes?" he said irritably.

"President Bishop on line one, Mr. Pruitt."

A rush of adrenaline, and a little fear. The first morning of the new crisis and the president was calling already. Nestor stared at the blinking light on the phone, thinking what to say.

When he'd gotten his job, he never thought he'd be talking to the president almost every day. His wasn't an especially important position, as assistant director of the federal Task Force for Disaster Control. As head of President Bishop's party in Oklahoma, Nestor had carried the state for him in the election, so they had to reward him. But his religious views weren't popular with the rest of the new president's aides, and Sloane, the chief of staff, made sure

Nestor got a position with no real power. The whole idea of the task force was a gimmick, anyway, a campaign promise to combine the federal bureaucracies that handled disasters in order to save the taxpayers money.

But that was all right with Nestor. He knew he wasn't as smart as some of those people in Washington. Besides, he didn't want power, just a little recognition, and he'd gotten that, along with credit for bringing the task force headquarters and all the federal jobs that came with it to Oklahoma City. So he was perfectly happy, until nature began to act up. Earthquakes in San Francisco and Los Angeles, floods in the Midwest, forest fires, new diseases—the list got longer every month. Nestor found himself with more work than he wanted, forcing him to work eighteen-hour days, and weekends like this one.

That would have been OK, too—he was willing to work—as long as Gibbs, the director, was there to tell him what to do and take responsibility. Gibbs was smart and he knew how to use power. When the country was swept by all those disasters, Congress had stopped feuding long enough to fund the task force at a level higher than even the president had sought. Gibbs had wasted no time expanding his power, arguing successfully that in a national emergency other agencies, including the Centers for Disease Control and Prevention in Atlanta, should be brought under his authority.

Then Gibbs had died in a one-car rollover.

And now the president's nomination of the new director of the task force was tied up in committee. In the meantime, Nestor was stuck as acting director. He was in over his head, and he knew it.

He cleared his throat and picked up the phone. "Good morning, Mr. President."

"Pruitt, what the hell's going on out there in the Gulf? You hear about that?"

Nestor glanced at the file on his desk. "Yes, sir."

"Well?"

"My analysts are working on it, Mr. President. Some sort of fish kill."

"No shit, Sherlock. Half the fish in the Gulf of Mexico are dead and you say there's a fish kill."

Nestor suppressed his irritation at the profanity. "We have the best chemists in the business analyzing water samples, sir, and biologists running tests on hundreds of specimens. We should know in a few days what caused it, Mr. President. God willing."

"God's not in charge of this," the president said. "You are. You have a plan for what happens when all these fish drift ashore? You know how many electoral votes Texas and Florida have?"

"Yes, sir, I know. And we're working on a contingency plan to evacuate the coasts."

There was silence on the other end. Then, "Evacuate. You mean you plan to move everybody on the Gulf Coast inland? Are you crazy? You know what that'll do to me?"

"That's only a contingency, Mr. President. I've called the governors of those states, and they've alerted their national guards. We don't plan to move anyone unless we have to, but they tell me there's a chance all those rotting fish could cause a disease outbreak. And the stink may make people sick. But first, we're going to try to get rid of the carcasses as they drift ashore."

"Well, you do what you have to, by God. Just make sure you do it quick. And don't scare people. The other side's howling for my ass already. As if this were my fault. I don't intend to be a one-term president; you understand?" The line went dead.

"Yes, sir," Nestor said as he hung up the phone. "You blasphemous backslider."

He stared at the file, but there were no answers there, only flat descriptions of hundreds of square miles of ocean clogged with dead fish. Jargon like "major marine ecological disturbance" and "cause unascertained."

He sighed again. He needed help. There were dozens of experts he could consult, but he didn't know any of them very well. He needed an adviser he could trust and understand. He tried to think of someone among his friends and acquaintances who could make sense of what was happening, but there was no one.... Wait. Last year at a hurricane conference in Florida he'd met someone, a woman scientist he had liked and could actually understand. What was her name? Sanchez? No, Soares, that was it. Annie Soares.

He reached for the phone.

•••

Saturday, December 23, 11:48 A.M.

In Montana, Michael Walker woke with a glacial hangover and the sound of a horn honking outside his RV trailer. For an instant, panic seized him and he jerked upright, but then he relaxed. When they came for him, they sure as hell wouldn't honk to let him know they were there. Anyway, the horn sounded familiar. A moment later he recognized it and swung his feet out of bed, filled with apprehension and eagerness.

His head throbbed and he winced. Since he'd already been fired, he'd seen no reason to quit drinking—all the more reason, in fact, to get blasted. He stood, mildly surprised he was still dressed.

As he stepped through the bathroom, he caught a glimpse of his face in the mirror. "My God." He stopped, raked his fingers through his unruly hair, put his hand to his mouth, and breathed on it. "My God."

The honking had stopped. Someone began pounding on his door. Michael groped under the tiny sink, found a bottle of Listerine, and swilled a mouthful. The pounding grew louder.

" 'eah, 'eah, don't get 'er panties in a wad." He spit in the sink, took a deep breath, and opened the door.

The woman on the step said, "About damn time." She was small, with dark brown eyes and long black hair that was swept up under a sheepskin cap. The flaps were down over her ears. She also had a smile that, Michael suspected, could boil water and a laugh pure enough to drink. But right now she wasn't smiling or laughing.

"Morning, Darby," he said. "My wake-up call?"

She eyed his rumpled shirt. "It's noon, Matthew. And that looks like you slept in it."

It took Michael an instant to remember his alias. "Like to iron it for me?" A gust of wind banged the door against the side of the trailer, and he reached out to grab it.

"Why do you keep moving this tin tent? What are you hiding from? I had a hell of a time finding you."

He glanced at the deserted fishing access site and the Yellowstone River beyond. The river, normally ice-choked in December, was a now a trickle that barely covered the rocks. "Women. They won't leave me alone."

"Well, you don't have anything to worry about from me. I'm here on business."

"Wanta come in?"

She glanced into the trailer, eyes narrowed, then stepped in warily.

He stood back to let her by. "Pigeons?"

"What? Oh." She put her hand up to the fluffy cap. "I was working on my new concerto. Etta's kids were noisy. Jeez, Cooper, you haven't cleaned this place since I moved out."

"I have, too. I shampooed the upholstery." He didn't mention he'd done it to get rid of the faint smell of her perfume, which had haunted him.

"That was a year ago."

"That long? Time flies . . ." He looked around. The place *was* a little grungy. "Well, at least I put up the outdoor Christmas decorations."

"Beer pop-tops on a dogwood bush. I'm overwhelmed."

"Uh, you want some orange juice or something?"

"I'll pass. What's that awful noise?"

Michael listened and realized his Willie Nelson CD was playing. It had been, as far as he knew, all night. "That's Willie. Would you rather hear Garth?"

"No. How can you listen to that stuff?"

"What's wrong with it?"

"It all sounds alike, for one thing. Same words, same three chords."

"Thank you, Darby Mackenzie, head-banging master of metallica."

"Look, I just came to give you a message."

"First, have a seat. I've got coffee."

She sighed and nudged a mildewed bath towel off his only chair, then sat gingerly. "Christ, Matt, you look like hell. What happened to you?"

"Gee, I'm glad we're having this talk, Darb." Embarrassed, he emptied the drip basket, threw a handful of fresh coffee into a filter, and poured water in to brew. "I, uh, quit last night. So I celebrated." He put the pot on the tiny stove and lit the gas.

"Troxel fired your butt?"

He shrugged.

"Uh-huh. And you're drinking now, too?"

"I had a few. Medicinal purposes only." He shoved aside a stack of *National Enquirers,* glancing at one he hadn't had a chance to read. " 'Holy Shroud of Turin Stolen by Aliens,' " he read aloud, and gave a low whistle.

"Look, do you want to hear this or not?" she said.

"Only if you take that stupid hat off." He sat down on the sofa across from her.

She reluctantly pulled off the cap and shook out her long hair.

Michael tried not to stare, fought down the surge of want, the feeling of emptiness he felt every time he saw her. She glanced at him, then away.

"Uh, coffee's coming." He jumped up and rummaged in the cupboard for a paper cup.

"Why are you doing it, Matt? Why are you self-destructing? You didn't drink when we lived together."

Maybe if you hadn't left . . . "Just trying for a few laughs." Hot coffee splashed his fingers as he poured it. He sucked on them, then turned and handed the coffee to her. "But hey, you didn't come here to talk about me. What's the message?"

She took the cup and studied him, frowning. "Your sister called."

For a moment he was lost. He only had one sister, and she was in California and never called him. "Ursula?" he said.

"That was the name she gave. You never told me you had a sister."

"Didn't I?"

"She asked for someone named Michael first. Etta said she didn't know any Michael. Then this Ursula asked for you."

"What did she want?"

"I don't know. She wouldn't say. She sounded upset." Darby sniffed the coffee suspiciously, tasted it, looked surprised, and took another sip. "Who's Michael?"

"I don't know."

She pulled a scrap of paper out of the pocket of her oversize plaid shirt. "She wants you to call her."

"OK."

"Right away." She handed the number to him. "What do you suppose it could be?"

"How would I know?"

She sighed and stood. "Right. The Great Stone Face." She set the coffee on the dinette table and walked to the door. "I'm glad you wouldn't marry me; you know that? I don't know what I ever saw in you."

"Really, I have no idea, all right? If I knew, I'd tell you. Um, can I borrow your phone?"

"It's not mine. It's Etta's. Ask her."

"Let me change first. I'll be right there."

"Suit yourself." She stalked down the metal steps and strode to a battered blue van with the words DARBY'S BAKERY hand-painted on the side.

He watched her, eyes on her faded jeans. "Darby," he said.

"Yeah?" She turned as she opened the door of the van.

"Thanks."

Without answering she got in and drove away, trailed by a plume of dust.

•••

Saturday, December 23, 1:05 P.M.

Etta Snowgrass lived with her husband in a rented farmhouse west of Sweetwater. She was a magnet for orphans and foundlings of all species, the most important of which, to Michael, was Darby Mackenzie, who had lived with Etta since moving out of his trailer, sharing a room with the oldest daughter.

As Michael drove into the yard a one-eyed horse watched him over a fence rail and a goat with three legs hobbled around the side of the house, an evil look in his eye. Michael opened the door and got out, ready for the inevitable charge. Bacchus was slow, but he could do damage if he took you by surprise.

The goat charged, a determined wobble. When he reached Michael, Michael stepped aside, grabbed the goat by the horns, and threw him on his back. Bacchus lay still for a moment, then struggled to his feet, shook himself, and extended his head for a scratch, a changed goat. Until next time.

From the seat of his pickup Michael picked up the sheepskin cap Darby had forgotten, threaded his way through the chickens pecking on the lawn, and headed for the house. On the porch a black dog so old its muzzle had turned pure white opened its eyes as he climbed the steps but didn't otherwise move. In the backyard he heard the happy shrieks of children playing. He opened the screen and went in without knocking.

"Hey, Etta!" he shouted.

"Kitchen!" she shouted back.

He walked through the worn parlor. "Smells good."

Etta was kneading bread dough in a washtub on the kitchen table, her brown skin white to the elbows with flour. With seven adopted kids, she said, there was no point in making small portions. She herself was large economy size, at least 200 pounds and six feet tall. He looked around for Darby.

"She's in the barn," Etta said without looking up. "Making her music."

"Oh, I was, uh, looking for Clayton. He around?"

"Fixin' fence. Don't that beat all this time of year?" She looked up and gave him a grin. "Why don't you two get back together?"

"Clayton and me? He's not my type, Etta. Besides, you're already married to him."

"Smart answers ain't gonna get her back, Matt."

"Darby said my sister called. Can I use your phone?"

"Long-distance?"

"Yeah. But I'll call collect."

"In the parlor."

As he left the kitchen, she called after him, "You still love her. Otherwise you wouldn't have brought her cap back."

He looked at the cap, then threw it into a chair and dug into his hip pocket for the scrap of paper. When he glanced at the number his heart fell. It was his sister's home phone. He'd told Ursula to call him only from a pay phone. For a moment he thought about driving into town to use the pay phone by the drugstore, but if his sister's phone was tapped, the damage had already been done. He smoothed out the paper and punched zero into the phone, then the numbers Darby had scrawled. When the operator answered, he said, "Collect call, please."

"Your name please?"

He hesitated, then in a low voice said, "Michael."

Saturday, December 23, 1:10 P.M.

Waiting for her brother to call, Ursula Walker stared absently at the television, some soap opera. She'd phoned in sick this morning, hearing the inevitable pregnancy joke from Hoffman and another congratulation for her win. She hadn't even considered telling him about being followed; it would be a sign of weakness. A woman associate was supposed to be able to handle her own problems. Especially a pregnant woman. Especially a single pregnant woman.

She had, however, called the San Francisco Police Department. They were sympathetic. They would send a patrol car by her house once a day for a week or so, but without a license number there was little else they could do. She felt chagrined about not thinking to get the plate number, she who prided herself on her powers of observation, on staying cool in the courtroom. *Not good, Urs.*

She hadn't slept at all. But in the morning things looked better and she was able to dismiss the feeling of foreboding that had grown in the dark, even to convince herself she'd been imagining things. Then the white Buick drove by her house again.

She panicked. She called the police once more, then locked herself in her bedroom, crying, wishing for the first time since she had decided to have a baby that she were married.

After she stopped crying, she went into her study and looked out the window. Down the block a police car was parked, its engine idling. The Buick was gone. She ran through a list of everyone she knew, trying to think of someone who could help but came up blank. With a shock she realized that among all her acquaintances, all her so-called friends, not one of them could help her in a situation like this.

Which left her brother Michael.

She hadn't seen him in . . . what? four years? The last time was at Mom's funeral, she guessed. Even James had been there. She'd briefly considered calling him, too, a mark of her desperation. But he'd gotten so strange lately, some kind of political zealot. And even if she had felt comfortable around him, she didn't think he'd come to San Francisco.

Michael might, though. She just wasn't sure he'd be much help. As children they'd been close, and as adults they'd stayed in touch for a while, with occasional phone calls and cards at Christmas. Actually, it was Michael who had stayed in touch, she admitted. A year or so ago he had stopped calling her, perhaps sensing her coolness, and she never tried to reestablish contact.

She wasn't sure why she hadn't. She liked him. He was just such a screwup, flunking out of Stanford, then that other college, what was it, Iowa State? Then when he joined the army it looked like he'd finally get it together, even though he wasn't an officer. Instead, he wound up in prison. And when he got out, he just disappeared. How like him. His last call came from somewhere in Montana.

"Don't tell anyone else where I am," he had said, "not even good old James." He gave her a phone number and told her to ask for Matt Cooper when she called. And to call from a pay phone. She shook her head, wondering what kind of trouble he'd gotten into this time, but for some reason she'd kept the number in her billfold. This morning she'd dug it out and called it.

She quit trying to concentrate on the soap opera and pulled herself up to go to the bathroom. The phone rang. She lunged for it, answering it in the middle of the first ring.

"I have a collect call from a Michael: Will you accept the charges?"

"Yes, of course. Thank God."

"Hi, Urs. This is your home phone, isn't it?"

He sounded older, tired. Now that she heard his voice, she had second thoughts. Maybe she shouldn't have called him.

"Yes, of course. Why?"

"Why don't you call me back from a pay phone? I'll wait here."

"I can't, Michael. I'm afraid to leave the house. Someone's following me."

"Who is? How do you know?"

"I saw him. In a white Buick." She described the incident. "He followed me home, Michael. He knows where I live. I didn't even go to work today."

"Did you call the cops?"

"Yes, of course. There isn't much they can do."

"Any idea who it could be? An old boyfriend?"

"No. I don't have any weird boyfriends or anything. I'm a nice person. Why would anyone stalk me?"

"You're a lawyer, Ursula. Believe it or not, a lot of people hate lawyers. Why don't you hire someone to protect you? A bodyguard. I'm sure you can afford it."

"I don't want any strange men living in my house. I'd be wondering who'd protect me from them."

"What would you like me to do?"

"Can you come to San Francisco for a little while? Stay with me? It'd be nice to see you, anyway."

He hesitated. "I'm not sure that'd be a good idea."

"Please, Michael. I don't know who else to call."

There was a long pause. She pictured him with that faraway look. He always drew into himself to think. Finally, he said, "Yeah, sure. If you need me. The thing is, um, I'm a little short of gas money."

She heard his embarrassment and felt protective, as she had when they were kids. Her little brother. She also felt scorn: a man his age, broke. "Fly, Michael. I'll wire you the money."

"I don't know if I can get a seat this close to Christmas."

"I have some connections at Delta. Just get here as soon as you can, please."

5

As the Boeing 737 descended toward San Jose International, Michael stared at the darkened window, trying to ignore the crying baby in the seat behind him and the vitamin salesman beside him who was talking about a topless bar Michael had to see.

Michael wasn't in the mood for topless bars; he was wondering how much trouble he was flying into. But he couldn't refuse to come if his sister needed his help. Unfortunately, even his sister's airline connections couldn't get him a ticket yesterday.

He hoped he hadn't endangered Darby and the Snowgrass family, too. He didn't think so. If Ursula's phone was tapped, the people looking for him would know he was coming to San Francisco. They'd look for him there.

Truth was, though, he'd stayed in one place too long. He should have left Montana months ago. The problem was Darby—he'd refused to marry her because he couldn't put her life in danger, but somehow he could never quite talk himself into moving away, either.

After he had hung up the phone, he'd picked up Darby's cap and walked out to the old round-roofed barn she used as a studio to tell her he was leaving. And to pry a thanks from her for remembering the cap. From the hayloft came the sound of electronic music. Although she ran a bakery to make a living, music was her passion. Even when she'd lived with him, she'd loved that music more.

He opened the Dutch door and stepped into the gloom of the barn, startling a pigeon, which circled once, cooing, then landed in the eaves. As he climbed the steps to the loft, the dry, sweet smell of hay brought back memories of last summer. He and Darby had helped stack it, working side by side, laughing, enjoying just being together.

He stepped up onto the loft floor and paused as the music assaulted him. Nearby, a space had been cleared of hay and swept clean, the hay bales replaced by synthesizers, extension cords, and strange electronic equipment and by the tarp she used to keep it all covered. Even when they'd pooled their money, every spare dollar she made went for equipment. Admittedly he had a tin ear, but people who knew something about music told him she was very good. Jealous, he watched her, a rapturous look on her face as she coaxed sounds from the keyboard.

When the music paused he cleared his throat. She glanced up, then back at the keyboard.

"I brought your cap back," he said. He held it up.

She nodded, didn't speak. A harsh chord came from the synthesizer.

"Can I talk to you a minute?"

"I'm busy, Matthew." The chord changed into one even worse.

"I'm leaving."

She nodded.

"Leaving town."

She looked up and the music stopped. "Yeah?"

"I need you to look after Jack for a little while, will you?"

"How long?"

"I don't know. Couple days. Week or two."

She looked at him, waiting for an explanation. When he said nothing, she looked down and resumed playing.

"Will you or not?" he shouted.

She stopped. "Look, if you want my help you'd better come across with a little information."

"It's my sister. She needs me to come to California for a while."

"Why?"

"I don't know. Says she's in some kind of trouble. Somebody's following her or something."

"How long will you be gone?"

"Just until this thing blows over. Unless I decide to move out there." He watched her reaction, hoping for an expression of dismay.

She only shook her head. "You're not sticking me with that tomcat. If you're not back in two weeks, he goes to the pound."

"Nice to know you'll miss me."

"I'm trying to work here, Cooper."

"Will you watch the trailer, too?"

She raised a hand in assent and bent over the keyboard again. Dismissed, he hung the cap on a guitar neck with a sigh and left.

The seat belt light came on with a *ding*, and Michael drained his 7UP. Planes gave him claustrophobia and he just wanted to get off and breathe fresh air. He threw the plastic glass in the trash bag as the steward went by.

With a chirp of tires the plane bumped down. The baby behind him reached up and pulled his hair. "When you go there," the salesman was saying, "be sure and ask for Holly Hooters. Holly Hooters, don't forget. Tell her Carl said hello."

They crawled toward the terminal and stopped, waiting in line for a gate. As a precaution, Michael had flown into San Jose, instead of San Francisco, planning to rent a car and drive to Ursula's house. But she wanted to meet him, so he'd wired her his arrival time and the gate number. He felt a thump, heard the whir of hydraulics as the ramp attached itself to the plane. People jostled into the aisles, and Michael, pushed ahead of the baby's crying, inched his way to the doorway and down the long tube to the terminal.

A cluster of people waited. He looked for his sister but didn't see her. He scanned the crowd again. A blond, very pregnant woman in an expensive-looking maternity dress smiled. His glance slid past her, then back. "Ursula?"

She leaned forward as he approached and pecked him on the cheek. "Thanks for coming, Michael."

He stepped back and examined her as people flowed around them. She looked tired. "I didn't know you were married."

"I'm not."

His eyebrows involuntarily rose. A pair of passing nuns turned and looked, frowning.

"I just never found Mr. Right, Michael. I couldn't wait any longer. I want a child. Why shouldn't I have one?" She steered him away from the gate.

"So, who's the father?"

"A lawyer at the office. A decent man. He's OK."

Michael looked at her.

"What? It's not like that. Even if I'd been married, I couldn't have had children without in vitro help. This is the twenty-first century. A lot of women are doing it."

"A lot of women are not my sister." He felt grouchy and tired, and the last thing he needed was to learn his unmarried sister was pregnant with a test-tube baby.

She took her hand off his arm. "You sound just like Mom. Against everything new."

"Well, maybe she wasn't always wrong." He caught himself. He also didn't need to start fighting with her the minute they saw each other. "Sorry, Urs. It's your life."

"You're right." But she smiled a little and took his arm again. "You have bags?"

"One. I tried to carry it on the plane, but they made me check it."

"It may take a while, then." She guided him toward the baggage claim area.

"So how've you been?" she said as they waited among a crowd of harried businessmen and holiday travelers loaded with gifts.

He shrugged. "I'm surviving."

"Are you working?"

"Not at the moment. You look like you're doing well, though."

"My career's going very well for me. Oops." She put her hands on her stomach and bent forward.

"What's the matter?"

"I need to sit down."

He led her over to a row of black plastic chairs, and she sank into one. "It's all right. A few twinges. I've been having them all day. I checked in with my obstetrician and he said it was just Braxton-Hicks contractions."

"You sure you're OK?"

"I'm fine. I'm not due for two weeks."

He sat down beside her. On the fringes of the crowd a handful of young people in dirty green robes were ringing tiny bells and begging for money, receiving mostly curt refusals.

A girl of about eighteen, a brass bell tinkling in one hand, came over and thrust a basket into Ursula's face. "Help support a Christian youth organization?" Her long dark hair was plaited into a braid, her face fixed in a smile. Her eyes looked like poached eggs, the pupils large and round.

Ursula pushed the hand away. "No."

The girl stuck the basket into Michael's face. "Help support a Christian youth organization?" Same tone of voice, same lack of expression.

"I gave at home." He watched as she turned to a man next to

them. "Ringers," he said. "You have those here, too, huh?"

She glanced at them, uninterested. "Yes. All over. I thought Montana would be the one place without them."

"No such luck. They have a place in the mountains near Sweetwater. New Jerusalem of the Church of True Atonement. Everyone just calls it the Ringer ranch." He and Darby had moved to Montana, in fact, to be near Ringer headquarters. Or rather, Darby had, and he'd gone with her. He wondered now if they had done the right thing.

They'd been living together in his trailer near Santa Barbara then. She was working full-time in a Sam Goody's, which was where he'd met her. Darby had baked a huckleberry chocolate cake for the residents of a rest home, and apparently Mother Mary Grace, the leader of the Church of True Atonement, had visited the rest home looking for converts, eaten a piece of the cake, and liked it so much she'd gotten Darby's phone number and called her, offering to hire her as the church's baker. Darby had declined, wanting to pursue her music. Mother Mary upped the ante. If Darby would bake for her and her inner circle, the church would pay her enough to support herself while she composed music. She didn't even have to live at Ringer headquarters.

To Darby the offer was tempting. The baking would only be part-time, and the rest of the day would be hers. The only drawback was that she'd have to move to Montana. She talked to Michael. To him, Montana was as good a place as any to hide, maybe better. He agreed to go with her. She accepted their offer.

In the airport, a male Ringer a little older than the rest was staring at Michael and Ursula as he tinkled his bell. Michael returned the stare.

Suitcases began to tumble onto the carousel. "There's my bag." He stood and pushed through the crowd, grabbed the canvas duffel, and hoisted it onto his shoulder. "Where's your car?" he said as he helped his sister to her feet.

"I took a cab. It seemed safer."

"Good thinking."

They walked through the automatic doors onto the sidewalk, toward the row of waiting taxis. Michael sniffed the exhaust fumes. "Ah, it's wonderful to be back."

"Sarcasm doesn't become you." She walked toward the nearest cab. The driver opened the trunk, and Michael threw his duffel into it, then climbed in the backseat beside Ursula.

"Where to, please?" the driver said, sliding behind the wheel. His license gave a Lebanese name. The dashboard was covered with small plastic statues of Jesus and the saints.

"San Francisco," Ursula said. She gave him the address of her house on Waller. The driver whistled in surprise or pleasure, then gunned the engine and sped away from the curb.

Michael looked at her, smiled, unable to think of any small talk. He started to ask her about being followed but decided to wait until they were alone.

"Are you prepared?" the driver said, watching them in the rearview mirror.

"What?" Michael said.

"The world," the driver said, flashing a grin. "It is ending. Are you prepared?"

"Ready as I'll ever be," Michael said.

"That is good," the driver said. "You are believers then?"

"I'm an atheist," Michael said, hoping to shut him up. He'd been too busy with his own problems to think much about God.

It was the wrong thing to say. The driver's eyes grew wide and he began to lecture them, his attention on the rearview mirror instead of the expressway. "The end is coming. For a young couple like you," he said, "there will be hard times. Very bad."

Ursula elbowed Michael, giving him a scowl. "Thanks a lot."

He smiled. "See, and you think you have troubles now." He

leaned back against the seat and closed his eyes, feigning sleep, leaving his sister to listen to the sermon.

The driver droned on, reminding Michael of a cell mate he'd had briefly, an Algerian who'd been transferred out after only two days in Oakdale. For a while Michael fought the memories, but as drowsiness overtook him he gave up and let them turn over in his mind, swirling like the snowflakes in a glass paperweight.

When he stepped through the prison gate onto the sidewalk, a man in a Hawaiian shirt handed him a plane ticket, then turned and walked away.

"Hey, wait!" Michael shouted, but the man got in a car and drove off without looking back.

The ticket was first-class, the destination Denver. At Denver International, James was waiting for him. He led Michael into the parking garage, to a black Pontiac Grand Am. "Your new car. Like it? Get in; I'll drive. I'll show you your house, a nice little place on West Eldorado. Nothing ostentatious, but good enough. Plus ten thousand dollars to get you started. Better than prison, huh?"

Michael said, "I appreciate the help. But you haven't told me what I'm supposed to do."

"No. I haven't."

Cruising along Interstate 76, James said, "This is your last chance to back out, Michael. I want to be fair. You have doubts about this, we can turn around right now. You go back where you were and everything's the way it was. Once I tell you about your job, it's too late. You hear me?"

Michael pictured ten years in Oakdale. "I'm here. What do I do?"

"Serve your country, the way you've been doing. America still has a lot of enemies, Michael. Some of them are right here. You're going to help protect us from them."

"You work for the CIA?"

James sneered. "The CIA couldn't carry our ditty bags."

"So who do you work for, then?"

"We're an arm of a group of people who belong to several different government agencies, a specialized resource arm. Let's just call it the Arm. See, some of America's enemies have to be removed from time to time. It needs to be done. Most of the time we can arrange an accident, but once in a while we want to make a statement, or there isn't time to set up an accident, and that's where you come in. We call them closings." He smiled at the real estate terminology. "We give you a deal, you close it. Simple, eh?"

"I don't want to kill any more people."

"You've already killed a dozen. What difference does a few more make? It's for your country."

But it did make a difference. Every person he had killed in the army had made a difference. "I don't own a weapon," he said.

"Yes, you do. A Wilson's Stealth forty-five ACP with suppressor. In the trunk. Seven-shot box magazine. More than you need, a good shot like you."

Michael said nothing. He'd made a commitment, but he was beginning to wonder if there was something worse than ten years in a cage with Lorenzo Rey.

James clapped him on the shoulder. "Just think of this as a continuation of your military service, Michael. No difference. We need you. This is still a war, only closer to home. You either fight or you're a deserter." He glanced at him. "You're the only closer who knows who I am. You understand what that means?"

He nodded.

They drove a few more blocks and James said, as if he wasn't sure Michael really did understand, "We shoot deserters. Just like the army."

His new house was ranch-style fifties, with walnut paneling and green shag carpet. Two bedrooms, a finished basement. Michael stood in the kitchen and looked out into the backyard, at the maple tree and rose garden. "Who owns it?" he asked.

"You do," James said. "Edward Harvey." He reached into his blue Armani suit and pulled out a handful of cards. "Driver's license." He flipped that onto the table. "Social security card." He flipped that onto the table, too. "Visa card, don't get carried away." Flip. "Birth certificate. And season tickets to the Rockies. A new life, Michael You're a lucky man."

"Yeah."

"Oh, and by the way, your first job? It's tomorrow morning." James took three color snapshots from his coat pocket and handed them to him. "Here's what he looks like. When you're through looking give them back to me."

He looked at the face in the photo. Latino, maybe forty, nice smile. He didn't look dangerous. He looked like your next-door neighbor. "Who is he? What did he do?"

"He's an enemy, that's all you need to know. Now, tomorrow morning at seven you go to the Texaco station on the corner. There'll be a gray van parked in back, keys above the visor. Use it. At nine, be on the thirty-six hundred block of Eliot, out by Mile High Stadium. The target will be walking the street, going from house to house. Return the van to the gas station. I'll check back with you tomorrow afternoon. Maybe we'll take in a baseball game."

Smiling, he went out and shut the door behind him.

The man's name was Salazar, Michael found out later. An activist priest running for Congress. According to the *Denver Post*, an innocent American citizen gunned down in a drive-by as he was campaigning door-to-door.

James had thoughtfully provided a bottle of Jack Daniel's as a housewarming present and, the night before his closing, Michael drank it all, numbing his conscience and the feeling that something was very wrong. When he picked up the van the next morning and drove toward Mile High Stadium, he tried to put his mind safely beyond reach and let his reflexes take over. Found Eliot Street, didn't see the target, drove around the block. His mind was trying to warn him about something. There he was. Michael raised his pistol. Fired a single round that dropped the man in his tracks, blood seeping onto the sidewalk.

And he knew as he pulled the trigger who had set him up.

Sick, he drove the van to a shopping mall on Colfax, left it in the parking lot behind a Sears store, went inside, through the mall, and out the other end, then caught a city bus. At the Greyhound bus terminal he bought a ticket to Duluth.

The drone of the cabdriver's voice faded, and Michael dozed. Ursula's gasp brought him awake. She grabbed his arm and pointed out her window. A black Toyota raced alongside the taxi in the fast lane. Its front window was down and in the shadows Michael saw the driver raise his right hand. A pistol barrel glinted.

The cabdriver slowed.

"Keep going!" Michael shouted. "Don't stop, for Christ's sake!"

"He must have followed me!" Ursula said.

He pushed her down onto the seat and crouched over her. A pop sounded and the cabdriver jerked, then slumped against the wheel. The taxi swerved.

"Oh, my God!" Ursula screamed.

The cab careened across the highway, plunged over an embankment, and bounced down a wooded slope. Michael leaned over the seat and groped for the steering wheel, but the driver's body blocked it. The cab skidded sideways and ricocheted off a live oak tree, threatening to roll over, but the rear end clipped another tree and they spun around and came to a stop, upright.

Ursula cried out and grabbed her belly.

"Are you hurt?" he said.

"My water broke. I think I'm going into labor."

6

In the Toyota, the man who called himself Jerry Manning drove on. This was where he had planned the closing, exactly this spot, and the results were what he had expected. No surprises in his jobs. He didn't like surprises, so he planned. Even rush jobs like this one, which had interrupted another one in Seattle.

He didn't know much about the target, just some renegade closer, finally found after a two-year-long tap on his sister's phone. That was more than Manning usually knew. By telling him that much, his employers, he knew, were making a point, making sure he understood how long their memories were. And what happened to closers who tried to quit.

That was OK. He didn't plan to quit. He liked his job, hated it when there was no work for him. He wasn't sure exactly what he liked so much about it. The closings were all right, though the truth was that killing people wasn't all that exciting; just pull the trigger and watch them twitch and die. It was something else. Maybe the way he felt himself change when his name changed. Jerry Manning now, computer programmer. He liked that, for now. He barely remembered his other names, his other selves.

At a gravel road connecting the north- and southbound lanes he slowed and, ignoring the honk of the car that swerved around him, turned onto it. AUTHORIZED VEHICLES ONLY. He smiled. He waited at the southbound lane for a semi to pass, pulled onto the highway, and drove back along it until he reached the place where he calculated the taxi had stopped. He would have to kill all of them, of course. No witnesses.

Braking, he pulled onto the left shoulder and stopped, then set the emergency brake. From the seat he picked up a Wilson's Stealth fitted with a suppressor. He tucked the pistol into a holster beneath his sport coat, opened the door, and got out. For a moment he stood listening. OK, over there. People moving.

He took a step toward the noise, and headlights glared behind him. A car slowed, pulling onto the shoulder. Highway patrol? More likely some Boy Scout citizen. He stepped off the pavement out of the direct glare of the lights and turned, waiting.

The door of the car, a black Jeep Cherokee, opened and a very short man in gray sweats and running shoes stepped out. "Any trouble? You need a lift?"

"No trouble," Manning said with a smile. "Just relieving myself."

"Oh. Sorry. Thought you might need help." The man chuckled; his hand lifted from behind his leg; metal flashed. Manning heard the shot and at the same time felt a terrible impact crush his chest. He staggered backward, hand groping for his own weapon. In the seconds remaining of his life his former identities seemed to peel from his mind like the skin of an onion, Jerry Manning, Oliver Sonnen, Paul Snider, R. T. Buell, and he felt an instant of regret that he would die before they reached his real self. He was trying to remember who that was when the darkness came.

●●●

In the backseat of the taxi Michael sat up and looked around. They had come to rest in a median strip several hundred feet wide. Through a gap in the trees he could make out the outline of rolling hills west of the freeway and the scattered lights of houses.

"Is he dead?" Ursula said.

He glanced at the driver. "Yes."

"I think the baby's coming. Michael, I'm scared."

"Hold on a little while, can you? This isn't a great time to have it." He tried his door. It wouldn't open. He eased over her and opened her door. "Come on."

Pale and shaken, she took his hand and climbed out. Traffic hummed past on both sides, and he caught an occasional glimpse of headlights through the trees.

In the southbound lane below them a car slowed and stopped.

"Let's get out of here." He led her away from the cab.

"Wait wait," she gasped. "A contraction . . . I've got to sit down."

"Not here. Someone may be coming."

"Michael, I have no choice."

He glanced toward the highway. Were those voices? "OK, here." He led her to a live oak tree, eased her down against the trunk, and knelt beside her. "Can you keep your legs together or something?"

She smiled weakly. "This isn't what I had in mind, exactly. I was thinking more like the university medical center."

From the direction of the highway a shot sounded, deafening in the relative quiet.

Ursula screamed. A door slammed and a car sped away.

"Quiet. Shh, shh. Stay here." He rose and ran down the slope.

At the edge of the trees he crouched and scanned the area. The black Toyota was parked on the shoulder of the highway. Nothing else. No, wait. That thing at the edge of the weeds. He waited, but it didn't move, and after a long moment he stood and walked over to it.

It was a man, young, twenty-five, maybe, lying on his back, eyes and mouth open in surprise. Dark stain still spreading over his chest.

With his foot Michael nudged the body, and the coat fell open.

He sucked in his breath. Shoulder holster and the grip of a pistol. He stooped to look and saw the Wilson's Stealth. An Arm assassin. Oh, shit! They'd found him.

He glanced around. Whoever had killed this man must have been in the car that drove away. But who? And why?

He shook his head, tried to concentrate on one problem at a time. First, his sister. He didn't know anything about delivering babies. OK, get help.

On the highway a car rushed toward him, twin cones of yellow light. He climbed the shoulder and waved his arms, but the car whizzed past without slowing, its sound receding. He ran north along the edge of the pavement. Maybe a call box.

But there wasn't one.

Finally, winded, he stopped and ran gasping back up the wooded slope. He didn't see Ursula. "Urs," he said. Then louder, "Urs!"

"Here. Hurry, please."

He ran toward the sound, found her with her knees up, head between them, panting. "Oh, God, Michael. Do something. The baby's coming."

"Aren't you supposed to know what to do? Didn't you take a class or something?"

"I was planning to . . . take Lamaze, but I got too busy."

"Come on." He stooped. "I'll have to carry you."

"I'm too heavy."

"Hell, I used to carry you around the house when I was ten. I can still do it." He gathered her into his arms and struggled to his feet.

"What was that shot?"

"They're gone. Don't worry about it."

"Where are we going?"

"There are lights across the road. Maybe we can find a ranch house or something." He stumbled down the slope toward the freeway with Ursula in his arms, swinging wide around the assassin's body. A semi hurtled past, its wind lifting his hair. Behind it was a gap in traffic, the highway dark.

He hurried across the warm asphalt, his arms like lead, his sister moaning, her hands clutched around his neck.

"Christ, wouldn't you know it? A fence." He stopped at the four-strand wire. "I have to put you down. Can you crawl through if I pull the wires up?"

She nodded. Sweat trickled down her face. "Why did he kill the driver? Who was he? It's so awful."

"Don't worry about it now. He's gone." He set her down and pulled up the lowest wire. "Careful, it's barbed."

On her hands and knees she tried to crawl beneath the fence. "Ow, ow. I can't do it."

He looked over his shoulder. A string of cars approached from the north, spotlighting them. "Try. You have to. There's a house up ahead. We'll try to get you there." He pulled harder on the fence wire.

She tried again and this time she made it. He heard her dress tear.

When she was through, he scrambled over and gathered her up again and struggled toward the nearest house, guided by a mercury vapor light glowing orange in the yard.

Ursula moaned again. "She's coming. I can't wait. Put me down."

They weren't going to make the house. "Just a few more steps," he panted. "There's a . . . barn right here. Almost . . ."

A small horse barn loomed in front of him, its stall doors marked by white Xs. As he reached it, lights under the eaves flashed on, blinding him. He fumbled open the nearest door and carried her in. At the house a dog started barking.

The stall was empty, its floor lined with clean wood shavings, and he laid her gently down. She shrieked and lay back. Across the aisle a horse nickered, nervous.

He stood helplessly. "What can I do?"

"Catch her when she comes."

He knelt and watched the baby emerge, headfirst, slick and red, and he put his hands under it. Ursula screamed again as the head came through, then the baby slid out into his hands.

A light went on in the stall. A man and a woman stood in the stall door, their faces frozen in surprise.

"It's a boy!" Michael said.

7

In Boston, Linda Bach poured water into the coffeemaker, noticing the water looked a little rusty. Someday they'd have to replace the pipes in this old house. Right now she was more concerned with what she should wear for the presentation today. Maybe the camel blazer.

As she put bread in the toaster, her husband wandered into the kitchen. "Have you seen my blue shirt?"

"Hanging up in your closet."

He disappeared. She felt a wet nose on her leg and pushed it away. "Max, no, these are new panty hose. Jason," she shouted upstairs, "feed Max, will you? And give him some fresh water."

"In a minute."

Her husband came back into the kitchen. "Have you seen my checkbook?"

"On the washing machine. You want toast?"

"I knew I had it somewhere last night; I was working on it."

"Jason!" she shouted, then gave up and pulled the Purina sack from under the sink and poured food into the dog's dish. Wagging his tail, Max sniffed and began crunching kibble, and she ran tap water into his water bowl and set it down.

"Is Megan up?" she said, but her husband had disappeared again.

Linda finished making the coffee. Behind her the dog started lapping the water, then jerked back. Whining and shaking his head, he trotted out of the kitchen.

She climbed the stairs. Her daughter was still in bed, the covers over her head. "Come on, you have ten minutes if you want to ride with me. Right now!"

"All right, all right." Megan swung her legs out of bed, disgust written on her face.

"Mom!" Jason yelled from his room. "Max just spewed on my math book."

"Well, what was your math book doing on the floor? Get a paper towel and wipe it up."

"It stinks."

Linda hurried back downstairs. Her husband was sitting at the table reading the paper, a cup of steaming coffee in front of him. "You read 'Dilbert' this morning?" he said.

"I haven't had time." She pulled the toast from the toaster and scraped butter on it.

He took a sip of coffee and spit it on the newspaper. "Yuck!"

"What's wrong?"

"The coffee. What'd you put in it?"

A scream came from upstairs.

She ran up, her husband close behind her. Megan was standing in the bathroom, still in her Megadeth sleep shirt, scrubbing at her mouth with a towel, a toothbrush in her other hand.

"What's wrong?" Linda said.

"Eeuww! Gross. I'm trying to brush my teeth, and the water. You gotta be kidding. You expect me to brush with that?" She scraped at her tongue.

"It's bitter," Linda's husband said.

Linda stepped over to the sink and turned on the cold water. Bent down and sniffed. Strange odor. She cupped her hand under it, touched her tongue to it. Jesus! Was it ever! "Well, just leave it for now. Get dressed. We're late."

"I'm calling city hall," her husband said behind her as she went down the stairs.

In the kitchen he picked up the phone. "What's the number?"

"Look it up."

He pawed through the book, mumbled a number, and punched it into the phone. Then he looked at her, frowning. "Line's busy."

8

Michael lounged on the hotel sofa, drinking scotch and flipping the TV back and forth between a video of famous hockey fights and live female mud wrestling. For now, Ursula and he were safe and he was allowing himself the luxury of getting a little drunk. On the sofa next to him lay a newspaper he'd bought to see if there was any mention of the shooting, but there wasn't. A lot about fish kills in the Gulf of Mexico and other places around the world, but nothing about the taxi driver or the other body he'd found on the interstate. He wasn't sure if no news was good or not.

He glanced at the fire in the wood-burning fireplace, then at the fancy paintings on the wall of the suite. He would have chosen a Motel 6 to hide in, but Ursula had insisted on someplace with class, and it was her money. She had picked the Hamilton Hotel, and they'd been here two days.

The owners of the barn had called an ambulance, which took Ursula and Michael to the university medical center. He'd lied to the farm couple, told them he had been driving his wife to the hospital and his car broke down. He wanted no questions from the San Mateo County sheriff. The couple seemed unaware of the killings on the highway, and by the time the sheriff's office contacted them, if they ever did, Michael planned to be long gone.

Sedated, Ursula spent the night in the hospital under observation, but there were no complications. He spent a nervous night in the waiting room, trying to erase from his mind the images of the dead taxi driver and the assassin. In the morning he cautioned his sister not to mention the drive-by shooting.

"Why on earth not?" she said.

"I can't get involved. I'll explain later."

"But, Michael—"

"Please."

She looked at him skeptically but did as he asked.

Now his sister came in from the kitchen, carrying the baby. He switched the channel to Oprah. "Should you be up yet?"

"I feel fine. Hold him, will you, Michael, while I warm his formula?" She laid him in Michael's lap.

His drink sloshed on the end table as he set it down. "Hey, wait; wait. I don't know anything about—"

"Oh, he won't bite. Just don't drop him." She disappeared into the kitchen.

Uncomfortable, he made a barricade around the kid with his arms.

The baby began to cry.

"Hey," he said. "Knock it off. I won't bite, either."

The baby stopped fussing and watched him silently with dark, solemn eyes.

In the kitchen of the suite Ursula filled a bottle with Similac and put it in the microwave to warm. While it did, she peeked around the corner to make sure Michael didn't drop the baby.

When she'd first seen him, a boy, brown-skinned and black-haired, when she expected a blond, blue-eyed girl, she'd been shocked and outraged. She'd chosen the father carefully, not only for intelligence but also for physical appearance. She'd always pictured herself the mother of blond children. Not only wasn't this baby blond, he looked ... well, Mexican. And they'd promised a girl! She'd sue them, put the baby up for adoption.

But in the hospital, she was amazed how quickly the infant had come to seem a part of her. He was a sweet baby. Anyway, he didn't look *that* foreign. So when she got out of the hospital she put off calling the clinic about their mistake, for a day, then another day. Now she wasn't sure she'd ever call them.

The microwave beeped and she took out the bottle, screwed on the nipple, and tested the temperature of the formula on the inside of her arm. She wished Mom were here to see the little guy.

She went into the living room and caught Michael smiling at the baby, his tiny hand wrapped around her brother's index finger. For a moment jealous, she picked up her son and laid him gently against her shoulder, rubbing his back and cooing to him, and he made contented smacking noises.

As Ursula sat down at the other end of the sofa, Michael glanced over, watching as the kid helped guide the bottle into his mouth with tiny, eager hands. "I thought breast-feeding was healthier."

"I suppose so," she said, "but it's just not practical. I'll be going back to work in a few weeks."

"You decide to keep him?"

She sighed. "I think so. There was a contract, of course. I'm sure I could get my money back, but—"

"What would happen to the kid?"

She looked at Michael, troubled. "Legally, that's a gray area. I suppose I could put him up for adoption. The sperm donor might have a claim if I did that, though."

"You mean that lawyer friend of yours?"

"No. I don't think so. This guy doesn't look like Jack Somerset at all. There must have been a mix-up of some sort." She tickled the baby's nose with her finger and he grinned a toothless grin, milk running down his chin. "I don't know. I guess it doesn't matter, anyway. I think I'll keep him."

"Hmm." He watched her. "Then you'd better give him a name."

"I know; the nurses were after me to do that. But I'll have to think about it. I had lots of good girls' names. But boys . . . Somehow he just doesn't look like a Joe or a Mike."

"For God's sake, don't name him Mike."

"Oh, I think you have a good name. It just doesn't fit him." She looked up and smiled. "Thanks for being there. I don't know what I would have done if you hadn't been with me."

He smiled, feeling guilty.

"I was planning to hire a nurse to take care of him during the day," she said, "but with what's been going on, I'd feel safer having you here, too. Will you stay a while longer?"

He sighed. Time to confess. He finished his drink to fortify himself. "Um, well, I need to talk to you about that. I may be making it more dangerous for you if I stay. I think maybe that guy who shot the cabdriver was after me, not you."

"You? Why would he be after you?"

"It's a long story." He got up to pour himself another scotch, wondering how much to tell her. She'd never been very close to James, but they always seemed to get along well enough, and Michael wasn't sure how much she'd believe anyway. "It goes back to a job I took when I got out of prison. I did some things that were . . . well, illegal."

"What kind of things?"

"I'd rather not get into that right now."

"You mean you're still a criminal? Is that the reason for the phony name? You told me the police weren't after you."

"They're not. Someone else is." He sat down again. "I think maybe they found me through you. Probably by tapping your phone."

"*My* phone?" She stared at him.

"It's possible."

"You mean they've heard everything I've said?" Her voice rose.

"Maybe. I'm sorry, Urs."

"But they were following me. Why?"

"I don't know, maybe they thought you'd lead them to me."

"Michael, I could have been killed! My God, why didn't you tell me?"

"I had no idea they were doing it or I would have." He drank off half his scotch.

"Oh, great. This is just great. I call my brother for help and find out he's the one who's causing my problem in the first place. Thanks a lot." She stood and stalked toward the kitchen.

"I'm sorry," he said again. "Look, I've decided to leave tomorrow. I think it'd be safer if you disappeared, too. Come with me, Urs. I don't think they're after you, but who knows?"

She stopped and turned. "With you? Are you serious?"

"Why not?"

"Michael, I've got a job here. A baby. I can't just pack up and go off to Sweetriver, Montana."

"Sweetwater. And we wouldn't be staying there."

"Where would we be going?"

"I'm not sure."

"Great. I just can't do that, Michael."

"Would you rather get shot?"

"You said yourself it was you they're after. When you leave I'll be fine." She looked down at the baby, biting her lip. "Although maybe I *will* hire a bodyguard."

He started to tell her it wouldn't do any good, that if they wanted her dead, she'd be dead, with or without a bodyguard. There were so many ways. She wouldn't even know they were there. The killer could shoot her from a hundred yards away with a scoped rifle or from a passing car or walk up behind her in a crowd with a knife. So many ways. It was nothing personal, the way they killed, very detached, very clean. And the advantages were all with the hunter. But telling her that would only frighten her more. He shuddered and finished his drink.

". . . should, Michael?"

"What?"

"I said, do you think I should? Hire a bodyguard?"

"I think you'll be safer coming with me for a while."

She studied him, angry and worried. The baby's bottle was nearly empty, and he blinked his eyes sleepily. Finally she shook her head. "I think I'd better hire someone. And I don't feel right not calling the police. Shouldn't we tell them these people are after you?"

"I told you, I did some illegal things. I'd just as soon the cops didn't know about them."

"Does James have anything to do with this?"

The name jabbed him like electricity. "Why?" he said, staring at her. "Has he asked about me?"

"No, not lately. He called a couple of times, a couple of years ago, but you told me not to tell him where you were. I even took your number out of my address book."

"Thanks." His shoulders sagged with weariness. "I'm sorry I got you into this."

"You should be," she snapped. Then she sighed. "No, I'm sorry, Michael; it's my fault, I guess. I shouldn't have bothered you in the first place." She drew the nipple of the bottle gently from the baby's mouth. "I'm going to give him a bath, then put him down and take a shower. Will you listen for him, in case he wakes up?"

"Sure."

She smiled wanly and carried the baby out.

Michael rose to pour himself another drink. He looked at the bottle of Chivas Regal, set his glass on the cabinet, and carried the bottle back to the couch. It would take more than a glass to numb the guilt. He should have stayed in Montana; all he'd done was make things worse. Why did he always figure out the right decision after he'd already made the wrong one?

He went to the door and checked the lock, then fastened the security chain. He didn't think there was any way James could track them here, but why take chances? He went back to the sofa and flopped down.

Half an hour later the bottle was empty. He had flipped back to the hockey channel, where a fistfight was in progress between Stu "the Grim Reaper" Grimson and Todd Ewen. Before Michael passed out, he was thinking it was ironic they'd ended up playing for the same team.

•••

At the door the short man named Salway glanced around. Except for the backup behind him—a woman and another man—the hallway was empty. He drew a key from his pocket and inserted it in the door lock. The dead bolt slid back with a satisfying snick, and he turned the knob.

It had been easy to get the key. People would do anything for money. Salway waited, listening for sounds on the other side of the door. When he heard none he pushed the door silently inward. It opened two inches, then stopped against a security chain. He gestured to the man behind him, who placed a slim, long-handled cutter in his hand. Carefully Salway slid the cutter into the opening, clamped its titanium jaws around the chain, and squeezed. The chain fell apart like string.

Drawing his gun, he beckoned to the man and woman behind him to follow, then stepped inside.

"Housekeeping," he said softly, smiling.

The television was on, but no one was here. Wait. He stood on tiptoe to see over the back of the sofa. Someone was lying on it. An empty liquor bottle lay on the floor. He walked over to the sofa, put his gun to the ear of the drunken man, and nudged him with it. No response. How contemptible.

He signaled and the three of them walked into the master bedroom. Behind a closed door he heard water running. That would be the woman, then, in the bathroom. He might not have to kill her.

Beside the bed stood a crib, and inside it slept the baby. He motioned to the woman, and she stepped forward, bent over the crib, and gently picked the child up. The infant, his eyes screwed shut, frowned and made sucking noises but went on sleeping. The woman wrapped his blanket around him and looked at Salway, waiting for orders.

He smiled a bit to show he approved of the manner in which she handled the child, then turned away. The other two followed him out of the bedroom and through the living room, past the drunk on the sofa, now snoring.

Behind them the door closed with a quiet click.

9

In the shower Ursula thought she heard something and stopped rinsing her hair to listen. The noise of the water was too loud, and she shut it off. "Michael?" she shouted. "Is the baby fussing?"

No answer.

She shrugged. Must have been imagining things. Still . . . She stepped out of the shower stall and put on her robe. Maybe Michael had picked up the baby to play with him or change his diaper. As much as Michael was drinking, she wasn't sure that was a good idea. She went into the bedroom to check.

The baby wasn't in the crib.

She walked into the living room, where the television was playing some hockey game. "I'll take him now, Michael, thanks."

For a moment she didn't see anyone and she stopped, confused. Then she saw her brother passed out on the sofa, the empty scotch bottle on the floor.

"Michael?" She shook his shoulder. "Where's the baby? Michael?"

He groaned a little but didn't move.

Alarmed now, she looked over the room, but the baby wasn't there. She hurried into her brother's bedroom and checked it. The baby wasn't there, either. A cold wave of fear passed up from her bowels.

She looked in her brother's bathroom, then the kitchen. She must have missed something. He had to be here! Terror slurring in her blood, she checked the crib again. It was empty.

She screamed.

When she ran back into the living room, Michael was trying to sit up, looking groggy and confused.

"Where have you put the baby? Where is he?"

"Wha . . . ?"

"The baby, Michael! Where is he? Oh, my God, someone's taken him. How could you?" In shock, she snatched her car keys from an end table and ran for the door. "Please, Michael! Wake up. I need you. Shit!"

"Urs, don't. Stay . . ." He sagged back onto the sofa.

She wrenched open the door, thinking she should get her purse—it had her driver's license—but there was no time; she ran to the elevator and punched the button. And kept punching it, thought she could take the stairs, but that was so slow, and then pounded the elevator door with her fist, sobbing.

The elevator finally arrived. The doors opened and an older woman in a business suit raised her eyebrows, then stepped out, edging past her.

Ursula knew her hair was dripping and her feet were bare and she wasn't interested. "Did you see a baby come by here? Anyone with a baby, just now?"

The woman frowned, shook her head, and walked quickly away.

Ursula got into the elevator and punched the button for the lobby, holding it down, hoping the elevator wouldn't stop at any other floors.

The door opened in the lobby. Except for a handful of businessmen checking in at the registration desk, it was empty.

She ran toward them. "Did anyone see a baby?"

The men turned and stared. The clerk, a young Oriental woman, raised her head.

"My baby's been kidnapped. Did anyone see someone carry a baby through here? Just now?"

Several of the men shook their heads. Some turned away.

The receptionist looked alarmed. "I think I did. A few minutes ago. Should I call the police?"

"Please, please! Where did they go?"

"Let's see; I didn't . . . Into the parking garage, I think. There were three of them, and I thought, *Isn't that cute, three men and a baby, like the movie?* Except one was a woman, the one carrying it."

"Call the police!" Ursula shouted and ran toward the doors leading to the parking garage.

Michael sat up again, part of his mind trying to get a message through, something about the baby, but his brain wasn't working right. Diapers. Sick. No, gone. The baby was gone? How could that be? Ursula would keep him. . . . That wasn't right. Urs had told him; she had run through . . . had to wake up. He got to his feet, weaved into the kitchen, and stuck his head under the tap. Baby gone. The idea finally registered and the thought chilled him, sobered him a little. The baby was gone. How? Who?

Anger. Then shame. Michael, the noble guard. *A fucking poodle could have done a better job. You stinking, worthless . . . Got to help.* He drew his head out of the water and shook it. *Think.*

But all he could come up with was, *Go after them.* He tried to run to the door, but his legs still weren't working right and he staggered. Somehow he made it to the door.

Ursula sprinted to her car, the concrete cold on her bare feet. She backed the Saab out of its space and with a squeal of tires raced down the ramp to the exit.

The long-haired attendant glanced at her, then did a double take, smirking.

"Did you see three people drive out of here with a baby? Two men and a woman? Please!"

He looked at her, amused, then nodded. "Might have been a baby. In an Olds, I think; no, a Buick. A white Buick. But there was only two of 'em."

"Which way did they turn?"

"Hell, I don't . . . Uh, that way, I guess, down Lombard. I need your—"

She pushed the ticket at him and, when the barrier slowly raised, gunned the engine and darted out onto the street, cutting off a green Mercedes, which honked at her. The light was green, please God, a little help. A white Buick. She knew the one, the bastard. *I'll get you, you sonofabitch. Hang on, sweetie.*

Down Lombard, two blocks, three, and the lights were with her. Then she saw it, a white Buick, the one that had followed her; she was sure of it. Why? Why were they doing this to her?

It turned left on Van Ness, heading north, and she sped after it. Squealed around the turn on a yellow light, cutting off two cars, leaving angry honking behind her.

She was gaining on them. At Francisco only four cars behind. Lane-surfing, she cut the gap to three, then two. She could make out the license now, 1AM1862. *Gotcha, you bastards.*

The Buick turned right onto Bay, and if the light held she could . . . *Shit!* Yellow, then red. Ursula slammed her fist against the steering wheel, then decided to run the light. But as she reached the corner a group of Japanese tourists stepped off the curb, laughing and talking. Honking, she inched forward, trying to move through them.

In the left lane a Jeep Cherokee eased to a stop beside her.

Sitting on the pillow he used to see over the steering wheel, Salway pushed a button, and the tinted passenger window of the Cherokee rolled down. The woman was agitated, he could see that, and he didn't blame her for it. But she was too close. He was right to have covered their retreat.

Feeling an instant of regret, he raised the pistol in his right hand and fired one shot, the pop muffled by the silencer. A small hole appeared in the window of the Saab, a spiderweb of cracks radiating out from it. The woman's head snapped to the side and blood spattered the window. The Saab lurched ahead a few feet; then the engine died.

Salway pushed the lever and the window of the Cherokee rolled up. When the light turned green he pulled out onto Bay Street, turned left, and accelerated smoothly into traffic.

By the time Michael reached the corner of Van Ness and Bay his legs were working reasonably well. Small crowds had gathered on all four corners, and he pushed through the people blocking his view. Ursula's Saab was in the intersection, flanked by police cars with flashing lights. What was going on?

A knot of cops stood clustered beside the car. Behind it stood an ambulance, and as he watched, two white-uniformed attendants opened the rear doors and pulled out a gurney, opened it, and rolled it toward the Saab. She was hurt!

He ran into the street toward the car, but an officer in uniform spotted him and hurried over, waving him away.

"Go on about your business, sir. There's nothing to see."

"Is she all right? What happened?" He tried to sidestep the cop.

"Do you know this woman?"

"She's my . . ." Then his brain kicked in. "No, I guess not. Thought I did. Is she alive?"

The cop frowned. "Please stand over there on the sidewalk."

The attendants were lifting Ursula out of the Saab. Her head, God, the blood. Shock drained all feeling from him, and his mind went white and empty.

The cops were talking, and through the numbness he heard some of the words.

". . . drive-by . . ."

". . . third one this year . . ."

"... like that one in Chinatown?"

"Witnesses?"

"None that ... Random, maybe. At least ... not dead."

Not dead? He raised his head, hoping.

A radio crackled. "Central to Thirty-nine."

One of the cops by the Saab walked over to his patrol car, reached in, and picked up the mike. The ambulance attendants pushed the gurney into the ambulance, climbed in after it, and pulled the rear doors shut. Michael knew he should be doing something. *They shot Ursula!* Then he remembered her baby.

Roof lights whirling, the ambulance pulled away from the curb.

He stared at the bloodstained window of the Saab. "They're getting away with her baby," he mumbled.

The cop had walked away a few feet to move a teenage boy back onto the sidewalk and was heading back toward Michael. He looked surprised before recovering his impassive cop face. "What did you say?"

"I, uh, did she have a baby with her? I thought I saw one."

"Sir, if you know something about this, please step over there and talk to Lieutenant Chen. Otherwise, get off the street. Right now."

"No. No, I don't know anything." He turned away, aimed toward the crowd on the sidewalk. A tow truck drove slowly past him.

He walked back toward the hotel. One foot in front of the other. Should be people crying. Something.

One step at a time. Don't hyperventilate. He thought, *Don't be sick ... don't be ...*

He turned and retched into the gutter.

10

The personal secretary for Nestor Pruitt, acting director of the Task Force for Disaster Control, knocked once, opened the door, and stuck her head in his office. "They're waiting in the conference room, Mr. Pruitt. All but Dr. Soares. She's stuck out at Will Rogers."

Nestor glanced at his Rolex. "It's five past. I don't dare wait for her." He pushed back his chair and stood, smoothing his pompadour. "Call Hemi's for some sandwiches, won't you, Cyndee? We may be in there awhile."

As he walked down the corridor to the conference room he popped two Rolaids into his mouth. Six more fish kills in the last twenty-four hours. The president on his back—

"Forty-eight hours, Pruitt," he'd shouted at him. "I want some answers by then. Forty-eight hours." And hung up. Good gracious.

The buzz of conversation subsided when he came in. Nestor stood a moment watching them, a little intimidated. Eight, no, nine scientists around the table, all but Soares. Fish pathologists, marine biologists, behavioral neuroscientists. Ph.D.'s, stacks of papers, reports—all these brains. A Baptist country boy from Oklahoma was out of his league here. But he had to show them he was in charge.

"Good morning, gentlemen," he said. "Coffee up and let's get to it."

He sat down at the head of the table and waited for them to get settled. Then he nodded at a young man with a black beard and a bald head. "Dr. Brauss, you're in charge of this team. I hope you have some answers for me."

Brauss cleared his throat, fiddled with some papers. "As you know, Mr. Pruitt, there've been an unprecedented number of major marine ecological disturbances, MMEDs, in recent days, perturbations in fish populations worldwide."

Listen to him. With language like that, how did his wife and kids ever understand him? Nestor held up his hand. "Now, I know you all have the training to follow this line of jargon, but I'm just a politician. Speak English, won't you?"

Brauss frowned. "I'll try to make this as plain as I can, sir, but unavoidably there'll have to be some technical terminology. Now then, at last word we've had massive fish die-offs in the Gulf of Mexico, Santa Barbara Channel, Baltic Sea, Dutch Wadden Sea, North Sea, Gulf of Thailand, and Tolo Harbor." He glanced at Nestor. "That's Hong Kong."

The door opened and a tall woman, about forty, with short graying hair, strode in carrying a stack of papers up to her chin. "Don't forget the Kattegat Strait," she said.

Brauss glanced up at her, nodded slightly. "I was going to mention that."

"Gentlemen, Dr. Annie Soares," Nestor said. "She's from the Marine Research Institute, Florida Department of Natural Resources, that right, Annie? Met her at a hurricane conference last year, so I asked her to sit in."

Soares smiled slightly and set her papers on the table, then sat in the empty seat as the men around her made room.

"The die-offs in the affected areas are nearly total," Brauss continued. "To this point it's estimated that approximately thirty percent of the coastal fish population has been impacted. Fish tissues from most sites have been assayed for a variety of toxins. Tests revealed the presence of synthetic organochlorine pollutants in almost all fish tested, including dieldrin, T. nonachlor, and hexachlorobenzene, as well as PCBs, DDEs, and DDTs. Concentrations of two or three hundred parts per million were typical."

"Is that high?" Nestor said.

Brauss shrugged. "Human tissue rarely contains greater than three parts per million."

"It's extremely high," Annie Soares said, "but unfortunately, these days it's not uncommon."

Nestor turned to her. "High enough to be fatal?"

"Generally not, not on this scale and not with this suddenness."

Brauss looked at Soares. "May I continue? Heavy metals . . ." He glanced at Nestor. "That's mercury, cadmium, lead—"

"I know what metal is," Nestor said.

Brauss's scalp turned pink. "Heavy metals were also present in all samples, but not in lethal concentrations."

"What are you saying?" Nestor said. "That this stuff is always in fish?"

"In varying quantities . . . yes, nowadays it is. But I want to emphasize I do not think these contaminants were the ultimate cause of the perturbations."

"They're not? Then why am I listening to all this?"

Annie Soares said, "Because this stuff made them more vulnerable to what did kill them."

"And what was that?" Nestor said. Now he remembered why he liked this woman. He could understand her.

Brauss cleared his throat again. "If I may? Tests for brevetoxin—the red tide—were positive in most of the tissue samples. *Ptychodiscus brevus*, the algae associated with red tide formation, is common in the Gulf of Mexico. It's the consensus of the research team that blooms of algae are the most likely precipitating events leading to the deaths."

"All of them? All over the world?"

"Yes. Different algae, of course, bloom in different areas. There are brown algae, blue-green algae, any number of toxic varieties. Red is the one you're probably most familiar with. Bear in mind, Mr. Pruitt, that fish die-offs are not a new phenomenon. There've been many precedents in recent years: the die-off of bottle-nosed dolphins along the East Coast of the U.S. in 1987, the black sea urchins in the Caribbean, several others. With the continuing deterioration of the oceans, blooms of toxic algae are increasing dramatically, and many algae that have never bloomed before are doing so now. In some places it happens up to three or four hundred times a year."

"Three of four *hundred?* That often?"

"Yes, but not that often in lethal concentrations, of course."

"The heck. So what causes it?"

Brauss looked uncomfortable. "Well, there is no single causative factor, so far as we can tell. Detergent additives have been associated with some blooms. Other pollutants enrich the nitrogen and phosphorous—"

"We're causing it," Annie Soares said. "Human overpopulation and pollution."

"Well, that's true, of course . . . ," Brauss said.

"I agree with what Dr. Brauss has said so far," Annie said, "but there's something about these blooms that bothers me."

"What's that?" Nestor said.

"May I?" She looked at Brauss.

He nodded grudgingly.

"Well . . . I'm not sure." She tapped the stack of papers thoughtfully. "I only had time to scan these reports quickly on the plane up here, and I'd like more time to study them. The pattern seems a little unusual."

"Unusual?" Brauss smirked. "Of course it's unusual, Dr. Soares. That's why we're here."

Annie flushed.

Nestor said, "I can't give you any more time, Annie. The president wants an answer today. The rest of you guys agree with Dr. Brauss? Algae blooms with no—what'd you call it?—single causative factor, are responsible for the die-offs?"

Heads nodded.

The door opened and Nestor's secretary burst in, her usual wiggle almost gone in her haste. "Mr. Pruitt, the president called again. Excuse me." She handed him a pink message slip.

It said: "Drinking water supplies of New York City, Boston, and D.C. contaminated. Prez says call him *NOW!*"

"Dr. Brauss," Nestor said, "write up the report, if you will. Excuse me, gentlemen. I have a phone call to make."

11

In the ICU waiting room in the California Pacific Medical Center, Michael sat with his head in his hands. A TV was babbling on a wall above him, some game show giving away huge amounts of money. Every few minutes the shiny aluminum doors of the elevator across the alcove would open with a *ding* and a nurse or doctor would get out and walk briskly down the hall, through the steel doors that barred the way into the intensive care unit. Somewhere behind those doors, in a glass chamber, Ursula was fighting for life, hooked to what seemed like a dozen different machines.

Michael had pretended to be her fiancée, making up some name that, at the moment, he couldn't even remember. The doctors wouldn't talk to him at all, and the nurses couldn't tell him much, only that Ursula was still alive but in a coma. She'd survived the bullet being removed from her brain, but they didn't know when she would regain consciousness or how much functioning she would lose if she did.

Miserable, he picked up the front page of the *San Francisco Chronicle*. Maybe there was an article about Ursula's shooting. He scanned the headlines, but there was no mention of her, although the stories he did see were frightening—forest fires in the West, contaminated drinking water in the East, massive fish kills around the world, even a rash of burglaries at blood banks in the Bay

Area. Weird. He wondered if that was responsible for the hospital's supply of fresh blood being low. It worried him. Would there be enough for Ursula? He'd donated two pints for her himself, which made him feel marginally better. But not good enough to read those headlines. He turned the page.

At the bottom of page 5 he found a tiny article about the shooting. A drive-by, the paper said, with no information on the person responsible. He ripped out the article and tossed the paper back on the table.

From a speaker in the ceiling a woman's voice briskly told Dr. Singh to call extension 42. The ICU doors opened and a middle-aged man stepped out and looked around, bewildered. He trudged into the waiting room and sat in a chair near Michael, giving him a tentative smile. A husband, maybe, or a father. A fellow sufferer. Michael tried to return the smile, unsuccessfully. The man turned away and stared vacantly at the television, the studio audience laughing in glee at something the host had said.

Michael tuned out the noise. His head hurt and he felt the weight of his guilt like chains tied to his ankles and wrists. The damage he had done he couldn't heal; the hurt he'd caused he couldn't even share. He tried to think, to make sense of what had happened. Ursula had been shot, and the baby had been kidnapped. Why would the Arm kidnap the baby? There was no point. Shoot Ursula, possibly, to pay Michael back for killing their assassin. They could've thought that. Might even kill the kid, too, and leave him there as a statement; oh, yeah, the bastards would do that. But as far as Michael knew, the baby hadn't been killed. So why kidnap him? They didn't work that way. And why, he wondered, didn't they kill me when they had a chance? Jesus, they must have walked right past me. For that matter, why didn't they kill Urs in the hotel room?

Because it wasn't them, he realized. The Arm didn't do it. Somebody else must have.

Who? Why?

He started over. The baby might still be alive. His sister's baby. Since Ursula was unable to care for him, did that make Michael the infant's guardian? He wasn't sure. Who else would there be? Who cared about the kid, other than him? Did *he* care? He didn't even know who the father was. It was just another baby. He looked at his finger, saw the tiny hand wrapped around it. Somebody had kidnapped the little guy. What chance would he have now?

Michael couldn't heal the damage he'd caused, but maybe he could lessen it.

He could find the baby.

Fear blew through him. *No way! I'm no hero. I've got no special strength or virtue. I hate pain. I'm afraid of fear.*

Who else is there? the voice in him said quietly.

Shit.

A moment of panic made him dizzy. He let it pass, then stood and walked toward the elevator doors.

As he descended to the lobby he thought about what he should do next. Before he came to the hospital he'd packed his duffel, gathered Ursula's things, and checked out of the fancy hotel. James, he knew, would still be looking for him.

He couldn't afford another hotel—he had less than a hundred dollars on him, and his MasterCard was maxed out. But if he was going to look for the kid, he needed a car to get around.

The doors slid open and he stepped into the lobby. Two cops stood at the registration desk, a uniform and a detective in a burnt orange blazer. Michael turned back into the elevator, his knees nearly buckling, and punched the button for the second floor. Were they looking for him? He went into a newsstand, pretended to browse through the paperbacks for ten minutes, then walked down the stairs to the lobby again. The cops were gone.

As he came out the entrance a raw wind slapped rain into his face. Somehow it seemed appropriate. He pulled his jacket tighter around him and walked away.

Down the street he found a Budget Rent-A-Car and rented a Ford Escort, telling the clerk he'd pay cash—he couldn't risk James tracking him through his credit card. The clerk insisted on taking an imprint of his card anyway, and he gave her Matthew Cooper's MasterCard.

Feeling lost, he got in the car and wiped his face, watching the rain sheeting down the windshield. What next? He remembered a name Ursula had mentioned: Somerville or Somerset, something like that. The sperm donor. If Michael was going to do something, it was a place to begin. He started the engine.

Ursula's law firm occupied three floors of a glass tower on Sacramento. High ceilings, walnut paneling, and maroon leather wing-back chairs.

Michael didn't own a suit, but he'd put on what Darby called his concession to respectability: chinos, a Polo shirt, and a Minnesota Vikings jacket he'd bought in Duluth. He didn't have a plan, either; he was no detective. He'd been running so long he wasn't sure how to change gears and become the hunter.

The receptionist didn't look up from her desk. He stood in front of her a moment, and when she finally glanced at him, he said, "I'd like to see Mr. Somerville."

She scanned his purple Vikings jacket, wet from the rain, and flashed him a frosty smile. "I'm sorry; we have no Somerville."

Something beeped on her desk. She spoke softly into her headset while Michael waited, trying to remember the man's name.

When she was finished, he said, "I meant Somerset. Jack Somerset."

"Have you an appointment?"

"No."

"May I tell him what it concerns?"

"It's personal business."

She took his name and suggested he have a seat. It might be a few minutes.

He sat in a leather chair and waited. The opulence of the office intimidated him, which, he suspected, was its purpose. Occasionally people, mostly men in gray or navy suits and shiny black shoes, walked past him without a glance.

Forty-five minutes later the double oak doors shielding the inner offices opened and Jack Somerset came out with his hand extended, a professional smile in place. *Yeah, I can see why you picked this guy, Urs,* Michael thought. Six-two, six-three, a young, blond Robert Redford. He stood and shook hands.

"Mr. Walker? What can I help you with?"

He glanced at the receptionist. "Maybe it'd be better if we talked in your office."

The smile didn't waver. "Of course. Come this way, won't you?"

He followed the lawyer through a wainscoted corridor with expensive-looking oil paintings hanging on the walls. Third office on the left. Smaller than he expected, with no view. A computer on one side of the desk, files stacked high on the other side.

"Have a seat, won't you?" Somerset picked up a pen, held it poised over a yellow pad. "Now what can I do for you?"

"My sister picked you to be the father of her baby."

The smile developed rigor mortis. "Excuse me?"

"I'm Ursula's brother."

"Ursula? Walker? You are?"

"I am. Unfortunately for her." How much to tell him? The basics, at least. "Ursula was shot yesterday."

"She's on maternity leave."

"She was shot in her car. Chasing the bastards who stole her baby. What I want to know is, what did you have to do with it?"

Was that the way Joe Leaphorn did it? Probably not, but Michael didn't know the right way.

Somerset stared. "Ursula?"

He nodded.

The lawyer laid the pen carefully on the pad. "Are you sure? I just . . . She was . . ." He was trying to be cool. He wasn't succeeding.

"She's in a coma."

"Christ Almighty." The professional facade fell away completely, and under it Michael saw a tired, fearful young man. "Who did it?"

"I don't know. That's why I'm here. She told me you were the father of her baby."

"Well, I . . . not the father, really. I . . . donated the sperm. It was all legitimate; it's done pretty often these days."

"Did you love her?"

He frowned. "This is rather personal, isn't it?"

"Attempted murder is personal."

"All right. No. I didn't. I mean it wasn't a matter of . . . It wasn't like that. For her, either. We weren't involved. Ursula just wanted a baby, and she was . . . very practical about it. She asked me would I donate, no strings. I suppose I was, um, flattered. You know?"

"I guess."

"Will she live?"

"They don't know."

He put his head in his hands. "Damn. Ursula Walker." After a moment he looked up at Michael. "You say somebody kidnapped our . . . her . . . the baby, too?"

"Yes. Do you know anything about that?"

"No way. I would never do that. I've already got two kids. I signed a waiver of parental rights."

"My sister said someone had been following her. Do you know any reason why anyone would do that?"

"Following her? I don't think so. She was in our insurance defense department. I mean, I suppose it's possible she could have offended someone—clients do get upset when they lose. But I can't see that. And she got along with everyone here. She was . . . OK."

Michael was trying to dislike this guy. A six-three blond, rich lawyer, who wouldn't? But he was having a hard time of it. The man's suffering seemed genuine. Michael glanced at the stacked files, the top ones about to fall off the desk. He had the impression Somerset was over his head, just hanging in there.

"Have you called the police?" the lawyer said.

"The police are on it," Michael said. "So, how does this work, this in vitro thing? Did you use a hospital or what?"

"A private clinic. A laboratory, actually, out in Livermore. Ursula did some insurance work for them, I think, was how she found them. Expensive."

"Yeah? Like how expensive?"

"Thirty-five thousand, I think she said, and no guarantees."

Christ, he had no idea she wanted a baby that bad. "What's the name of this place?"

"Genetics . . . something or other. I have it here somewhere." Somerset swiveled his chair, picked up a Rolodex from his credenza, and plunked it on the desk. He flipped through it. "Here. Genetics Utilization Flexibility Research, Inc. Genflex." He turned the Rolodex around for Michael to see.

"You have a piece of paper?"

The lawyer gave him one and he copied down the address and phone number. "Who were you working with out there? Anybody in particular? Technician, I mean."

"Reproductive endocrinologist." Somerset smiled, proud of his vocabulary. "Uh, some woman. Yates, I think her name was. Jerilyn, no, Jocelyn Yates. Supposed to be one of the best, according to Ursula." His smile faded. "I hope this doesn't get back . . . I mean, I'm married."

"Yeah?"

"My wife doesn't know. It would upset her."

"I'll bet," Michael said.

Outside, the rain had settled into a relentless drizzle, the sky sealed by massed gray clouds. Michael found a lunch counter down the street and went in. He ordered coffee and sat hunched at the counter, hands wrapped around the cup. He warmed his hands on the coffee, stared out the window, and thought. He missed Darby and he missed Ursula, more than he would have believed. He'd never felt more alone. He finished his coffee, left a dollar on the counter, and walked out.

It took him four hours to get to Livermore, partly because on the way there he had an attack of guilt and shame. Ursula was lying in a coma and might die, and it was his fault. The torment was nearly beyond him, and he had to pull over to the side of Interstate 580 and stop. Hundreds of white windmills covered the hills near the highway, looking like giant seagulls, their blades revolving slowly. He sat staring at them. The hills around him were brown and treeless, like the pictures he'd seen of Spain. It made him feel like Don Quixote in hell. Finally the pain receded enough for him to drive on.

The clinic he was looking for was in a long one-story building that seemed to be a warehouse. He wondered why a fertility clinic needed a building that size; the parking lot wasn't even half-full. Maybe they just rented space. He parked the Escort and got out.

After five minutes of searching, he found the entrance, a green steel door with small lettering: GENFLEX.

The reception room was tiny and spartan, the receptionist a twenty-something man with muscles Michael thought would look more at home in a health spa. A plastic name holder on the bare desk said his name was Jacob. As Michael came in, Jacob lifted his crew-cut head and watched him.

"Afternoon," Michael said.

Forced smile.

"I'd like to see Dr. Yates, please."

"Dr. Yates isn't in. Sorry."

"Oh. So am I. I came a long way to see her. When will she be back?"

"I have no idea."

Silence.

"Can you find out?"

Reluctantly Jacob picked up a phone and punched a button. "Someone here wants to know when Dr. Yates will be back." He listened, keeping his eyes on Michael. "Long hair, about six feet. Dissipated, out of shape."

Michael straightened his shoulders.

"OK." Jacob set the phone back in the cradle. "What do you want with her, sir?"

"Business. The wife and I want a baby and, well, you know, my sperm count's down a little. I think it's working around radiation so long—Hanford, see—but the wife, she wants a kid, and we heard she's the best."

Jacob nodded, as if his guess was confirmed. "Dr. Yates quit. She doesn't work here anymore."

"Oh. Well, do you have an address for her? It's important."

"No."

"No? How do you know? Can I talk to the person you just had on the phone?"

"Sorry. He's tied up."

"What's his name, at least?"

"Sorry, I'm new here." His eyes were fixed on Michael, a small, tight smile on his face.

Michael returned the smile. "It was obviously your warmth and charm that got you this job."

Pink crept up the man's neck.

"You're not going to tell me a damn thing, are you?"

Jacob's smile widened.

"Well, thanks for your cooperation." Frustrated, Michael walked to the door. Schwarzenegger would have pounded the information out of the man. At the door Michael turned, briefly considering that approach. The man would go six-four, easy. Now cracking his knuckles. Or maybe not.

He left.

12

On the plane back to Tallahassee, Annie Soares wondered why Nestor Pruitt had bothered to ask her to the fish-kill conference if he wasn't going to listen. Then she told herself to be fair. After all, she hadn't disagreed with the consensus, not really. As far as it went, the report was accurate. And she understood why Pruitt couldn't give her more time to examine the data; he must be under incredible pressure to come up with fast answers. But the pattern of the algae blooms bothered her. The timing, for one thing. This wasn't the season for red tide in the Gulf.

She decided to go over the reports again this evening—wait, no, she couldn't; she'd promised Nicky she'd watch his soccer game. Well, Saturday, then. No, she had to work; she was behind on that Okeechobee pollution study. Sunday? Oh, hell, she had to meet with Ronald about child support.

Unwillingly her thoughts were pulled to her ex-husband. Amateur suffering poet and professional womanizer. The graduate student he'd left her for had moved out, she'd heard, but it hadn't taken him long to find another one. Philandering jerk. If he'd spent as much time with his sons as he did proving his manhood, maybe they'd still be married.

Hey, that's life, Annie, she reminded herself. Bitterness only made things worse. She pulled her thoughts back. May as well use the few minutes she had. She opened her notebook computer and inserted the disk with the algae bloom data.

•••

Thursday, December 28, 4:45 p.m.

Depressed, Michael drove back to San Francisco, wondering if he should try to break into the fertility clinic to look at Ursula's records. The trouble was, he knew nothing about computers and probably wouldn't be able to find the records or decipher the information if he found it.

By the time he reached the city it was dark and he was hungry. He exited and found a bar, parked, walked in, and ordered a burger and a draft. The beer-stained front page of the *Chronicle* lay folded on the bar. Michael glanced at the headlines: "HEPATITIS OUT-BREAK. BOIL ORDER IN EFFECT." All the more reason to stick to beer. When it came he paid, reached for it, then heard Ursula's voice: "How could you?" and pulled his hand back.

He told the bartender he'd changed his mind, ordered boiled coffee, and tried to think.

The phone book, dummy.

On the back wall he found a pay phone with the San Francisco white pages hanging from a chain beside it. Yates, Yates. A lot of them, but no Jocelyn. No J., either, for that matter.

Information had no listing for a Jocelyn Yates in San Francisco or any of the surrounding towns. Oakland had one, but it turned out to be a seventy-three-year-old retired librarian who didn't want to let him hang up. He promised to call her back sometime.

Tired and out of change, he wandered back to the bar, thinking he should find a safe place to park the car for the night if he was going to sleep in it. He ate his hamburger, which was burned, and tried to think of another option.

He could stay in his sister's house, of course. Her garage door opener and spare house key were in her purse; he'd already searched the purse for Yates's address. But by now the Arm would know their closer was dead and have sent someone else looking for Michael. And they'd start with his sister's house. He didn't feel suicidal enough to stay there.

Her house. He stopped chewing. Of course. She could have Yates's address in her address book.

He put down the burger, no longer hungry.

On his way into the city he stopped to check out a Rodeway Inn, but they wanted eighty-five dollars for a single. He drove on.

In San Francisco he took Fell to Waller and followed it to Ursula's house, a federal blue and gray Victorian, three stories with a garage beneath, the tallest house on the street. He drove slowly past it, looking for anything suspicious, but it was too dark to see much. The cops would probably have been through it, and they might have it staked out. So might the Arm. But if those guys were around, he knew he wouldn't see them.

A half-block beyond Ursula's house he drove into the parking lot of Buena Vista Park and turned off the lights. He waited. If he went into her house now, he'd need a light to see, a dead giveaway to anyone watching. If he waited until dawn he just might catch any watchers napping. Or not.

The only other car in the parking lot was an ancient station wagon. An old woman sat behind the steering wheel, muttering to herself. Inside the park he could make out two men sitting under a tree near their sleeping bags, passing a bottle back and forth. Any of them could be cops, Michael thought. Any of them could be Arm. Most likely they were homeless. A lot of that going around.

He smiled at the woman, but she didn't look at him, just kept muttering. Finally, he pushed the seat back as far as it would go, pulled up the headrest, and tried to sleep.

He couldn't. He passed the night watching a sliver of moon make its way across the sky. Near midnight the men with the bottle crawled into their sleeping bags. The woman in the station wagon had disappeared into the back.

Time crept.

He opened his eyes to find the sky around him lighter. It was time. The men were asleep, the woman, he assumed, still somewhere in the wagon. He took a deep breath and started the car. With his lights off he cruised toward Ursula's house.

As he turned into her driveway, he punched the garage door opener. The door slid up. In the garage a light flashed on. Swearing, he drove inside, and the door closed behind him.

He got out and listened but heard nothing. The stairs into the house were behind an unlocked door. He turned off the garage light and groped up the stairs in the dark, the steps squeaking. At the top was another closed door, and he paused at it to listen again, but he heard nothing except his own ragged breathing. He turned the knob. Locked. He fumbled the key out of his pocket and opened it. Faint gray light from a window showed him he was in the kitchen. The air was stale and smelled faintly of Ursula's perfume.

Where do you keep your address book, Urs? In your study? Probably. Now where would that be?

He decided to start at the top. As quietly as he could, he groped through the dining room and living room, found the carpeted stairs, and went up. Second floor, bedrooms. The doors stood open, except for one. He hesitated, then opened it. Bathroom.

A steep set of hardwood steps led upward, and he climbed them. Pentroom. Ursula's study. It was lighter outside now, easier to see. Hardwood floors, clipped ceiling, white leather sofa, bookshelf, desk, computer. And hands. Michael stopped. A half-dozen sculptured bronze hands in various poses, scattered around the room. He picked one up, studied it, wondering if his sister had modeled for it. It didn't look much like her hand. Unattached body parts made him nervous, and he put it down.

He scanned the room. If the cops had been here, they'd been careful. Everything organized, everything in its place. He wondered what kind of impression Ursula had of him. A slob, probably. A failure. He decided he'd clean up the trailer when he got back.

A blinking light near the phone caught his eye. Of course, her answering machine. Why hadn't he thought of that? He hurried over and pushed the message retrieval button. There was a sound of faint hissing—an open line—then a click. Another open line and another click. Two more clicks sounded before the machine stopped. Hang-up calls.

Michael looked over the bookshelves. Self-help books, how-to-get-rich books, law books, a few computer books. A shelf full of romances. *Really, Urs? Maybe you're still looking for Mr. Right after all.* But no address book.

None on the desk, either. He looked at the computer, wondering if she'd programmed all her addresses into it. She would have done that. Ursula was a believer in technology. Wishing he had enough time to read the manual, he sat down and turned on the computer, then the monitor. That about exhausted his knowledge.

The machine whirred and a series of images flashed across the screen; then the picture settled into a blue field with a dozen or so icons on the left side Now what? He examined them. One was a letter with wings. Was that E-mail? Maybe Ursula had corresponded with Dr. Yates. Worth a try.

He fumbled with the mouse until the little arrow covered the letter. Then he was supposed to click, wasn't he? He did. A series of beeps came from the computer, like a telephone dialing, then a rush of static. A message appeared on the screen: "Welcome to Oracle On-line. Please enter password."

Uh-oh. He thought a moment, then, using his index fingers, typed in: "Ursula."

The words "Invalid password" blinked on and off.

Try her address. He typed it in.

"Invalid password."

He sat staring at the computer. *Think. If I were Ursula Walker, my password would be* . . . He typed in her personalized license plate: "U 2 TOP."

A list of choices appeared on the screen. "Help." "Compose." "Mail Index." "Folders." "Addresses." "Other." "Quit."

"Addresses," that was it. This was easy. The instructions on the screen told him to press "A" on the keyboard, and he did. Her address book appeared, a list of names with strange characters. He glanced down the list for a name he recognized and found one: "bobhoffman32@aol.com." Hoffman was her boss, he knew, but he had no idea what the other characters meant. His optimism evaporated.

He scanned the list for the name Yates, but he didn't see it. No Jocelyn, either. The only other name he recognized was James@probe.net. His brother? He felt his stomach flip. James was a common name, but there was no last name. Could James be eavesdropping on him now? He'd read about computers being hacked into. With a shiver he punched a key. The main menu appeared on-screen again.

He reached up to shut off the computer, then stopped himself. *Don't be paranoid. Even if James was eavesdropping, how could he know who was using the computer? Relax.*

He glanced at the menu again, noticed the "Mail Index" entry and beside it: "Folder Inbox, 3 messages."

He pressed "I" as instructed.

Another list, this one three items long:

N1	Dec 27		(296)	Urgent
N2	Dec 26	Jack Somerset	(723)	What's up?
N3	Dec 26	Ronda Marx	(1569)	Lunch

Urgent? Michael fumbled with the mouse until the little arrow covered "N1." Then he clicked. Text appeared on the screen: "Judah 850, F2F:−<"

Judah. Was that a Bible verse? Had Ursula gotten into some sort of religious study group? She'd never been religious while they were growing up, and he'd seen no sign in the last two weeks that she'd changed her views. What was it then, a message? Some sort of code? The other messages had a sender's name, but this one didn't. Why the anonymity?

He got up and checked the bookshelves for a Bible but found none. He sat down again and stared at the words.

Outside, a car door slammed. Startled, he ran to the window and looked down. Just a neighbor going to work. The man started his car and drove away. Michael scanned the street. In the park the sleeping bags had been rolled up and the men were gone. The dilapidated station wagon was still there, the old woman back behind the wheel.

Speaking into a cellular phone!

His body cold with fear, he ran to the computer and jerked the cord from the wall, then bolted down the stairs. How long would it take for a closer to get here? He'd been in the house a half hour, no longer. But that could have been too long.

He wrenched open the door to the garage and scrambled into the car, punching the door opener. With a squeal of tires he backed out. He threw the Escort into first, expecting the shot from a parked car, a bush. Nothing happened. He hit Masonic doing fifty.

Slow down, he thought. *Don't attract attention*. But now they knew his car, he had to get rid of it.

He drove toward Budget Rent-A-Car. At Haight a white Buick pulled in behind him and he panicked and floored the accelerator. But the Buick turned right on Page and he drew a deep breath, forcing himself to relax and slow down. He reached the car rental agency without anyone following him, as far as he could tell.

Which was small comfort. If they were there, he probably wouldn't know it.

He dropped off the Escort, walked out, and caught a bus, not caring where it was going.

An hour and three transfers later, still on a bus, he finally felt calm enough to think. He considered the message on the computer. Judah? What was that? And the squiggles at the end must mean something, but he had no idea what. He thought of Darby. She was always fooling around with computers; she might know what they meant.

The bus drove past an Avis car rental outlet. He got off at the next stop, walked back to Avis, and rented a brown Chevy Lumina with Ursula's cash. Then he drove to the nearest pay phone and called Etta Snowgrass's number.

13

Inside the U-Haul trailer Darby Mackenzie set a rocking chair upside down on top of the kitchen table; then she stepped out, trying not to show her anger. The few flakes of snow that fell were melting as they hit the ground. "Getting pretty full," she told Etta Snowgrass.

Etta came around the old International pickup, its springs sagging under its load and the weight of the trailer. She had a floor lamp in one hand and an end table under her arm. "Always room for one more thing," she said. She grinned. "We're gonna fill it up, though."

"How can you be so cheerful? Don't you want to kick that jerk's butt?"

"Sure." Etta set the lamp down beside the trailer and peered inside for a place to stash the table. "But it don't help anything. Things are what they are. We've got a place to live; that's what counts."

"I think you should sue him. You had a two-year lease. Saying Clayton isn't keeping the place up. Bull."

Etta spotted an empty niche and stuffed the end table into it. "Waste your life doin' things like that, suin' people."

"It's not fair." Darby began to cry and turned away.

"Oh, honey." Etta gathered her into her plump arms. "We'll be all right. That new place Clayton's uncle found, he says it's got good water. And the house is big."

"I know," Darby squeaked. "But it's clear out in South Dakota. It's just—"

"Here I am thinkin' about us," Etta said, "and you're the one who don't have a place to live. Why don't you come along? You know you're welcome."

"I know. But my business is here. I can't afford to leave it."

Etta gave her a squeeze. "Well, at least you can stay in the house for another few days. Give you a chance to find another place."

"I'll be OK. It's just that I'll miss you. You're my family."

Etta pushed her away and held her at arm's length, giving her a mock frown. "You got another family. Why don't you get back together with him?"

"Because he lies and needs to grow up. Anyway, he didn't want to get married. That's over, Etta."

"Not for him."

"Well, it is for me. Let's not talk about him, OK?"

"Where do you want this?" A fifteen-year-old girl struggled toward them, her arms wrapped halfway around a cardboard box.

"What's in it?" Etta asked.

"I don't know. Kitchen junk."

"Put it down right there. I'll find a place."

The girl, the daughter of Etta's cousin who had committed suicide, tried to ease the box to the ground. The bottom tore and pots clattered out. "Damn it!" She turned and ran toward the house.

"You'll like it there, Mary Horn!" Etta shouted after her. "You'll see!"

"All these kids who need you and you have to baby-sit me," Darby said. "I'm sorry. Let's go bring out that chair."

The screen door slammed and a boy of five ran down the porch steps toward them. "Darbee, you gots a phone call."

"Me? Who is it, Sam?"

"A man." Sam grabbed her hand and began pulling her toward the house. "He says it's urgent. What's that mean?"

"It means 'right now.' Who is it?"

"Don't know."

She let him tug her up the steps into the living room and over to the telephone on the floor. Looking important, he bent over and picked up the receiver with both hands and handed it to her.

"Hello?"

"Darby? This is Mi . . . Matt."

She felt relief mixed with anger, and a half-dozen other emotions she chose not to examine, feelings she could never separate when she talked with her former lover. "What do you want?"

" 'Why, Matt, how nice to hear from you,' " he said. " 'Gee, thanks, Darby. Nice to talk to you, too.' "

Sam was looking up at her, his mouth open. She made a face at him and a shooing motion with her hand. He turned and scampered away. "Knock it off, Cooper. I'm busy. I'm trying to help Etta move."

"Move? What happened?"

"She's been evicted. That jerk Troxel. His kid comes back from the army and wants the farm and all of a sudden Clayton's a lazy Indian who's not keeping the place up. Goddamn you men."

"Whoa, whoa! I didn't do it. And Clayton's a man, too."

"You know what I mean."

"No, I don't. But I don't want to get into that. Where they going?"

"South Dakota. The Badlands."

"South Dakota? As in South Dakota? Why there?"

"Because Clayton's uncle found them a farm there, and this time they're going to buy the land so some landlord can't kick them off again."

"You're not going with them, are you?"

Because she was angry at men in general and at him in particular, she said, "I don't know, maybe."

"What about your business?"

"I can sell it."

"Oh." She could tell he was trying not to sound disappointed. She felt guilty but satisfied she'd scored. "So what do you want?"

"I, uh, have a question for you," he said.

"Make it quick."

"It's about a computer message. I need to know what it means."

"What are you talking about?"

"Well, I saw an E-mail message on this computer and it had some squiggles at the end of it, and I thought you might know what they mean."

He sounded sober. Was this some new line? "How'd you get hold of a computer?"

"Ah, I just thought I should learn about that stuff. So I've been doing some studying."

"Come off it, Matt. You hate computers. And you don't study anything that requires heavy thinking."

"Ouch. Are we out of sorts today?"

"I'm busy. I have better things to do than listen to your bullshit." She started to hang up.

"Wait!"

Her hand paused over the cradle. There was real panic in his voice. Slowly she brought the receiver back to her ear.

"Can you just give me five minutes?" he said. "Is that too much to ask?"

She sighed. "All right, all right. Tell me why you want to know."

"I told you—"

"No, Matt. Either be straight with me for once in your life or I hang up. Right now. You hear me? I'm sick of this." She didn't realize she was shouting until two children appeared in the kitchen doorway, watching her.

For a moment she thought *he* had hung up. Then his voice, faint, said something like, "My sister's been shot."

"What? Ursula? Are you serious?" She was instantly sorry she'd shouted.

"They shot her in her car. It's my fault."

"Oh, Matt! I'm so sorry. Who did? Why?"

"You remember when she called? You brought me the message."

"Of course."

"Well, she was being stalked. She wanted my help. Protection, right? That's a good one. Well, I come down here, she's pregnant. We move into a hotel because these guys know where she lives—"

"What guys?"

"I don't know. That's the thing. I thought I did, but it turns out I don't. I don't have a clue. Anyway, she was being followed, so after she has her baby, we move into a hotel—"

"Ursula had a baby?"

The two kids in the doorway exchanged glances.

"Yeah," Michael said. "The night she picked me up at the airport. We were . . . Well, that's another story. Anyway, she was in the shower in the hotel and some bastard comes right into the room, must have had a key or something, and steals her kid. Can you believe that?"

"Oh, my God, Matt. That's awful. Where were you?"

Silence.

"Matt?"

"You want to know where I was? I was drunk, Darby. I was lying on the sofa in the hotel room, blind, stinking drunk. Hammered. They probably walked right past me. Then when Urs chased them, they shot her. They shot . . ." There was a muffled sob.

She waited, not saying anything, not pushing. Shocked by what he had said and by what he had done—*oh, Matt, how could you?*—

but finding herself relenting a little, too, touched by an emotional nakedness she had never heard in him before, she bit her lip and didn't say anything.

"Well," he finally said with false heartiness, "you wanted to know."

"Is she alive?"

"Barely. She's in a coma. It doesn't look good."

"What about the baby? Have the police found it yet?"

"No."

"That's horrible. Why would anyone do that?"

"I don't know."

"What are you going to do, Matt?"

"Try to make up for blowing it. That's why I'm calling. I found this message on the computer at Ursula's house. I was looking for the address of her technician."

"Her what?"

"Her technician, the one she was seeing at the fertility clinic. About the baby. See, I went to talk to the woman, only she's disappeared. I thought you might—"

"Just a minute, Matt." She glanced at the kids in the doorway and made a writing motion with her hand. The older one disappeared and came back with a pencil and an envelope from an old propane bill. "OK, read it to me," she said into the phone. "I want to write this down."

"All it says is, 'Judah eight-fifty, F-two-F,' and then some squiggles."

Darby scribbled on the back of the envelope. "The 'F-two-F' means face-to-face."

"Face-to-face?"

"Yeah, it means the sender wanted to talk to your sister in person."

"What about the squiggles?"

"What do they look like?"

A woman's voice said, "Please deposit two dollars, eighty-five cents for the next three minutes."

"Damn. Just a minute." Wishing he had a phone card, Michael counted his change on the phone booth shelf, two dollars and ten cents. He stuffed it in the slots, still embarrassed by his breakdown. *Bad form, Michael. Just get through this conversation.*

"Please deposit an additional seventy-five cents," a mechanical voice said.

"Darby, I don't have any more change. I'll have to go get some—"

"Why don't I call you back?" she said.

"Yeah, thanks." He gave her the pay phone number and hung up.

Feeling exposed, he glanced around him. The neighborhood was a seedy street of topless clubs, bars, and pawnshops. Down the sidewalk two shabby men stood talking, occasionally glancing at him.

The phone rang.

He picked up the receiver. "Hello?"

"What do the squiggles look like?" Darby said again.

"They look like a colon, a dash, and that thing like a parenthesis, only pointy."

"Which way is it pointing?"

"It's, um, pointing toward the dash."

"They're called smiley faces, Matt. This one means the sender's very upset."

"Upset. How about the name: Judah? Is it a Bible reference?"

"No. There is no book in the Bible called Judah. Jude and Judith. No Judah."

"Really? How do you know that?"

"Because I had to memorize all that stuff in Sunday school. I hated it. You said this was on your sister's computer?"

"Yeah."

"What was the date of the message?"

"Uh." He thought. "December twenty-seven."

"E-mail can be traced," she said. "That might be why the sender didn't sign his name."

"Well, if it isn't a Bible reference—wait just a second." He laid the receiver down on top of the paper, then ran to the rental car and rummaged in the glove compartment. A map of San Francisco. There should be one . . . aha!

Map in hand, he ran back to the pay phone as a bearded man in a ragged sport coat stopped in front of it, waving a barely legible sign, something about the end of the world. "Repent, sinner!" he shouted at Michael.

"I already have," he said, squeezing past the bearded man to pick up the phone. "Darby?"

"I'm here."

He unfolded the map and scanned the legend. Josiah, Joy, Juan, Juanita—yeah, there it was. What do you know? "That's it!" he said. "There's a Judah Street in San Francisco. Maybe it's an address. Whoever sent the message must have wanted to talk to my sister there."

"That's possible," Darby said.

There was an awkward silence; then she said, "Be careful, Matt, will you?"

"Yeah. Darby?"

"What?"

"Are you really moving to South Dakota?"

She hesitated, then sighed. "No."

14

When James Walker walked at a fairly fast clip, as he was doing now, his left knee clicked. On the sidewalks of Washington, D.C., it wasn't noticeable, but in the lobby of his office building the clicking seemed to reverberate from the marble walls. It annoyed him a little, but his knee had done that since he'd been hit in a football game his senior year in high school, and he'd gotten more or less used to it.

He could remember the game, remember the exact play in fact, when it happened, a fifty-seven-yard run that had started with a shot to the side of the knee by that big clown, what's his name, who had a scholarship to Ohio State, and ended with a touchdown because James had stayed on his feet and kept his legs moving, even though the grinding started about his third step. Put his team up by six and they should have won the game. They hadn't, only because most of the twits on his team weren't willing to give up their bodies.

He stepped into the express elevator. His mother had been at that game, another reason he remembered it. It was the only one she ever came to; said she didn't like football, was afraid he'd get hurt. The door slid shut. Always went to little Michael's science fairs, though. Not that James gave a rip. But it said something about women, didn't it? He punched the button for his penthouse office.

He'd stayed in the game after the injury so his mother wouldn't know he was hurt. His coach knew, though. Took him aside at halftime and told him, "Look, Walker, I know you're hurtin', but we have to win the conference championship. We deserve it. That team is the enemy; get my drift? They'll do anything they can to keep us from gettin' what we deserve. So we have a right to do whatever we can to them. The end justifies the means; remember that. Now, that kid that hit you is their best player. Take him out and we win the game; get my drift? It's payback time."

Fourth quarter, James on defense this time. He smiled, remembering. The big guy swinging wide to set up a block for a screen pass, James working his way behind him, then lowering the hammer, throwing himself at the guy's knees from behind. Cost them fifteen yards for clipping, but it was worth it. Guy never played for Ohio State. Still walked with a cane, James understood.

He whistled softly as he rode up the elevator, reviewing the day's business. The Chicago project—he needed to call Roper, rattle his cage. Those Miami Beach condos—should go down there; he didn't trust that spic construction company he'd been forced to use. All routine business of his cover realty company, smelling only of money.

But there was something worrying at him that wasn't routine, and he finally focused his attention on it. Arm business. Manning. His report was overdue, and James sensed problems. If Michael had been closed, he should have heard.

James had to admit that he'd misjudged Michael. He thought the army had turned him into a conscience-dead killer, the perfect qualification for a closer. But it was obvious now he didn't have the stomach for the work. At first James had considered finding him and talking to him, persuading him to come back. James didn't like the thought of killing family, even a screwup like his brother. But reluctantly he'd decided he had to sacrifice Michael. The people James answered to were intelligent and ruthless, and they didn't tolerate mistakes. And Michael had been one, James had to admit. Anyway, since he had committed himself to the Arm, he'd gained a new family, a family made up of a small number of individuals within the CIA and other agencies of government who felt as he did: that America had lost its way. And they believed, as he did, that it needed stern correction to force it back to the right road.

Now it looked like Manning may have failed to close Michael. James assessed the implications for himself. Not serious, not yet anyway, but it could get serious if Michael wasn't closed soon. James had pulled strings to get his brother the chance in the first place, choosing Miami as the place to set him up because federal prisoners from there would be sent to Oakdale, where a federal judge who believed in the Cause sat on the sentence review board. James's supervisor had opposed bringing Michael on board. If he found out Michael had defected, James himself could be in trouble.

The elevator doors opened into a teak-paneled corridor. On the mahogany doors across the hall, gold lettering said: POTOMAC REAL ESTATE. Putting on his public face, James strode into the suite and gave a cheery greeting to a dozen secretaries at computers.

In front of the door to his office sat an antique desk, almost a barricade. At his approach, Margaret, the private secretary provided by his employers, looked up without a smile.

An antique, too, he thought. *Gray-haired old fossil.* Must have been something in her time, though, judging by that tattoo on her calf she tried to hide with support hose. And she was efficient; he had to admit that.

He paused at her desk and leafed through the pink message slips she handed him. All routine.

"There was also a call from San Francisco," she said. "White line."

He glanced at her, wanting to ask if it was Manning, but they didn't discuss white-line business out here.

"They'll be calling back in five minutes," she said.

He nodded and went into his office.

A mug of Egyptian coffee was steaming on the inlaid desk. He glanced at the brass-bound glass cabinet against the wall, full of artifacts he had personally collected, most of them from sites of his real estate developments. Small printed signs labeled them as Anasazi, Mayan, Greek, and in one case just Ancient. His employers had chosen the decor to add to the cover and he supposed it did make the office look more like a capitalist real estate company, but his own tastes were more ascetic and the office made him a little uncomfortable. Sometimes the whole business of making money made him uncomfortable.

He picked up the mug and stood at the floor-to-ceiling windows, sipping at the coffee and gazing at the city spread out on the horizon, the White House, the Washington Monument, the Potomac River beyond them, a view he normally enjoyed. But this morning the smell of trouble ruined his enjoyment.

The call came in less than five minutes. It rang only on his private phone, and as he picked it up Margaret pulled the massive oak door shut from outside, creating a soundproof chamber.

"Yes?" James said.

A woman's voice said, "San Francisco. Manning is dead."

He knew it. "How?"

"Nine-millimeter in the chest. His body was found on Interstate Two-eighty north of Woodside."

"Suspects?"

"None. No witnesses."

"The target?"

"Arrived as scheduled."

"Where is he now?"

A hesitation. "The sister's house is empty. We've checked all the maternity wards. She was in the university medical center for two nights but was discharged."

"You lost him."

"We think he's still in the city."

James thought. How could a beginner like Michael take out Manning? It surprised him and made him angry as well, partly because good closers were hard to find and expensive to train, but mostly because his brother had beaten one of his best men. James had to remind himself that Michael hadn't beaten him, personally, which would have been unacceptable.

The secure line hummed very faintly as San Francisco waited for instructions.

"You have twenty-four hours to find him," James snapped, and hung up.

He strode to a computer desk on the far side of his office, booted up the computer, and punched in a password, then a second. Then a third, very carefully. If this one were wrong, the entire disk would be erased.

On the screen appeared a file name, Ursula, then a string of numbers. Phone calls made by his sister from her house during the last six months. He scanned the list for a number he'd noticed earlier. There, third from the bottom. When she finally called Michael. December 23 to area code 406. Montana.

James called up another program and ran a search for the prefix and number. A few seconds later the information appeared: "Sweetwater, Montana. Residence. Clayton Snowgrass."

He began to whistle.

•••

Friday, December 29, 9:23 A.M.

Michael discovered that Judah Street was out by Golden Gate Park. He drove slowly west along it, 700 block, 800; there it was: 850 A church? The signboard read: ST. MARGARET OF THE SUNRISE CATHOLIC CHURCH.

He drove past, made a U-turn at the next intersection, and parked across the street from the church. It had to be the place. Whoever had sent the E-mail wanted to talk to Ursula about something face-to-face. Maybe he or she had wanted to meet Ursula here. But why a Catholic church?

Michael studied it, a tan brick building with twin rectangular bell towers. It looked like there was a school playground behind it. A few cars were parked on the street nearby. One of them, a red Subaru station wagon, had a man behind the wheel. Probably waiting for a worshiper, Michael thought.

After a few minutes he shut off the rental car, got out, and walked across the street to the front entrance. He didn't know who he was looking for, and it wasn't likely the person would still be here anyway. But he didn't know what else to do. He tried one of the massive front doors and it opened.

The vestibule smelled like incense and old candle wax. He paused to let his eyes adjust to the gloom, then pushed open a swinging oak door in the front of him and stepped into the sanctuary, easing the door closed behind him. The high-roofed room was mostly empty, with only a handful of people scattered through the pews.

He sat down in an empty pew near the back and scanned the people in the sanctuary. Most of them were women. The only man in the place sat in the back row, staring straight ahead. In a dark suit with his sandy hair buzzed short he looked somehow familiar, but Michael was sure he'd never seen him before. An old woman in black sat in the front pew fingering her rosary beads as she mumbled to herself. A few rows behind her, a trio of stout Hispanic women prayed silently with their eyes closed. At the far end of Michael's pew, in the aisle beneath a stained-glass window of Jesus walking across water to a boat, a woman in a wheelchair sat with her head bowed, also praying. Maybe he should do the same, Michael thought. But he didn't know how, and he wasn't sure whom to pray to anyway.

He waited, hoping something would happen that would give him a clue to the identity of the person who had sent the message to Ursula, but nothing did. Ten minutes passed. Twenty.

He looked at his watch. He was wasting time.

The man in the back pew rose and walked forward to the woman in the wheelchair. He bent forward and murmured, "Time to go, Dr. Yates."

Michael blinked in surprise.

"Five more minutes," the woman said. "Please."

The man reluctantly backed away and sat down.

Michael studied her. She was fifty, maybe, with long gray hair and a strong, almost masculine face that had become too thin.

Michael got up and walked to the end of the pew and sat beside her. Her head was bowed and her lips were moving. A long black coat nearly covered her withered legs.

He said softly, looking at the altar, "Dr. Jocelyn Yates?"

Her back stiffened, but she didn't look at him. She said nothing.

"Dr. Yates," he whispered. "My name is Michael Walker. My sister, Ursula, was your client."

After a moment the woman turned slightly toward him, peering at him with gray eyes that had yellow-green smudges of exhaustion under them. A pair of wire-rimmed glasses hung on a gold chain around her neck, and she put them on to examine him. After a moment she nodded slightly, as if she could see the resemblance, and let them drop again. "Where is she?" she said.

"Ursula was shot. She's in a coma."

The blood drained from her face. "Oh, my God in heaven." She looked away. After a moment, she whispered, "I suspected, when she didn't come. I've been here every day. Did they take the child?"

"Someone did. Who did it? Can you tell me where he is?"

Her shoulders sagged. "That poor baby."

"Why? Who did this?"

She shook her head. "It's too late. There's nothing you can do now."

"My sister's baby has been kidnapped," he whispered angrily. "Don't tell me there's nothing I can do."

"Shhh," Yates said.

"I want to know what's going on."

She hesitated, then fumbled in her purse and drew out a scrap of paper and a pen.

Footsteps came down the aisle behind them. He turned to see the man who'd approached her before hurrying forward.

She scribbled on the paper.

The man reached them and grasped the handles of her wheelchair. "Time to go, Dr. Yates." This time it was a command. He stared at Michael, then turned the wheelchair and pushed it up the aisle.

Michael caught up with him. "This woman was talking to me. If you don't mind, we'd like to finish our conversation. In private."

The man smirked. "Would you now? And who might you be?"

"Please, Mr., uh, Samuels," Yates said to Michael, "I have to go now. We'll finish our talk about angels some other time."

"Do you need help?" Michael said.

"Oh, no. This gentleman is my escort. Please don't interfere."

"Shall I call the cops?"

She made a weak attempt at a laugh. "Of course not. There's no need for that. Now please step aside."

Reluctantly he did.

The muscle wheeled her quickly past him toward the door.

"Where can I reach you?" Michael said.

She glanced back and shook her head, a pleading look in her eyes.

He waited for the vestibule door to close behind them before he followed. He wasn't about to let Yates disappear.

As he started up the aisle, the vestibule door swung open again and a short, bald priest stepped in, scowling. He spotted Michael and steamed toward him. "Is that you making all this noise? I won't have that in the sanctuary."

"Sorry, Father," Michael said. "I ran into someone I know."

"Well, take it outside. There are people trying to pray."

"That's just what I'm doing." He tried to step around the priest but he blocked the aisle.

"Do I know you?"

"No," Michael said. "I'm from out of town."

"From where? Are you Catholic?"

"No. I—"

"What's this?" The priest bent down, then straightened, a scrap of paper in his hand.

The paper Yates wrote on! Michael snatched it from his hand. "Thanks; I dropped that."

"Young man, you are rude."

"I know. Sorry." He stuffed the scrap into his pocket and headed for the door.

As he stepped outside, the red Subaru station wagon pulled away from the curb, Yates sitting in the back.

Michael ran for his car.

He reached it in time to hear air still hissing from his tires.

●●●

Friday, December 29, 11:21 A.M.

On a farm three miles from Marietta, Ohio, Luther Bos looked up from the dead steer as Doc Wilmot's truck turned into his farmyard. With a growing uneasiness, Luther stood and watched as the veterinarian made his way past the house and machine shed toward the feed lot. He'd put off calling the vet as long as could, knowing in his heart this wasn't bloat or scours or any other normal cattle disease. But he was afraid to find out what it was. He spit a stream of tobacco and watched the truck stop.

Old Wilmot got out. "Morning, Luther. That the one?"

Luther nodded and stood aside as the vet hobbled up with his cane and looked down at the steer.

"How long's he been dead?"

"About twenty-four hours."

Wilmot looked at him. "Why'd you wait so long to call me?"

Luther shrugged, uncomfortable. "You know how it is. You get busy. Couldn't do anything for him anyhow, he died that quick."

"How'd he act before he went down?"

"Well . . ." Luther tried to remember. "Nothing real noticeable. I come out to feed him yesterday and he was normal. Come back a couple hours later to fix that waterer and he was down. Died right while I was standing here."

The vet poked the carcass with the end of his cane. He frowned and turned the cane around and hooked a hind leg with the crook. He pulled. The leg bent easily.

"How long you say?"

"Twenty-four hours, Doc."

"Should have rigor mortis by now. Mmp . . . I'm gonna take a blood sample."

Doc Wilmot limped back to the truck and a moment later came back with a syringe and rubber gloves, a white mask over his nose and mouth. He laid the cane down and knelt beside the carcass, his knees cracking, and worked the latex gloves over his roughened fingers. "I don't want you touching this carcass without gloves and a mask; hear me?" His voice was muffled. He jabbed the needle into the skin. A stream of chocolate-dark blood filled the syringe. "Uh-oh."

"What's the matter?"

The vet got to his feet, his forehead wrinkled with worry. "I think you got trouble, Luther."

"What is it?"

"Won't know for sure till I take a peek at this." He eyed the syringe. "But if I'm right . . . There's only one thing I know of will keep an animal from getting rigor. Same thing that turns their blood this color." He glanced at Luther. "You may have anthrax."

For a few seconds, Luther couldn't breathe. He struggled to make his lungs work, but he had forgotten how. His mind worked, though, and while he fought for breath, it calmly calculated that he was finished. The bank would never carry him another year. His farm, his life—gone. Then his lungs started to work again and he drew a quick intake of air.

Doc Wilmot was watching him, sympathy on his face. "We'll have to quarantine you, Luther."

Luther nodded, his face, he hoped, calm. "I expect." He spit.

"Where's the rest of your animals?" The vet looked around.

"I didn't know anything was wrong, Doc. There was no sign at all till this one kneeled over. Saved it back to eat ourselves."

A look of horror was growing on Wilmot's face. "You shipped already?"

Luther nodded again. There was a ringing in his head that wouldn't go away. "Four days ago. Three hundred and forty-eight steers. Can people catch it from the meat?"

"They sure as hell can. It's a nasty way to die. Who'd you sell them to?"

"They've been contracted for a year."

"Who to, Luther?"

"Burger Meister. The hamburger chain."

15

The note said only: "New Jerusalem."

Michael stared at it a long time, knowing what the words meant but not sure how to interpret them. He'd heard Darby use the term. New Jerusalem was the headquarters of the Ringers, the Church of True Atonement. Was Dr. Yates telling him she was going there? Did she have some connection to the kidnapping?

By the time he'd gotten the tires on his rented car repaired, she'd been long gone. He'd driven the streets of San Francisco for a while, illogically hoping to spot the red Subaru that had driven her away from the church. When that didn't work, he'd staked out the church, but she hadn't come back.

Or was she trying to tell him that the cult had taken Ursula's baby?

A bead of sweat trickled down his rib cage. That seemed more likely. Yates didn't want him to follow her, so why would she give him her destination? But if the baby had been taken to New Jerusalem, Michael knew he'd never get him back. And from what he'd heard about the Ringers, he'd die if he tried.

Maybe she was just trying to scare him.

Well, it was working.

Still, if the kid was there—if there was only a chance he could be there—Michael had to try. He couldn't live with himself if he didn't.

Desperately he tried to think of an alternate explanation for the note, but he couldn't. He had to go back to Montana.

On the bus Michael had time to think about a lot of things, including riding on buses, which he hated because they made him feel helpless and exposed. He could have used one of Ursula's credit cards for plane fare, but he suspected the Arm would be watching the airport. Instead, he caught a ride to Oakland with a trucker named Norm, whose wife had just left him and who needed to talk it out.

In Oakland, Michael spent his last ninety dollars on a bus ticket to Sweetwater. If there was any consolation in going to New Jerusalem, he thought as he boarded, it was that James and the Arm wouldn't be looking for him there.

He'd almost rather face them.

He slumped in his seat, his mind churning with questions.

Why had the kidnappers chosen Ursula's child?

When he thought of his sister he felt a stab of guilt for leaving her. He'd gone back to the hospital to say good-bye, but there was little change in her condition and he doubted she heard anything he told her. He worried that the Ringers, or whoever had shot her, would come back to finish the job. But logic told him they wouldn't. Apparently they had what they wanted.

The bus ride was long and during most of it the air outside was smoky and full of ash from the forest fires that were raging from California to Colorado and north into Canada. Behind him the sunset was an open wound between horizon and black sky, and an orange glow grew brighter ahead.

A few miles east of Reno, Nevada, the bus slowed, then stopped.

Michael, on the verge of dozing, jerked awake. Flashlights approached the front of the bus. For a moment panic overtook him. Had they found him? He peered out to see a uniformed highway patrolman in earnest conversation with the driver.

A moment later the driver turned to the passengers. "We have to detour onto Fifty-A. He says there are fires blocking the interstate. Trip's gonna be a few hours longer than planned. Sorry, folks."

In the seat across the aisle a five-year-old girl glanced at her mother. "Mommy, will we be all right?"

"We'll be fine," she said. She glanced at Michael, worried.

He smiled and winked at the girl, echoing her mother's words. He hoped he wasn't lying.

There were no more delays, though, and the bus pulled into Sweetwater at 1:30 Monday morning. It wasn't until Michael got off that he realized he'd spent New Year's Eve on a bus. Whoopee.

The Whoa and Go Café that Rimrock Stage used as a bus stop was closed, the lights dark. Michael was the only passenger to get off, and the new driver, surly because he had to open the luggage compartment, dug out Michael's duffel, threw it on the ground, and drove off without a word.

Grubby and exhausted, he glanced around at the deserted street, wishing his trailer were closer to town. He could call Darby, but he didn't want to wake her and didn't want to expose her to the danger anyway. By now, Arm may have located his trailer and could be waiting for him.

A gust of wind sailed a plastic grocery bag across the street and flattened it against the window of the café. He watched it a moment, then sighed, threw his duffel over his shoulder, and began walking.

●●●

Monday, January 1, 1:45 A.M.

Hoping he wasn't getting cow shit on his new boots, Vic Lopak squatted in the dark and watched a light in the farmhouse. The blue glow of a TV screen was visible through a crack in the curtains. One person inside, as far as he could tell; he could only see a silhouette. Could be a woman, but he hoped it was Michael Walker. Vic wanted to have a little talk with him before he killed him. Why'd he go and leave a great job like this? He was glad the house was a mile away from the nearest neighbor. No one would hear the screams when he had his little New Year's Eve party.

He pushed up the brim of his new Stetson, checked his watch, the luminous dial faintly green in the moonless night. It was time. He was relieved, thinking he'd probably catch his death of pneumonia out here like this. It was the climate change; he always caught a cold when he left Florida. And going from that to this, January in Montana . . . Bar maid last night told him it was the warmest winter on record, people walking around in shirtsleeves. Hell, it was only forty degrees. In a down parka he still felt cold.

He scanned the yard a final time, no one outside, checked for car lights on the country road—none—then stood, stamping blood back into his feet. He walked toward the light.

A half hour later he opened the front door and stepped out onto the porch, light from the living room throwing his shadow in front of him. He left the door open while he checked his hat for blood spatters. He'd taken off his jacket but left his hat on, liking the feel of it. No stains, he saw with relief. Blood was hard to get out, and there'd been a lot of it.

Unfortunately, it wasn't Michael Walker's blood. Some kid named Troxel, claimed not to know Michael Walker or anyone named Matt; he'd just gotten out of the army. And, reluctantly, Lopak had to believe him, because no one lied under that kind of pain. Said the Snowgrass family had lived there, but they'd moved. Didn't know where and didn't care. Just some Indians.

Lopak tugged down the sleeves of his jean jacket and brushed off his new Levi's. Dead guy might be right about that. The Indians didn't figure into this, far as he could see. Walker was probably just using this address. Made sense; moving around like he was, running like a rabbit, he'd need a place to get his messages.

S'OK, Michael. Not this time, but I'll find you.

"Sorry to bother you," he said to the corpse. "Happy New Year."

He switched off the light and locked the door behind him.

•••

Tuesday, January 2, 12:40 P.M.

After he moved his trailer, Michael drove into town for supplies. While he'd been gone, he'd run out of propane. Fortunately, the weather was so warm the pipes hadn't frozen, but the food in the fridge had sprouted molds of interesting colors. Come to think of it, maybe some of those colors had been there before he left.

At Marvin's IGA he charged a can of orange juice, a bag of cat food, and some chili fixings. As he drove to the gas station for propane, he noticed Darby's delivery van parked outside the Whoa and Go. He pulled in behind it.

When she came out few minutes later, an empty caramel roll pan in her hand, he was leaning against her van.

She saw him and stopped, her face lighting up for an instant before the shutters came down. Her expression carefully blank, she walked toward him. "About time. I was going to take that tomcat to the pound today. You're out of cat food."

"Jack can fend for himself," Michael said. "He caught a four-pound trout at the river this morning. How are you?"

"OK." She looked at him, concern showing for a moment in her eyes. "I'm sorry about your sister, Matt. Really. Did you find out anything?"

"Yeah, some. That's what I need to talk to you about. Got time for a cup of coffee?"

She looked at her watch. "I've got a delivery to make in Bozeman. I'll be a couple of hours."

He was tempted to ask if he could ride along, but her tone didn't invite company. "Why don't you come out to the trailer when you're done? I'll cook dinner."

"Chili?"

"How'd you know?"

"That's the only thing you ever cook, Cooper." She hesitated. "All right, sure. I'll be there when I'm done." She opened the van door and put the pan inside.

"I moved the trailer."

"Again? Why?"

"Keeps the bill collectors away." He gave her the new location. "Etta leave yet?" He was reluctant to let Darby go.

"Yeah." She climbed into the van and slammed the door, then rolled down the window. "Kids weren't happy."

"I don't blame them."

"I gotta go." She drove off.

●●●

Tuesday, January 2, 1:25 P.M.

Vic Lopak told the man on the other end of the line, "He's not here. He's in California somewhere." Lopak had learned that in the Stockman's bar, along with the phony name Walker was using, Cooper.

"Not anymore," the man said. "Michael turned in his rental car about forty-eight hours ago. He slipped the tracer, but we think he's headed your way."

Michael. Like the man knew him pretty good. Lopak wondered

what there was between them, if this Michael had screwed up one of his closings. The man seemed obsessed by him. Lopak wondered again who, exactly, he was working for. Not that it mattered, really, but it was interesting to speculate. Judging from the nature of most of his targets, he suspected his employer was part of some secret political organization inside the government. It was clear there was a political agenda. That was OK with Vic. One cause was as good as another as long as he got paid.

"I'll keep an eye out," he said and hung up.

He strolled away from the phone booth, toward his rented Suburban. He could watch the bus depot and bars. Sooner or later, Michael Walker would show up. But Vic was bored with waiting, and he'd learned something else at the Stockman's. Walker, alias Matt Cooper, lived in a trailer. No one seemed to know exactly where he kept it, but it wasn't in town. To pass the time, Vic thought he'd drive over to the forest service office in Livingston, get a map of the campgrounds in the area, then pay them all a visit, one by one. A little western scenery. He thought he'd enjoy that.

He stepped out of the path of an old lady, tipping his hat as he did. This western shit wasn't bad, kind of fun. He'd always imagined himself as a cowboy. He thought, *Hell, they got airports in Montana, too; I could live here as well as anywhere.* Maybe he'd moved out here after he closed Michael Walker. Get himself a horse. He grinned.

16

Michael stuck a candle in an empty Jack Daniel's bottle and put it on the dinette table, then stood back to examine his efforts. *Not bad. Let's see, matches.* He opened the drawer where he kept the matchbox and found a half-full pint of bourbon he'd forgotten to throw away. Holding it up to the light, he looked at it a moment, then, regretting it only a little, poured it down the drain.

A few minutes later Darby's bakery van pulled up outside his trailer. Jack the Ripper, who'd been hanging around just out of reach all day, as if even he had missed company, disappeared through the torn screen door.

"You're right," Michael said. "Stay away from women."

He went to the door and held it open as Darby came up the steps, a ceramic bowl in one hand and a plate wrapped in tinfoil in the other.

"I brought a salad," she said, holding up the bowl. "My diet requires more than meat."

"Hey, chili has beans in it, too. It's nature's most nearly perfect food. What are you keeping under cover there?"

"Cake."

"Not the famous Darby Mackenzie huckleberry chocolate?"

"I had some day-old." She came in and stopped short, gazing around the trailer. "My God. What happened?"

"Well, I freshened the place up a little. Dusted . . . you know."

"So that's what that pickup load was I saw going to the dump."

"Here, let me take that." He took the bowl from her and set it on the table, then put the cake on the counter.

Darby took off her jacket, started to throw it on the chair, stopped, and hung it in the closet.

Michael studied her. In faded jeans and an oversized plaid shirt with the sleeves rolled up she looked wonderful. But then, she'd look wonderful stepping out of a car wreck. His hands were sweating and he felt as nervous as he had the first time they'd made love—the closest thing to an out-of-body experience he'd ever had. He couldn't help it. He loved her. And he knew she loved him; at least she had once. When they'd met their hearts had fused in a rush, like two match heads struck together. He'd also known he couldn't jeopardize her by marrying her. But he couldn't bring himself to leave her, either.

"Isn't that the same outfit you were wearing when we met?" he said.

"I don't want to talk about when we met," she said. "Or where we met, or us at all, OK?" She eyed the candles suspiciously. "This isn't a date, Cooper. You said you had some things to talk about, that's why I'm here. Let's stick to that agenda."

"Whatever you say. Chili's ready." He lifted the pot from the stove, burned his fingers but refused to show it, and set it on the table. Darby dished out the chili and salad. He watched as she tucked her hair behind her ears and bent over her chili, poking through it with a spoon.

"Still inspect your food before you eat it, I see."

"Your trailer was always full of surprises. Besides, haven't you heard about the anthrax in hamburger?"

"Yeah, but they haven't found any in Montana, yet. Anyway, what do you expect to see, poking around with a spoon? If I'm feeding you anthrax-infected meat, you won't know it until it's too late."

"That's comforting."

The propane heater whuffed on, always just short of an explosion. The windows buzzed. Michael tried to think of harmless things to talk about, subjects that wouldn't remind her of the reason she'd left him. "Thanks for bringing the cake," he said.

She shrugged. "It'd just get stale."

"Give me the recipe?"

"Nice try, Cooper."

"I could write and ask Etta. She's the one who gave it to you."

"You've asked her before, remember? She won't tell you."

"I could steal it and sell it for big bucks."

"It's not written down."

"Bamboo shoots under your fingernails might loosen your tongue."

"Stampeding buffalo wouldn't loosen my tongue." She smiled a little and gave him a glance, swiftly withdrawn when she caught herself. "So what did you find out?"

He sighed. "Not much." He ate a spoonful of chili while he thought of how to tell her what he'd learned. "I think I found the person who sent the computer message to Ursula."

"Really? Who was it?"

"A woman by the name of Yates. My sister's fertility technician. A reproductive . . . something."

"Reproductive endocrinologist?"

"Yeah. How'd you know that?"

"I read. Go on."

"Her name is Yates. That's all I know. Except I think now she's been kidnapped herself."

"Another kidnapping?" Darby looked at him skeptically. "Are you making this up?"

"No. Why would I lie about something like that?"

"I don't know, sympathy or something. You've been making up stories ever since we met. You lie, you get fired, you lie about that. There isn't much you won't do, Matt, except tell me the truth. What I don't know is *why* you're saying all this, some kind of new line or what."

Annoyed, he dug his wallet out of his pants pocket. "Yeah, I invented my own sister's coma just to entertain you." He took out a creased copy of the brief newspaper reference to the attack on Ursula and tossed it to her. "Don't flatter yourself."

She read it, then looked up, her eyes troubled. "I'm sorry. I do believe your sister was shot and her baby was stolen."

"Yeah? Well, I also know I was sitting in a church pew with that Yates woman when she wrote me this note." He took the folded paper from his wallet and handed it to Darby.

She unfolded it and looked at it. "New Jerusalem?" Her face went pale. "The Church of True Atonement?"

"I think so. It's their headquarters, isn't it? I think it means either that Yates was going there or that the baby was taken to it."

"That can't be it, Matt. There must be some other explanation."

"What?"

"I don't know. Why would they go around kidnapping babies?"

"They're a religious cult, one of the worst. Who knows what they believe? Maybe they sacrifice children or something. Yates didn't have time to tell me before some muscle came up and wheeled her away. But they have something to do with Ursula and the baby."

"It could mean anything," Darby said. She pushed her plate away, but the look on her face told him she was reluctantly admitting the possibility that what he said was true.

"You know those people. I thought you could tell me about them."

She gave him a frightened look. "Why?"

"Because I'm going to try to get the kid back."

"I knew it." She scraped back her chair and stood. "I knew you'd go and do something stupid."

"Darby, if I hadn't screwed up, they never would have gotten the poor baby in the first place. I'm responsible."

"Then tell the police. Let them get him back." She was trying to keep her voice steady, but he heard the quaver in it. "Or the FBI or somebody. If they did kidnap him, it's a federal matter, isn't it?"

"There's no proof. Who'd believe me? I'm having a hard time getting you to believe me. Ursula can't talk. Yates is gone."

She was silent, her head down, fighting tears. "Don't do it, Matt. OK, I admit it. Those people are bad. I've heard all kinds of stories."

"You do business with them."

"Right. OK." She looked up at him, defiant. "You want me to tell you what I know? They scare me to death, that's what, and all I do is deliver bakery stuff to them. I couldn't make it without their business or I wouldn't do it. Their leader is Mother Mary and she's wacko. She's paranoid; I've talked to her. And I know they have guns at New Jerusalem, up at Heaven's Door, big ones, and worse. They believe the end of the world is coming and they have some plan to deal with it, and they'll take out anybody who gets in their way." She glared at him, her breath coming in small gasps. "Is that enough?"

"I still have to do it." He tried to keep his voice calm.

"Ahhh!" she shouted in exasperation. "You don't hear a thing I say. You never have!"

He looked down at the table. "I hear you," he said quietly. "I know I'll probably die, but I have to do it."

She glared at him a moment longer, then wilted. "All right, do what you have to do. Just don't tell me any more about it."

"What exactly is Heaven's Door?"

She sagged back into her chair. "It's Mother Mary's private

hideout. It's up on a mountain in the middle of their ranch. I can drive through the ranch, New Jerusalem, but at Heaven's Door I have to stop at the gate. They don't let any outsiders in. A guard takes my stuff the rest of the way."

He tried to give her an encouraging smile, but she wouldn't meet his eyes. She stood. "I have to go. I've got to finish a concerto. I've already spent the commission." She took her salad bowl to the sink. "Thanks for dinner."

"Any time."

She grabbed her coat from the closet, the empty hangers clinking in the silence as she put it on. At the door she hesitated. "Matt, look; I'm sorry about what happened in San Francisco. But getting yourself killed won't help the baby."

"I won't get killed," he said, trying to convince himself. "I won't be an outsider. I'll join them."

"Join them? Are you kidding?"

"I'll let myself be recruited. That way I can look around."

She shook her head. "It won't work. They're too paranoid for that."

"Sure, it will. I've seen them try to recruit a lot of people."

"Matt, don't do it. Please."

"It'll be all right. I'm lucky, you know me."

"Yeah. I know you." She turned away and opened the door, but not before he saw tears in her eyes. "That's the problem."

●●●

Wednesday, January 3, 9:18 A.M.

Vic Lopak drove slowly over the road, if you called this a road, that led from the highway to the Yellowstone River. He'd started east of Sweetwater and worked his way west toward town, checking every marked campsite and every unmarked spot he found along the river that could be used as a campsite, anyplace Michael Walker might be hiding. Nothing so far, but Vic knew the guy had to be staying somewhere in the area. He'd find him.

The road wound through a stand of trees, one of those scraggly kinds like cottonwood, and ended at the river's edge. Vic parked the rented Suburban and got out, looking around. A lot of tire tracks. For the middle of winter, the place had been used a lot lately.

Pretending he was a frontier scout looking for Indian sign, he made a circle of the campsite. This western shit was fun. Not far from the river he found a bush with a half-dozen beer can pop-tops hung on it. Whoa, somebody was bored. Near it were deeper tracks, the kind an RV trailer might make. And were those pickup tire tracks? A lot of them, leading to and away from the RV marks.

Is this you, Michael? Was this your last campsite, pardner? He squatted and felt the inside of the most recent tire tracks. *Been here in the last day or two, be my guess. Means you're back. I'm closing in on you, buddy.*

He stood. If Walker had just returned, he'd need groceries, supplies, whatever. A town this size, he'd be easy to spot. Vic thought maybe he'd drive into town.

●●●

Wednesday, January 3, 10:05 A.M.

Michael called the hospital in San Francisco to check on Ursula's condition. There was some improvement, they told him; she was responding to stimuli, and showed signs of regaining consciousness. Encouraged, he drove to the Diamond Years nursing home in Sweetwater.

It was the best place he could think of to let himself be recruited into the Church of True Atonement: The week he'd sold Christmas trees in the lot nearby, he'd seen Ringers go in and out of here every day. They weren't wearing their green robes, but with their shabby clothes and chronic smiles they might as well have been wearing signs. Most of them were children, really, with a terrible vacancy in their eyes. Once he'd stopped a girl and asked her what they did there. She focused on him long enough to say, "We bring cheer and comfort to the residents."

He opened the front door and walked in, waiting for someone to ask him what he wanted, but the overheated lobby was empty and the reception desk vacant. In a lounge off the lobby he could see three old women sitting in front of a television. Two of them were slumped in their wheelchairs, chins touching their chests; the third was staring at a rerun of *I Love Lucy*. From a room somewhere he heard moaning.

He walked down a long hall that smelled of urine and Lysol, past open rooms where old people, mostly women, lay on narrow beds or sat listlessly in Naugahyde chairs. Metal plates that had been slid into brackets on the doors gave their names. Martha Williams. Emby Mott. If he was challenged by any attendants, he thought, he'd tell them he was looking for his grandmother. But he didn't see any attendants.

He passed a room and stopped, then backed up and looked in. A pudgy youth with a Bible sat on the bed talking earnestly to a frail-looking woman who was nearly bald. As Michael watched, the youth patted her on the knee and tapped the Bible with his finger.

Michael ducked into the next room and found himself face-to-face with an ancient woman in a rocking chair. She was creaking back and forth, pushing the chair with a slippered foot that barely reached the floor. Her short white hair, as fine as thistledown, waved gently as she rocked.

Michael said, "Oh, excuse me, Miss, uh, Mrs—"

"Where's your Bible?" she snapped.

"What? Oh, I'm not with them. I just thought you might like a little company."

She stared at him with small, bright eyes. "Carl."

"What?"

"That's my name. Mrs. Charles Carl."

"Interesting name." Michael looked for a place to sit.

"It's a lousy name. I never should have married that old man. How'd you like to be named Mrs. Charles Carl?"

"I wouldn't. Can I sit here?" He pointed to her bed.

She shrugged. "Sit anywhere you want. Who are you?"

"Matt Cooper. I live in town and I just thought . . ."

"What're you after?"

"Nothing."

She stared at him shrewdly and rocked, clutching the arms of her chair with blue-veined hands that shook rhythmically. "You're after something. Nobody comes to see me unless they're after something. Like those Bible pounders."

Michael sat gingerly on the edge of the bed. "What are they after?"

"My money. They can't fool me. They say they're trying to save my soul, but what do they need with my annuity, then? Where's your Bible?"

"I'm not with them." He heard the youth next door reading a Bible verse, his voice loud and hearty. He needed to keep Mrs. Carl talking until the Ringer got to them. "How long have you lived here?"

"Do you really want to know?"

"Sure, Mrs. Carl."

"I should have kept my own name. Back in those days we didn't do that. We couldn't do anything like women can do today."

"What was you maiden name?"

"Mankowski. I got the Parkinson's, you know. That was after

Charlie died. Stroke. I told him, quit smoking, he smoked two packs a day, I told him, you're killing yourself, but he never listened. Men never listen."

"Uh-huh." Michael was trying to overhear the conversation in the next room.

"He drank, too, but not as much as he smoked. Now, I like a beer once in a while, that's a fact, but they won't let us have any in here. Do you drink?"

"Um, once in a while."

"Well, there's nothing wrong with a beer before dinner."

"Did you have any children?" Michael said.

"Hell, yes. My kids stuck me here. They didn't want anything to do with me, too much trouble. Charlie now, he farmed a half-section in Iowa. All he was good at, you see, was farming. Then he got it into his head he wanted to be a rancher, at his age. Can you imagine? He was sixty, no, let's see, sixty-three. So he went and bought that ranch out of Sweetwater. Silliest thing he ever did, a man his age."

She talked while Michael listened and waited. The Ringer next door finished the Bible verses and began praying. His voice grew softer and Michael couldn't hear the words, only a murmur, sounding urgent.

Then the voice said good-bye. A moment later the pudgy youth stuck his head in the doorway. "Mrs. Carl, how are we today? Oh, I didn't know you had company." He had a puffy face and red hair hacked into a crew cut and he wore ankle-length chinos and a checked sport coat that bore stains from the four basic food groups. His bloodshot eyes were always moving, and his smile seemed permanently attached. He couldn't be more than twenty, Michael thought. "I can come back."

"No, no, come on in," Michael said. "We were just visiting."

The young man focused on him for the first time, staring with interest. The smile never wavered. "We meet almost every day to talk about heaven and Satan and doing what's right, don't we, Mrs. Carl?"

"We do not," she said. "You do all the talking. I'm just stuck here, so I have to listen. Besides, I'm Lutheran."

"That doesn't matter. We all need to hear the truth." He came into the room and thrust a freckled white hand toward Michael. "Brother Jeremy."

He stood and shook hands. Brother Jeremy's hand was as soft and puffy as his face. "Matt Cooper. What are you a brother of?"

"The true church. We're all brothers there. Are you interested in the Bible, Mr. Cooper?"

"Oh, a little. I don't know much about it, but since my wife left me, I've been poking around in it a little. I can't make much out of it."

Brother Jeremy beamed at him. "Well, it really takes someone who's studied it all his life to interpret it for you." He was standing closer than Michael found comfortable, refusing to break off eye contact. And he smelled like he hadn't been near a shower in a month. Michael returned his stare.

"Tell you what," Brother Jeremy said. "Since you're interested, you're welcome to sit in on our Bible lesson today. You'll learn a great deal."

"Well . . . You're sure I won't be in the way?"

"Not at all." He sat on the bed and Michael moved over to escape the body odor. Brother Jeremy turned to Mrs. Carl. "Now last week, we were talking about stewardship, do you remember?"

"We were talking about my annuity. At least you were."

The youth glanced at Michael. "No, no, you misunderstood me, Mrs. Carl. I was simply telling you that earthly wealth endangers your soul. As Jesus told his disciples, 'Verily I say unto you that a rich man shall hardly enter into the kingdom of heaven.' But today,

I'd like to talk about something else, the Judgment Day. It's coming soon, Mrs. Carl. We must all be ready."

"Oh, fiddle," she said. "I won't be around to see that. Preachers have been saying that for years. Nobody knows when it is."

"We in the true church do, Mrs. Carl. Holy Mother tells us—"

"Who's Holy Mother?" Michael said.

Brother Jeremy turned to him in surprise. "Holy Mother is Mother Mary Grace, God's only living prophet. God has revealed to her the hidden knowledge of the future."

"Oh."

"Holy Mother tells us that the time is here, the delay is over. Soon, very soon, the living and the dead will be called in front of the throne to be judged. Whoever is not found written in the Book of Life will be cast into the lake of fire."

"Sounds scary," Michael said.

"It's a frightening time, Mr. Cooper."

"So who'll do the judging? Mother Mary?"

Brother Jeremy looked at him, alert for signs of scorn or disbelief. He tried to look earnest.

"God will, of course. But Holy Mother will be at his side to counsel him. Members of the true church will be first in the Book of Life."

"Oh. Well, is it hard to become a member?"

Brother Jeremy's smug smile widened. "It's not easy. 'Many are called, but few are chosen.' A novitiate must be totally committed, willing to give up every part of his Satanic life. But so few people are able to meet Holy Mother's high standards, God allows her to offer a place in the Book of Life to others who are willing to surrender all their worldly goods. As a sign of their sincerity."

"Who do they surrender them to?"

"Holy Mother."

"But I thought worldly possessions prevent you from getting into heaven. Doesn't that apply to Mother Mary?"

He shook his head. "Holy Mother is a saint. She's not tempted by Satanic wealth. Out of the purity of her heart she is willing to bear that burden for you."

Michael nodded. "Very interesting. Listen, I have an appointment, but do you have anything I could take with me to read about your church?"

"Of course." Brother Jeremy dug into the inside pocket of his sport coat and pulled out a slick green brochure titled *First in the Book of life.*

Michael took the brochure and stood. "Maybe I'll see you again."

"I'm here almost every day, Mr. Cooper. If you have any questions, I'm sure I can answer them."

"Will you be all right?" Michael asked Mrs. Carl. He liked the old woman and decided he'd visit her for real when this was all over.

"I can handle him. You get while you can, young man."

That night Michael studied the brochure, which told him only that the Church of True Atonement had been founded on God's command in 1988. Its remaining three pages were devoted to the saintly qualities of Mother Mary Grace and her prophecies of the end of the world.

The next day he found Brother Jeremy in a room with one of the three women he'd first seen in the lobby in front of the television. She was feebly signing some kind of document.

When Jeremy saw Michael he took the paper from her and folded it, then stuck it in his pocket. He smiled. "Well, Mr. Cooper. Did you read our literature?"

"Yeah, I did." He came as close to the Ringer as he could bear to. "I have to admit your Mother Mary seems like a remarkable woman. You know, a lot of these churches, they don't have any firm answers, kind of wishy-washy, you know? But Mother Mary sounds absolutely sure she's found the truth."

"She has."

"Well, I just thought if you didn't mind, I might sit in on another lesson."

Jeremy beamed. "Of course. Have a seat over there. We were just practicing our penmanship."

Yeah, right, Michael thought as he sat on the bed. In her checkbook. He tried to appear interested as Brother Jeremy read from the Book of Revelation. The old woman nodded off in her wheelchair.

The next morning Michael came back again, forcing himself to sit through yet another sermon in another room, this one occupied by an old man who wanted to talk about his daughter, who had moved to Australia. Or Austria; the man wasn't quite sure. Jeremy read a passage about the coming judgment.

"You say this is going to happen soon?" Michael said.

"Very soon."

"When, do you know?"

"Holy Mother does. She'll reveal it to us in due time."

"And we have to be members of your church before we appear in the Book of Life?"

"No. For those who are earnest but unworthy, turning over all of their worldly goods to Holy Mother may be enough."

"But church members are first? They have a better place in heaven?"

"That's true."

"Well . . . See, I'm not rich, but I've got a little money in the bank. I've been working hard for it. I've always thought, that's what it's all about, isn't it? Money. But, hey, money didn't keep my wife from walking out on me, did it? I might be willing to turn it over to Mother Mary, if there's no other way. But . . ." Michael scratched his nose in embarrassment. "I've always liked being first, you know? Um, is there some way I can learn more about this church of yours? Find out if I might be qualified?"

Brother Jeremy studied him, calculating. "Possibly. It depends."

"On what?"

"On your sincerity. There've been a few people who tried to trick us. Like that reporter for the *Los Angeles Times*. He lied to us, tried to join us under a fake name. All he wanted was a story. When she found out who he really was, Holy Mother was very upset. She prayed for God to punish him and he did. God killed him in a car accident a few months later."

Michael felt a sudden chill. "Well, I'm no reporter. I'm not even sure about joining you yet, but I'd like to learn more, if I could. But I don't want to cause any trouble."

Brother Jeremy thought a minute, then nodded. "Listen; we're having a retreat this weekend. My brothers and I have invited a few people who want to learn the truth. If you're really interested, you can join us for the weekend."

"Where's it going to be?"

"At New Jerusalem."

"Where's that?"

"Our little ranch in the country."

Michael pretended to hesitate, then said, "OK, sure. Why not?"

"Good. I'll pick you up at your house Saturday morning about ten."

"No, I, um, live out of town. Why don't I meet you in front of the bakery?"

"All right."

As he walked back to his pickup, Michael thought, *See, Darb? Nothing to it.* So why were his knees trembling like a flashlight in a dark cellar?

17

When the call came from Nestor Pruitt, the acting director of the Task Force for Disaster Control, Annie Soares was in the kitchen having a second cup of coffee while she waited for her ten-year-old son, Nicky, to dress for his soccer game. Zach, the seventeen-year-old, was still in bed.

As she sipped her coffee, she kept one ear on the radio for news. Dead fish had started to drift into shore in a number of places along the Florida coast. So far, disposal crews had been able to keep up with the mess, and it hadn't caused any disease outbreaks yet. But if the mass of rotting fish became great enough, that could happen. And the stench would be overpowering. The spokesperson for the task force had warned people that evacuation might become necessary.

Carmela, her housekeeper, answered the phone. Annie thought she knew what the call was about—she'd been studying the reports on the fish kills, and her misgivings had deepened.

When Carmela gave her the phone, Nestor said, "I need you to come back."

"Back? When?"

Nicky appeared in a red-and-white uniform with MICRONIX COMPUTERS on the back of his shirt. "Mom, I'm ready."

"Right away," Nestor said.

"No, I'm sorry, Mr. Pruitt. I can't. I have a family to take care of."

"Well, bring 'em along. I'm moving you up to Atlanta. I want you to be liaison between my task force and the Centers for Disease Control."

"I'm not an epidemiologist, Mr. Pruitt. Get someone from inside the CDC."

"Heck, those people are the reason I need you, Annie. Translate all that scientific jargon for me. You're the only Ph.D. I've ever been able to understand."

"I can't move the kids now. They're in the middle of a school year."

"Then we'll pay for someone to look after 'em. Your country needs you, Annie. The CDC's stretched to the breaking point. They tell me they're looking at more outbreaks than they've ever seen. Latest thing, they got this outbreak of anthrax; you been reading about that? Fourteen states, thirty-four hunnert people so far, you should see the pictures. Big ugly welts on the skin, with blisters. Then there's the hepatitis B epidemic in half a dozen cities from the water. You got that virus that causes blindness, cytomegalovirus—did I say that right? Used to affect mostly HIV-positives, but now it's spread. And some kind of mutant strain of cholera in Central America. There's food poisonings in New Jersey and New York from E. coli; there's a new kind of flu in China, Bolivian hemorrhagic fever—Annie, the list goes on and on. I need to know what's in all those reports, and you're the one can explain them to me. So I'm drafting you, honey. As of today you're attached to the CDC as my personal liaison."

She looked down at Nicky, his face beginning to fall. Why couldn't the world leave them alone for just a week?

Nestor said into the silence, "We all have families, Annie. Unless we stop these diseases there might not be a world for them to grow up in."

Damn it! "Well," she said reluctantly, "I suppose I could talk to my boss and see if I could get a few months' leave."

"I already called him. Says if we need you, he'll give you as much time as you need."

Thanks a lot. She sighed. "All right. I'll talk to my sons and fly up to Atlanta Monday."

Nicky turned away.

She hung up and tried to tousle his hair, but he broke away and ran down the hall to his room and slammed his door. She gave him a minute and then tapped on the door. No answer.

She tried the knob, but the door was locked. "Sweetie?"

Still no answer, but a few moments later the lock clicked. She opened the door and went to the bed where he was sitting. She took him in her arms and held him, comforting her son with inadequate words.

●●●

Saturday, January 6, 9:45 A.M.

Darby stood behind the display case in her bakery listening to one of her customers, Mrs. Pittman, tell about her son in Chicago, who'd gotten hepatitis from drinking the tap water. "When my Jake was alive," she was saying, "and we used to travel? Why, we used to feel so sorry for people in all those third world countries because you couldn't drink their water, do you remember, dear? Now we can't drink the water in our own cities. It's just terrible."

Darby wasn't listening, because through the front window she was watching Matt Cooper walking toward the bakery. What in the world did he want? "That's good," she said to Mrs. Pittman.

"Good? Are you listening to me, dear?"

"Hm? Oh, I'm sorry. It *is* terrible about your son." Cooper was carrying his duffel bag. Where was he going now? And why was he walking?

"It destroys your liver, you know," Mrs. Pittman said.

"I know. It's awful," Darby said.

Cooper stopped in front of the bakery, his back to her. She turned her attention back to Mrs. Pittman in case he looked in the window. What was he doing, leaving town? The bus stop was at the other end of Yellowstone Avenue. Then it dawned on her. The Ringer ranch. Jeez, was that where he was going?. *Oh, my God, Matt. Don't do it.* She had to go talk to him again, try to persuade him not to. Glancing out the window, she quickly untied her apron.

At that moment the man who'd been looking at bagels sauntered over to her. Not local, she could tell. A dude with a barrel chest who looked like he worked out a lot. Brand-new cowboy hat and boots. " 'Scuse me, miss." Smiling and waiting patiently.

"Well, I told him not to move to Chicago," Mrs. Pittman said as she turned away. She looked at the man. "You just can't live in cities anymore."

He smiled at her and tipped his hat. "No, ma'am."

"Can I help you?" Darby said.

"I hope so." His eyes ran down her body as far as he could see from the other side of the counter, then back up to her chest. "I'm looking for a man named Cooper. That ring a bell with you?"

She stared at him, wondering what Matt had done now. "Matt Cooper?"

"That's right." His smile widened. "You know him, then?"

"I know him. What's he done?"

"Not a thing. See, I'm a cattle buyer and my car broke down over on the interstate a few weeks ago? This guy, he said his name was Matt Cooper, I didn't get an address, he was kind enough to stop and give me a ride into Bozeman. And while I was waiting for my rig to be towed in, we had a few beers, you know, while we watched a football game. Colorado–Nebraska. Well, we made a little bet on it and he won. I owe him fifty bucks. I didn't have the cash then, but I always like to pay my debts. But, see, I forgot to ask him for his address; all's I know he lives in Sweetwater. About my height, little younger, sandy hair, likes to wear it a little long."

She opened her mouth to tell him Matt was standing right outside but stopped. All her internal warning signs were going off. Something didn't sound right . . . A football bet? That was it! Matt never made bets, not even for fun. She'd teased him about it once, and he'd been embarrassed, mumbled something about always losing bets to his brother when they were kids.

Besides, this man was no cattle buyer. He looked like he wouldn't know an Angus from an antelope.

"Yeah, I think I know who you mean," she said, going slow now, thinking it out as she spoke. Matt might be a jerk sometimes, but she didn't want this guy to find him.

"Where might I locate him?" The smile continued.

"Last I heard, he'd gone to California. For the winter I think."

"California." He nodded thoughtfully. "Whereabouts, you know?"

"No. I'm sorry." *Get the hell out of here, Cooper.*

"Any chance he could have come back, last day or two?"

"Not that I know of."

"Where does he live when he's in town, if I might ask?"

"That I don't know. Sorry." *LEAVE, damn you, Cooper!*

The stranger held her gaze. She felt like a rabbit in front of a cobra.

"Well, thanks, miss. Anyone else in town who might know?"

"Um, you might try Bruce Walden over at the bank." Doubting very much he would know Matt, who never dealt with bankers. "He knows pretty much everyone in town."

"Much obliged." Trying to sound western. Western New Jersey, maybe.

He touched his hat brim and turned away.

Darby looked out the window. Matt was still there, slouched against a lamp post, whistling. She had to stall this guy. "Listen; why don't you let me make a few calls?" she said. "Maybe I can locate him for you. Would you like a bagel while you wait?"

The man glanced out the window and stopped. "Oh, never mind, miss. I think I see him now." He turned and winked at her and walked toward the door.

18

Lopak opened the door of the bakery, his eyes on the back of Michael Walker's head. *Bang, Walker, you're dead.* He thought he'd do it right now, get it over with. Driving a rented car, with a fake I.D., no way they could trace him even if someone saw him.

He glanced up and down the street. Deserted. No, a couple of ranchers standing on the other side of that pickup truck, talking about the weather or some stupid thing. But they couldn't see him do it. Only witness might be that girl in the store. She knew more about Walker than she'd told him anyway. He might have to pay her another visit.

As he stepped onto the sidewalk he slipped his hand inside his coat, felt the crosshatched grip of his Wilson's Stealth. Walker turned and saw him and nodded but stopped whistling.

A yellow school bus full of people wheeled around the corner and rumbled toward them. Vic glanced at it, then sauntered past Michael Walker, returning the nod.

The school bus pulled up to the curb with a screech of brakes and the doors swung open. The words CHURCH OF TRUE ATONE-MENT were hand-painted in black on the side.

Vic kept walking, but out of the corner of his eye he saw Walker pick up his duffel and climb on the bus. *What's this? You got religion, pardner?*

Well, whatever. He'd follow the bus—hell, he could follow it on foot, be more of a challenge—and his chance would come. He'd seen Michael Walker in person now and knew he wouldn't be a problem. Vic had a hard time believing the guy had been a closer.

And after he closed Walker, Vic decided he'd pay another visit to the girl. The next one would be more fun.

Michael climbed the steps of the school bus as Brother Jeremy, who was driving, greeted him with a calculating smile on his puffy, freckled face. "Good morning, Matthew. Welcome aboard." He looked at Michael's duffel. "You have your sleeping bag in there?"

"Yep."

"Good. Stuff it under the seat and let's go, then. We've got so much to do this weekend!"

The duffel was only half-full and went under the seat easily. Michael had packed light, as if he were only planning to spend the weekend. He knew he probably should have brought a different bag, but he liked the duffel. It made him think of the one trip he'd taken with Darby, a flight to Portland to see Powell's, the world's largest bookstore, the destination being her idea. He'd taken the duffel. She'd carried a suitcase with a dirty sock sticking out of it. She always did that, she said; it kept her suitcase from being stolen.

There were a half-dozen other guests on the bus, most of them young, most of them looking lost. Probably students from Montana State University in Bozeman. Beside each guest sat a Ringer, each one wearing poorly fitting clothes and the same idiotic smile as Brother Jeremy.

Jeremy closed the doors. "Off we go. We have so much to do. You're on the inside track now for heaven."

As the bus pulled away from the curb, Michael glanced at the bakery. Darby was probably in there. He should have stepped inside to tell her where he was going, but he knew she would have argued with him. Still, part of him had hoped she'd see him and come outside. He should have at least left her a note. Well, it was too late now.

He wondered who the man who'd come out of the store was, maybe the lawyer he'd heard Darby was seeing. No, the guy didn't look like a lawyer. Something about him made the hairs on Michael's neck stand on end. He knew he'd been careless. He'd have to watch his back more closely.

The bus rattled through town, across the I-90 overpass, and headed south into the Boulder River valley, sun-bleached and snowless.

"I'm so glad you could join us, Matthew," Brother Jeremy said, his smiley face showing in the rearview mirror. "I'm sure you'll have the same reaction I did. As soon as I heard Mother Mary speak, I knew I was hearing the truth for the first time in my life. Then, when I came to a weekend retreat, I felt, well, just vibrations of love everywhere. Don't you feel it?"

"Uh-huh," Michael said.

Across the aisle sat a white-haired man about sixty years old, easily the oldest person on the bus. Michael nodded at him and the man smiled sadly. "My wife died," he said.

"I'm sorry."

"We were married forty years."

The man's escort, a tall, skinny youth with acne, tapped him on the shoulder and shook his head. "Sorry. No communicating with other guests. We need your full attention."

"C'mon, everybody; we're going to sing a song!" Brother Jeremy shouted. " 'Row, Row, Row Your Boat,' come on now; sing." And he led off in a loud off-key voice. "Row, row, row your boat, gently down the stream. . . ."

The cult members on the bus joined in loudly, and so did a few of the guests. Michael smiled, glancing at the man across the aisle, but the man was singing and didn't notice.

"I don't hear you, Matthew!" Brother Jeremy shouted. "You're not singing. Satan lurks in slacking minds. Come on now; sing!"

Michael began mumbling the words. He knew the purpose of

the singing was to instill obedience, to condition the guests to respond to the authority of cult members.

"That's right, that's right," Jeremy crowed. "You have a wonderful voice. Louder now."

After twenty minutes of "Row, Row, Row Your Boat," Jeremy launched into "My Bonnie Lies over the Ocean." Michael fell silent, but Brother Jeremy noticed immediately. "You're not siiiinging," he warbled.

Michael sang, thinking, *This is what it must be like to be in hell with Richard Simmons.*

They careened along a blacktop of crumbling asphalt and potholes, the bus bouncing and jostling the passengers against each other. Michael hung onto his seat.

Between songs, Brother Jeremy told them how lucky they were to be allowed a chance to visit the true church; that they were special, better than the unbelieving masses; and that if they worked hard this weekend and obeyed their guides, they might be allowed to stay another week, maybe even to join, to take their places in the Book of Life.

One hour and ten children's songs later, they slowed and turned off onto a gravel lane that sloped down toward the Boulder River. Around them mountains rose steeply. On both sides of the road ran a chain-link fence eight feet high.

The bus stopped at a locked gate.

A man in a white robe sauntered out of a tiny guardhouse and fumbled with the lock. He swung open the gate, and Brother Jeremy drove through with a wave.

"Welcome to New Jerusalem!" Jeremy shouted to the guests.

Beside the river sprawled a cluster of wooden barracks, all the same size, most of them dilapidated. Michael had heard that the Ringers were rich, but if so, they weren't spending their money here. Near the barracks were garden plots, fallow now in winter. Pairs of robed members walked quickly between the buildings.

There seemed to be three colors of robes, white, brown, and green, and Michael wondered what they signified. He looked for women carrying babies but saw none.

As they neared the barracks, a man wearing a crimson robe trimmed with purple drove past in an open Jeep. For the first time Brother Jeremy's smile faltered, and he pulled the bus as far to the side of the road as possible.

A few minutes later the bus squealed to a stop in front of an unpainted barracks. Jeremy set the brake, opened the doors, and stood, turning to the guests with his fixed grin. "Your host will show you where to bunk. Hurry and spread out your bedroll and then meet back here. We have so much to do this weekend, and so little time. Hurry now."

"Why do you have a fence around your ranch?" Michael said.

Jeremy shrugged. "We just like to be left alone. See that building over there?" He pointed to a huge log lodge with a spire on top. "That's Holy House. If we're lucky, Mother might let us show it to you this weekend."

He beckoned to them and clambered down the steps. Michael picked up his duffel and followed the others.

The air was cold and felt good on his face after the stale air of the bus. As he stepped onto the frozen ground he looked around. If Ursula's baby was here, where would he be? There didn't seem to be any private houses. A nursery, then? He didn't see anything that looked like a nursery, but it was impossible to tell from the outsides of the buildings.

He followed the other guests into one of the barracks. The inside smelled like old wood and unwashed bodies. At the far end Jeremy stood waiting.

"We'll bunk here," he said. "Just spread your bag on the floor anywhere."

"We?"

"Oh, yes, I'll be sleeping beside you."

"Great."

Michael watched as guests were told where to sleep, girls at one end, boys at the other. Beside each guest was a cult member.

"Hurry," Jeremy said. "No gawking. There's too much to do."

"No bunks?"

"Sleeping on the floor is good for you. It builds character."

"I think I've got all the character I can stand."

Brother Jeremy frowned at him. "Satan lurks in slacking bodies, Matthew. If you're serious about joining us, you'll have to learn that."

"Sorry," he said. He unrolled his sleeping bag.

The grin returned. "That's the spirit. We'll have you on the inside track in no time. All right, everybody." He stepped over to a small table and picked up a stack of papers and a bunch of stubby pencils. "Fill out one of these forms, that's it." He handed one to Michael. "Be sure and answer all the questions."

Michael began to fill out the questionnaire. "*Full name:* Matthew Cooper. *Address:* None at present time. *Place of birth:*" He wrote: "Duluth, Minnesota." He had chosen the name from Duluth court records, after he fled Denver. The real Matthew Cooper, he'd gathered, was a construction worker who had skipped town to avoid summons in a divorce case. "*Have you ever been arrested?*" He wrote: "No." "*Church preference:* None. *Bank Accounts:*"

"Wait a minute," he said. "Bank accounts?"

Brother Jeremy nodded. "Checking and savings."

"Isn't that rather personal?"

"We have no secrets from each other, Matthew. But if you'd rather not tell us, you don't have to. Of course, if you hope to become a brother, we expect complete openness."

On the theory that bank accounts would make him easier to trace, Michael kept none. However, he'd told Jeremy he had money. He wrote in the name of a bank he remembered seeing in

Duluth, Minnesota, inventing a savings account in the amount of $38,000.

"OK, everybody," Jeremy said when he'd collected all the questionnaires. "Time for the lecture. Follow me."

Michael fell in with the rest of the guests as they trooped over to another building. The robed drones he passed didn't meet his eye. None of them carried a baby.

The room they entered had metal folding chairs lined up facing a wooden lectern and a blackboard. Brother Jeremy motioned him to sit in the front row, then sat beside him.

When they were all seated, a side door opened and a small man in a business suit entered, blinking.

Brother Jeremy stood. "Brothers and sisters in God and honored guests, this morning we have a special treat. Our very own adviser to Mother Mary Grace herself has agreed to speak to us. Please welcome Dr. Salway."

The man walked to the lectern and climbed up on a wooden box. Even with the help of the box, Michael could barely see Salway's head over the top. *He looks harmless enough,* he thought, *but this is going to be boring.* He sighed and slouched in his chair, then caught himself and sat up again.

"Man has to suffer," Salway said, staring at his audience. "Man has to pay indemnity in penance for Adam's fall. And how is this indemnity paid? By hard work, discipline, and punishment. By suffering."

Suffering? Indemnity? Michael glanced around at the other guests. Most of their faces showed confusion. Wondering what they had gotten into. But a few of them were nodding in agreement.

"If you have an injury," Salway said, "or are hurt through punishment, it is because of your sins. God is giving you a chance to suffer as indemnity. But all the work you will do, all of your suffering, will add up, and when enough indemnity has been paid, we will be free. These are the last days."

He paused, then added softly, "You are fortunate indeed, for you are among the last outsiders who will have a chance to join the chosen. Very soon we shall have no further need to seek out new members. They will come to us. They will beseech us. They will be turned away. Even among you, I'm afraid, most will be turned away, for only a few of you will possess the dedication, the willingness, to put your Satanic existences behind you. And only those we accept will be certain of a place in heaven."

So that was it, Michael thought. Shrewd. Instead of the hard sell, make them want to get in by making the cult exclusive. A few good men and all that.

Salway glanced over the crowd, his expression impassive, bored. His eyes, cold and gray, flicked across Michael, paused, came back, then rested on him a moment, looking puzzled. *Uh-oh.* Michael lowered his eyes. Had Salway recognized him? Impossible. How could he?

Then Salway began to speak again. "There is only Mother Mary Grace," he said, "and Satan. And nothing in between. All worldly things are Satan's works."

His voice droned on and Michael raised his eyes to study him. He'd never seen the man before. Salway paid no further attention to Michael, and finally he relaxed. When the lecture was over, the man walked out without another word.

Brother Jeremy stood. "All right, everybody, time for discussion groups. Follow your guide."

"Where's the john?" Michael said, following him out.

"Can't you wait? We don't want you to miss this, it's very important."

"So's my bladder."

With a sigh, Jeremy swerved toward the first barracks. "I'll show you."

He led Michael into a latrine with a row of sinks beneath stainless-steel mirrors, a trough urinal, and a half-dozen stalls.

"Thanks," Michael said, expecting him to leave.

But Jeremy followed him to the urinal, keeping up a constant chatter as Michael peed. In front of one of the stalls, another cult member stood, chatting to someone inside. As Michael zipped and turned, the Ringer by the stall looked at his watch. "Five minutes," he announced to the person inside. "Time's up."

Brother Jeremy took Michael by the arm. "Hurry. We're late."

The guests who had come with him on the bus, together with their escorts, were sitting in a circle on the grass outside the barracks. The tall, acne-scarred youth, who had been introduced as Brother David, was saying, "Now, who took something away from that wonderful lecture to remember?" He looked at Michael. "Matthew?"

"Uh, suffering is good for us."

"Great, Matthew."

"What did he mean when he said we're the last recruits?"

Brother David stared at him. "That will be explained later. Anything else good to say? No? Well, keep trying. Anyone else?"

He went around the circle, cajoling, browbeating, repeating statements Salway had made during the lecture. A few of the guests asked questions, which were deflected or met with frowns of disapproval.

Finally Brother Jeremy sang out, "Lunchtime, everybody," and the group got to their feet.

Lunch was a peanut-butter-and-jelly sandwich, chocolate milk, and a Hostess Ding Dong for each person. Michael recognized the food for what it was, part of the brainwashing technique he'd learned about in the army—altering nutrition and sleep patterns to cause exhaustion and lower intellectual and emotional resistance.

"Any meat?" he asked.

"We don't eat anything with eyes, except potatoes," Jeremy told him.

As he ate, Michael thought hard. He needed to get into the other buildings. A brown-robed girl mechanically sweeping the floor of the lunchroom gave him an idea. "Say, Brother Jeremy," he said. "Do good works earn points toward heaven?"

"Oh, yes. If they're the right works."

"Like sweeping and cleaning?"

"Of course."

"Then I'd like to volunteer to clean the buildings."

Jeremy looked at him in surprise, peanut butter on his cheek. "That's good of you, Matthew, but right now it's more important to concentrate on your training. Later, perhaps, you can join the cleaning crew." He pushed back his chair and stood. "All right, everybody, it's game time."

In an open space outside the lunchroom, he said, "We're going to play Simon Says. Line up."

Michael lined up with the rest, forced himself to play the game, and managed to go out in the first round.

After Simon Says they played Hokey Pokey. Children's games, Michael thought, designed to make the recruit surrender control for five minutes at a time, then twenty minutes. Then permanently. Foolishness with a deadly purpose.

"You put your right foot in, you put your right foot out . . ."

After the game came another lecture by Salway, who droned on about Satan. He didn't look at Michael.

Following dinner—carrots and cooked spinach—came another indoctrination session, which lasted until nearly midnight. Guests who disagreed with the lectures were snubbed and ridiculed.

Finally, exhausted, they were allowed to go to bed.

Michael lay on the floor in the dim moonlight that filtered through the dusty window, ignoring the mumbling of Brother Jeremy, who was kneeling on his sleeping bag. He thought about the baby, wondering if he was even here. Maybe it was a wild-goose chase. He decided to wait until Jeremy was asleep, then have a look around.

A few minutes later, snores replaced Jeremy's mumbling and Michael slipped from his sleeping bag. As he stood, the door at the far end of the barracks opened, and he scrambled back into his bag. A white-robed figure stepped in and walked slowly down the rows of bodies. Michael closed his eyes, listening to the footsteps draw closer, pass him, then turn and go back the way they had come. He waited for the door to open again and the figure to leave, but nothing happened. He opened his eyes a slit. The figure was standing in front of the door, facing them. Holding an assault rifle.

19

Unable to sleep, Darby stood at the keyboard in her new apartment above the Ben Franklin store, surrounded by boxes she hadn't had time to unpack. The concerto was frustrating her. It was supposed to be in F major but instead kept modulating, like her thoughts, to minor keys. She finally swiped her fingers down the keyboard and turned away.

She wandered to the dusty window and gazed down onto Yellowstone Avenue, dark now except for a handful of street lamps. Her real problem wasn't the concerto, she realized. It was Matt Cooper. She was worried about him. Her stomach felt like a rag being wrung, and that made her angry at him. He wasn't her responsibility—he'd made that clear when he refused to marry her. In hurt and anger she'd moved out of his trailer and vowed to get on with her life. The trouble was, he wouldn't stay out of it.

Did she really want him to? *Of course, why wouldn't I? He's secretive, a slob, can't keep a job* . . . *What in the world did I see in him?* She went back to the keyboard and tried a few experimental runs. He was just a mistake, she told herself, one of those things she'd regret for the rest of her life. And she knew about mistakes; she'd made enough of them, running away from Cedar City, Iowa, to LA, seventeen, sick to death of parents, sick of church three times a week, of Bible lessons, of no movies, no dancing . . . no life.

She turned up the volume, hoping to drown out the memories. Freedom in California, she could taste it. Fame, writing music for movie soundtracks, stepping out of a long black limo in dark glasses at a premiere.

She gave a short laugh. Freedom? Two years on the streets was a kind of freedom, she supposed, if you could stomach the filth, the men who always wanted . . . Her hands came down on the keyboard, sending a crashing dissonant chord echoing through the building.

She didn't need the aggravation, damn it. She'd escaped the streets, hitchhiked to Santa Barbara, and started a new life. A good life—at least it could be. She had talent, she knew that, and now a commission from a real orchestra. It was a start. She could be somebody. She didn't need some jerk messing it up for her.

The trouble was, she . . . loved him. Damn it, somehow Matthew Cooper managed to be greater than the sum of his parts. And right now, she was worried sick about him. Most of the townspeople regarded the Church of True Atonement as just a bunch of harmless nuts wanting to be left alone, but she'd seen enough of them to know better. She regretted now getting involved with them. When Mother Mary had called her and offered her a good income to move to Montana and bake for them, she'd ignored the warnings her gut was sending her. All she had to do was deliver some of her products to New Jerusalem every week. So what was wrong with that? The Ringers bought things from other businesses, didn't they? What did their religious beliefs matter? And the money would let her devote more time to her music. She had said yes.

But then she began to learn about them firsthand. She hadn't realized they'd search her van when she entered the ranch. OK, they were a little paranoid, but she could live with that. But the guards, where did they get those people? Dachau? They treated her as if she were some kind of vermin. She started hearing rumors of people disappearing up there, of caches of high-tech weapons, but she didn't believe them until the day she followed a semi truck up the mountain to Heaven's Door. When the semi stopped at the gate, the rear door opened and two guards jumped out, pulling the door closed behind them. But not before Darby had seen what was inside, a huge gun of some kind. These people weren't a little paranoid. They were seriously paranoid. They were dangerous. And Matt was in the middle of them.

She kicked a box of books, thinking, *I can't afford to lose their business, and furthermore* . . .

Oh, shut up, Darby, she told herself angrily. *If Matt has the guts to go into the ranch alone and try to get the baby back, why can't you help? You go up there every week anyway.*

She sighed and drew the cover over her keyboard. OK, her next delivery was Monday, day after tomorrow. She'd do what she could to look for Matt. And she'd keep an eye out for the baby.

•••

Sunday, January 7, 5:30 A.M.

Michael was shaken awake by Jeremy. "Rise and shine. Lots to do today. Satan never sleeps."

He crawled out of his bag, looking for the man with the assault rifle, but he was gone. In the men's latrine Michael splashed cold water on his face and brushed his teeth as Jeremy did the same beside him. On his other side a chubby young man named Kevin stared glumly at the sink.

"Hey, last day," Michael said to him.

"Guests are not allowed to talk to each other," Kevin's escort said.

The day was a repeat of the day before, except that instead of Hokey Pokey, they played kickball with shifting sides and no apparent rules. Guests who committed some unknown infraction were shouted at and made to sit down, then, five minutes later, urged to get back in the game. Between games Michael looked for a chance to sneak away by himself to look for the baby, but he was never left alone.

After one of the lectures, Michael asked Brother Jeremy if he ever really thought about what Salway was saying.

Jeremy looked horrified. "Oh, no. You have to turn off your Satanic mind. Stay in the spirit."

"Oh." A few minutes later, he said, "I don't see any children. Are married couples allowed to join? Just in case my wife comes back to me."

"Oh, yes. But they sleep separately. Sex is the work of Satan. And children are raised by the church."

"Where?"

Jeremy looked at him. "You mustn't worry about it. If you need to know, you'll be told," and he began to chant, "When you think, think, think, then you stink, stink, stink, and you sink, sink, sink."

•••

Monday, January 8, 5:30 A.M.

Michael got up and began to roll up his sleeping bag, going through the motions of preparing to leave. He'd been told the bus would arrive at eight to take him home and he found himself worrying he might actually have to leave, although he suspected the cult wouldn't dismiss a potential recruit that easily. Even those with no money were useful. There was always a need for cheap labor.

As he tied his sleeping bag, Brother Jeremy squatted down and slapped him on the shoulder. "Matthew, congratulations! I've been talking with Brother John, our novitiate trainer. He agrees with me that you've done especially well this weekend and that you've earned the right to stay a whole week. You're on the inside track for a place in the Book of Life, one of the chosen few. I'm so proud of you!" He beamed at Michael, then leaned closer. "We're having a special workshop this week for the few who've been chosen. Shall I tell Brother John you'll stay?"

He pretended to think it over. Around him, other cult members were giving the same good news to their guests. "Well, I don't know," he said.

"C'mon; we have something really, really special planned for this week, and Dr. Salway will answer all those questions you had. You're a novitiate now. Don't throw away all your progress. What do you say?"

Michael smiled. "I suppose I could stay another week."

"Great!" Brother Jeremy beamed. "I'm so happy. We'll really strike Satan."

Near the front of the barracks, Kevin, the pudgy kid, was arguing heatedly with his escort. The cult member beckoned to Brother Jeremy, who hurried over and joined in the argument, backing Kevin into a corner. Kevin began to cry.

Michael watched a moment, then went over to them. "If he wants to leave, let him go home."

"No talking between guests," Jeremy snapped. "Please wait over there."

"You want to leave, Kevin?" Michael said.

The boy nodded.

Michael took him by the arm. "Why don't you wait out front? I'm sure the bus will be along in a few minutes to pick you up." He steered Kevin toward the door. "We'll get your stuff later."

Jeremy changed tactics instantly. "Of course you can leave, Kevin. We just wanted to make sure you know what you're going to be missing." He followed them out. "I'll contact you next week.

Maybe you can come back sometime." He glared at Michael.

Michael watched the bus pull up and Kevin get on, looking relieved. As it drove away he thought of the guard with the assault rifle and wondered if he'd have another chance, himself, to leave.

20

Monday, January 8, 8:00 A.M.

In Atlanta, the Centers for Disease Control and Prevention were in major-crisis operating mode. The director, Arnold Gehring, reluctantly gave Annie Soares a tiny office in a basement. He told her bluntly that, as far as he was concerned, the task force was a waste of taxpayers' money. He had no use for Nestor Pruitt, whom he considered to be a political hack, and she should stay out of his scientists' hair.

So much for my country needing me, she thought as she booted up her notebook computer. Well, she'd review the data, give Nestor a plain English summary of current disease outbreaks, then go home.

She had to admit, though, that the job had its intriguing aspects. The rash of cytomegalovirus blindness, for example. Always before the virus had attacked only people whose immune systems were weakened, mostly HIV-positives. Why had it suddenly spread to the general population?

There was a new theory among some microbiologists, who felt that microbes didn't mutate randomly at all. Instead, they sensed a threat in the form of, say, penicillin and mutated in a specific, directed way. They actually ordered their DNA to become immune to the penicillin.

If that theory was true, she wondered, how long would it be

before some brand-new, even more dangerous microbe would emerge to challenge the human race? Six billion humans, all interconnected through the global village. A microbe's promised land.

She picked up a report from the top of the stack. The epidemic of drinking water contaminations. It had happened in seven different cities now, including Boston, New York, and Chicago. Emergency room capacities had been overloaded to the breaking point. Hospitals in all seven of the cities were turning away patients. At first sabotage had been suspected. It seemed just too coincidental that so many water supplies would be contaminated within a few weeks of one another. But the origins of the still-unidentified contaminations were not the water-treatment plants—the natural targets of saboteurs. The ominous thing was that most of the water-treatment facilities affected were state-of-the-art, with the right amounts of chlorine, the water passed through efficient filtration systems and kept moving at a rate that made it impossible for sporulated bacteria to form colonies. Yet they had failed to prevent the outbreaks.

She made a quick trip to the coffee room for hot water, which was tested twice daily for contamination, and then dug a box of chamomile tea from her purse. Dipping the tea bag in the water, she stared at the stacks of computer printouts and reports. This could take a while. She sighed and set to work.

•••

Thursday, January 11, 5:30 A.M.

As he'd done every day that week, Brother Jeremy shook Michael awake. "Rise and shine, Brother. Busy day today. We'll get so much done."

"Get so much done," Michael mumbled, crawling from his sleeping bag. His week at the Ringer ranch had become a blur, filled with lectures, indoctrination sessions, and games. The busy-work that occupied every waking minute, coupled with lack of sleep and the poor, sugary food, had made it increasingly hard to concentrate. He had to force himself to stay alert.

"Strike Satan," Brother Jeremy said cheerfully, moving down the row of sleeping novitiates.

"Strike Satan," Michael said as he scrambled to get dressed and added a muttered, "Yeah, right." He grabbed a brown robe from the communal pile. Brown was for novitiates, he'd discovered; full members wore green. White robes were worn by Mother Mary's Holy Guards.

"Why does she need guards?" he'd asked.

Jeremy looked at him sadly. "Matthew, Matthew. The world is full of enemies of the truth. You must learn that. Satan has forces constantly at work against us. We have to protect ourselves."

"Do they carry weapons?"

"Hurry now. No time for questions." And Jeremy had rushed off to the next lecture.

Michael splashed cold water on his face, which cleared his head a little, and shaved. He still hadn't located the nursery, but yesterday he'd seen a woman carrying a bundle he was sure was a baby. Although he hadn't been able to follow her, he'd marked the building she'd gone into. Sooner or later he'd get a chance to look. He finished shaving and followed the others out.

After a breakfast of granola and chocolate milk and the morning discussion session, the novitiates lined up outside the barracks.

"Great news this morning," Brother Jeremy said. "Holy Mother herself is going to give an important speech. The whole world will see and hear her on television, so we have to build a big stage over in that field for her speech. We'll start by carrying lumber. Ready? Let's begin now."

With the other novitiates, Michael trooped over to a stack of lumber and picked up two heavy planks, hurried with them out to the field and dropped them, then hurried back for more. Like the rest, he fell into a rhythm: stoop, lift, carry, drop, run. Mindless work at a frantic pace. Some of the members began to chant to themselves, "Help me, Mother; help me, Mary; help me, Mother; help me Mary." As the energy of the sugary breakfast wore off and his underlying exhaustion surfaced, Michael found himself silently chanting his own mantra, *Remember the baby; remember the baby.*

On the fourth trip, he had hoisted two planks and turned away from the pile when boards clattered behind him. Brother Jeremy shrieked.

Michael turned to see him writhing on the ground, holding his foot. He dropped his load and ran to him. "Let me help you."

Jeremy broke into a smile. "God has given me a chance to suffer. Thank you, Lord." With Michael's help he struggled to his feet.

"You need to have that looked at," Michael said. "Where's the infirmary?"

"Over there." He gestured vaguely and tried to stand, but grimaced in pain.

"I'll help you."

They set off, Jeremy hopping one-legged, his arm around Michael's shoulder. Behind them the others kept working, their chanting a little louder.

The infirmary occupied a single room in the end of a building indistinguishable from the other barracks. For equipment it held two beds and a desk. Behind the desk sat a white-haired woman in a green robe, who stood with a frown as they came in.

"What's the problem, Brother?"

"God is permitting me to suffer, Sister Hester," Jeremy said. But his smile was drooping and beads of sweat had broken out on his forehead.

"Who are you?" Sister Hester asked Michael.

"Matthew is a novitiate," Jeremy said as Michael eased him onto one of the beds.

"I'll handle this," Hester said brusquely. "You get back to work."

"Yes, Sister." Michael backed out the door, closing it behind him.

Already conditioned, he found himself hurrying back toward the job site before he realized that, for the first time, he was alone. He slowed his pace and glanced around. The few cult members in sight were paying no attention to him. He stopped. Where had he seen the woman carrying the baby? *Over there, going into that building.*

He turned and hurried off toward the building, trying to look like he was on cult business.

But when he got there he wasn't sure it was the right one. It was one of a dozen long, single-story barracks, all unpainted. He hesitated, then opened the door and went inside.

It was a deserted sleeping barracks. Rows of sleeping bags were rolled up along the walls.

He stepped out the door and stood a moment, trying to orient himself. The woman had gone into a building in this area, he was certain. If not this one, then . . . that one over there? He strode toward it.

At the door he listened a moment but heard nothing. Opening it, he found himself in a storeroom crammed with cardboard wardrobe boxes. A narrow aisle led through the room to another door.

On the other side of the door a baby was crying.

He walked past the boxes, put his ear to the door, and listened. No adult voices, only the sound of the baby. He hesitated, then opened the door a crack and peered through.

It was a long room with wooden cribs along one wall and small metal beds along the other. All the beds were empty and neatly made, but in several of the cribs babies were sleeping. A tiny baby with wispy blond hair was crying in the crib nearest to him. He saw no one else.

He stepped inside and checked the first crib, but it was obvious the blond baby wasn't Ursula's. He bent over the next crib, but the infant in it wasn't the right one, either. The third was empty. Quickly he moved from crib to crib.

Ursula's baby wasn't here.

He paused, wondering what to do next. The door nearest him opened, and a young woman in a green robe stepped in, smiling, Eyes like Bambi, he thought, but there wasn't a lot there.

When she saw him her smile disappeared. "What are you doing in here?"

"I, uh, got lost. My guide, Brother Jeremy, dropped a board on his foot. I took him to the infirmary and made a wrong turn, I guess, coming back. I came in here for directions."

"This isn't the infirmary."

"I can see that. I'm new here. I just got lost. Can you tell me where Barracks D is?"

"That way." She eyed him skeptically. "What's your name?"

"Matthew. I've only been here a week."

"It's against the rules to be alone."

"I know that. Like I said, my guide—"

"I'll have to report you."

"Please. I've worked so hard this week to become a brother. If I'm expelled, I don't know what I'll do. Can't you overlook this one mistake?"

She looked horrified. "Rules must be obeyed. You should know that by now. Satan loves for us to break them, but he can't tempt me. If you ask me to break a rule, I have to report that, too."

Michael stared at her, knowing anything he said would only make things worse. "You're right, Sister. I'm sorry."

As he walked away from the nursery, he glanced back to see the girl hurrying toward the administration building.

21

Dr. David Cisneros whistled as he pedaled his bicycle down Main Street of Indian Springs, New Mexico. Any time he biked the two miles from his house to his office without seeing a single tourist, as he'd done this morning, it put him in a good mood. He waved to Mrs. Hougen walking toward the café. Used to be you only had to put up with tourists a few months out of the year. Now it was pretty much all year round.

Although he'd had to live in Chicago while he finished his medical training, he'd moved back to his hometown because he couldn't stand crowds. They seemed to be following him, though, city people who had discovered the clean desert air and the trout streams of the Sangre de Cristo Mountains. Commuting to town he'd begun, almost unconsciously, to count out-of-state license plates, his mood by the time he'd reached his office depending on the tally. This morning it was zero, only locals on the street, most of them parked in front of the café.

Was there something going on? Oh, right, the town meeting about the new sewer plant. He'd forgotten. Feeling only a momentary twinge of guilt for not being there, he launched into a whistled version of Mozart's Divertimento in D, only to let it die as he spotted a green Honda parked down the street from the café.

California plates. Rats. Still, one wasn't bad. He could live with that.

David banked around the corner and pedaled up Salazar. A block farther on he heard a pop behind him, a pistol maybe, or a firecracker. He quit pedaling and coasted to a stop, looking back toward Main Street, curious, wondering if it was worth turning around to check out, then decided it wasn't. Probably just a car backfiring. There, it did it again, over by the school. Well, if anyone was hurt, he'd hear about it soon enough. He rode on.

In front of a one-story adobe building with his name on the window in black letters—the DR. a little larger than the rest of his name—he got off and guided his bike into the rack on the sidewalk, feeling pleased he didn't have to lock it, not in Indian Springs, not yet. He went into his office.

Except for his nurse-receptionist, who was polishing her nails, the office was empty.

"Morning, Bobbi," he said, encouraged. A good day, for sure. Might even get to that *New England Journal of Medicine* article he'd been intending to read, a discussion of cytomegalovirus. His brow furrowed as he thought about it. A particularly nasty virus that caused blindness. Up to now it had been seen only in people with immune system deficiencies, but it seemed to have spread to the general population. There had already been three cases reported in Albuquerque and one in Santa Fe. His mood serious now, he went to his office in search of the journal.

Two hours later he'd finished the article and given Mrs. Ramirez an insurance physical and was pouring himself a third cup of coffee when the phone rang. He heard Bobbi answer it, and a moment later she stuck her head around the door. "It's Dolores down at the café. She seems pretty excited."

He picked up the receiver. "Morning, Dolores."

"Doc, we got a problem here. You know old man Loftus, lives

out toward the canyon? Well, he's collapsed. He was just sitting here having coffee and then he said he didn't feel so good. I gave him an aspirin and that didn't help and he started to leave, but then he started coughing up blood."

"What'd you put in the coffee, Dolores?" David instantly regretted the joke. "Can he walk?"

"Hell, no, Doc; he's laying on the floor. We didn't know if we should move him or not. He's breathing real rough. You want to come over and take a look?"

"Better bring him up here. I've got all my stuff here. Get a couple of men to help." He hung up, thinking, *possibly pneumonia, maybe influenza; it hits old-timers like Loftus hard.* Although there hadn't been much flu in the area this winter. He wished again there was a real hospital in Indian Springs instead of the four-bed clinic attached to his office.

A few minutes later the door burst open and two men shouldered their way in, carrying a grizzled old rancher with a three-day growth of beard. The man in front, Ed Peralta from the hardware store, wheezed, "Damn, Doc, I wish to hell you made house calls."

"Bring him in here." David led the way into a room with a high hospital bed. "Start an IV, Bobbi. Let's get some fluids into him."

They arranged the rancher on the bed. His eyes were wide with fear and he labored for breath, his lungs making sucking, gasping sounds. Acute Respiratory Distress Syndrome. "Let's get him on oxygen."

As his nurse scrambled to set up the oxygen tent, David opened Loftus's jacket and shirt and held a stethoscope to his bare chest. The lungs were filling with fluid. Lobar pneumonia then, maybe.

"How do you feel, Mr. Loftus?"

"Lousy," the old man said weakly. A trickle of blood emerged from his nose.

"Can you describe it?"

Loftus whispered something that David didn't catch. He bent toward his mouth to listen. "...pink smoke, and then..." The old man coughed, spewing blood and green mucus into David's face.

Alarmed, the doctor jerked back, grabbed a paper towel, and wiped his face. This wasn't pneumonia. He had to get Loftus to Santa Fe. He went to the phone and dialed the hospital in Santa Fe and asked for a helicopter, then strode back to Loftus.

One of the men watching coughed. David glanced up to see him grab his chest, gulping for air, then stagger over to a chair. "Doc?"

"Help me get him into the other room," he said to Peralta.

This man was a lot heavier than Loftus, and it took all they had to get him into the second room and onto the bed.

"Bobbi," David shouted, "get me—"

The phone rang.

"Never mind; I'll get it." Maybe this was hantavirus; it attacked the lungs. But this seemed a lot more virulent. He briefly considered cytomegalovirus but dismissed it. This was much worse. He checked Loftus. The old man's eyes were closed, and the gasping had stopped. David put two fingers on the neck, checking the carotid artery for a pulse. None. He lifted an eyelid. Pupil dilated.

Loftus was dead.

Bobbi hurried into the room. "Mr. Atwood's on the phone. Two kids collapsed on the playground. He wants to know what to do. And Mr. Peralta in the waiting room says he doesn't feel well." Her voice trembled. "What do you think it is?"

"I don't know." It didn't act like anything he'd ever seen. And it worked incredibly quickly, quicker than anything he'd seen. "I don't think it's a disease. No disease progresses this fast. Must be some kind of poisoning."

He thought a moment, staring at the syringe in his hand, then went into his office and sat down at his desk. He flipped through his Rolodex, got a number, and dialed the New Mexico Department of Health in Santa Fe. When a doctor came on the line he told him who he was.

"We've got some kind of an epidemic on our hands," he said. "Poison gas, maybe, although it acts like it's infectious." He described the situation. "Get a team up here ASAP."

The doctor on the other end told David he'd get on it immediately. David hung up and called the New Mexico state medical examiner and told him the same thing.

When he was finished, he pushed back his chair and went into the waiting room, filling now with townspeople coughing and gasping for breath. Some of their noses ran with green mucus; some coughed up blood. Some were bleeding from their noses and ears. All of them looked at him with fear.

"Help us, Doctor," a woman said. "What's happening?"

"I don't know." David's head had begun to ache. His hands were sweaty, and his body was cold with fear. "I've called the state health authorities. They're sending help."

He made his way back to the room where he'd left the second man who'd gotten sick. He was dead! How could that be? Too quickly, too quickly. No time for treatment.

Bobbi stood in the hallway, biting her lip and crying.

"Go home," he said. "There's nothing you can do here. Go home and stay there."

She nodded and hurried to collect her coat.

He felt feverish now and his muscles were aching, as if he were catching the flu. But his lungs were starting to feel dry and irritated and it was painful to breathe.

He went back to the waiting room to try to calm his patients. Several dozen people crowded into the room now, coughing, some of them lying on the floor or sprawled against the wall. Many were children.

When they saw him a chorus of voices shouted for his attention. "Help is on the way," he said. He realized there was nothing he could do, nothing else he could say to give them encouragement.

He went back to his desk. A part of his mind calmly observed his symptoms, and he made notes on a yellow pad. He coughed, then coughed again. He gasped for air. Hard to breathe. His lungs must be filling. Holding his hand over his mouth, he coughed hard and felt something warm and sticky on his hand. He looked down to see blood ooze through his fingers and drip on the desk.

He kept making notes of his symptoms until he was too dizzy and weak to write. Then, feeling as if he were walking underwater, he made his way to the couch and lay down and closed his eyes.

•••

Thursday, January 11, 11:46 A.M.

In the restaurant of the Holiday Inn in Bozeman, Montana, Vic Lopak drank his orange juice and watched the local television news crew, two men and a woman, finish breakfast. There should have been one more at the table, he knew, but the fourth crew person, the sound engineer, wouldn't be going out to cover that nutball religious woman's speech today. Right now he'd be in bed in his motel room, Vic suspected, with his knees drawn up to his chin. Between quick trips to the toilet.

As Vic watched, a waitress brought the woman a Styrofoam cup of coffee; then they all pushed back their chairs, gathered coats, and walked out of the restaurant. Through the window he watched them climb into the van with KCTZ painted on the side.

He sneezed, pulled a Kleenex from the small box he carried with him, and blew his nose, thinking he should be in bed himself; his head felt like a balloon. Colds weren't something to fool around with. His mother believed in raw onions for a cold and she was right about most things, but he knew the only way to get rid of a cold was to take lots of vitamin C and get plenty of rest. Which he intended to do as soon as he finished his closing. The cold was Walker's fault, making him wait around outside that ranch house the other night. He'd pay for it, though.

As the news van pulled out of the parking lot and turned toward Interstate 90, Vic stepped outside. He waited, giving them a twenty-minute lead—he knew where they were going—then drove onto the interstate and turned east, toward Sweetwater. *Damn, let's get some heat in here.* He flipped the fan to high.

An hour later he turned onto a two-lane road that soon became gravel and arrowed south into a mountain valley. OK, time for the Superman-in-the-phone-booth act. He pulled into a deserted ranch lane and stopped the rented Suburban. From the equipment bag beside him he dug out two magnetic bright red-and-blue KCTZ logos he'd made last night, and got out. He wiped the front doors with a wad of tissues, pressed the logos onto the doors, and drove back to the road.

Let's see; check the time—no problem there. Sneezing, he groped for a Kleenex. The Suburban hit a pothole and bounced. *Damn!*

Twenty miles later a sign by the road said: NEW JERUSALEM and Vic slowed and turned. Ahead of him was a gate with a guard post, and in front of the gate a car was being searched by three guards in white robes. He stopped. A few minutes later one of the guards signaled the gatehouse and the gate swung open.

The huge guard sauntered up to Vic's car.

Vic rolled down his window. "KCTZ News."

"Step out of the car, please."

Vic got out and looked up at him. Football player, he guessed. Linebacker, probably. The guard reached past him, plucked the keys from the ignition, and threw them to another white robe, who keyed open the trunk and lifted the lid while the third, his head shaved smooth, opened the passenger door and began rummaging through Vic's equipment bag.

"Who you say you're with?" the first one said.

"KCTZ News."

"KCTZ is inside already."

"That's the transmitter van. I'm John Clark, sound engineer."

"Why aren't you with them?"

Vic bent over and sneezed, then straightened. "Sorry. Just isn't room in the van for four." He blew his nose. "See all the equipment? Getting so automated they probably won't even need me, another year or two."

"ID."

Vic handed him the fake driver's license he'd made. The guard inspected it, looked at a list of names on a clipboard, and checked off the name John Clark. "Turn around and raise your hands."

When he did, the guard—on second thought he was too big for a linebacker, more likely a defensive tackle—ran his hands over Vic's body quickly and expertly, then watched as baldy ransacked the equipment bag, pulling out spare batteries, audio connectors and adapters, rolls of solder, and tools, tossing them onto the floor.

"Hey, hey, be careful with that stuff. Christ, I'll never find anything now."

"You watch your mouth," the tackle said.

The third guard finished with the trunk and joined in the trashing of the equipment bag. He turned it upside down and shook out the remaining contents.

"Shit," Vic said.

"One more word of profanity and you're staying out here; got it?"

"Yeah, yeah."

The bald guard tossed the bag back onto the seat, slammed the door shut, and nodded at the football player.

He handed Vic a pamphlet titled *First in the Book of Life.*

"Here's some literature you should read. Learn the truth." He turned and signaled the guardhouse, and the gate swung slowly open.

"Stay on the main road until you reach the parking area. If you enter a restricted zone you'll be evicted. Have a nice day."

"Thanks," Vic muttered as he got in. "I intend to."

The road led him between empty fields toward a steep wall of mountain. Dust ticked the windshield. A mile inside the gate another white-rober stood on the road, and Vic followed his directions, turning into a field covered with stubble like a military haircut. Twin tracks had been ground to dust by traffic. Other guards directed him to a parking space in the fourth row of cars.

He shut off the car, leaned over, and sorted through the tools and equipment strewn on the floor, looking for one adapter plug in particular, the two-and-a-half-inch Cable Craft; where was it?

He grabbed the bag and shook it, fighting down anxiety—he needed that plug—then found it under the seat where it had rolled. He picked it up with a grunt, then waited while another car parked beside him and the occupants, a Livingston radio crew according to the sign on their car, got out and hurried toward a huge stage erected in the middle of the field.

Vic unscrewed the plug end from the body of the adapter, took out the tiny needle inside it to make sure it hadn't been bent, being careful not to prick his finger on the tip, replaced it, inspected the firing mechanism and the CO_2 cartridge, and breathed a small sigh of relief.

He reassembled the adapter, put it in his Levi's pocket, got out, and headed for a line of portable toilets. When he found an empty one he went inside and locked the door, wondering when was the last time this thing had been cleaned out, thankful now he had a cold so he couldn't smell anything.

He shrugged out of his parka, ripped open the lining, and pulled out a thin green robe, knowing he'd catch pneumonia run-

ning around in this thing all day with no coat, Jesus, deciding he
didn't want to move to Montana; there must be warmer western
states. Why couldn't he have gotten a closing in Texas? Tore off
his tie but decided to leave his sport coat on—he needed *some*
warmth—then pulled the robe over his head and settled it into
place. Polyester, so the wrinkles weren't too bad, the green of the
robe more vivid in the weird green light in the Sani-Can. Then,
really regretting it, he crammed the parka through the toilet hole
into the sewage well and watched it slowly sink, weighted by the
solder and tools in the pockets.

Vic shivered, checked his watch, and peered out the screened
vent. A half hour till Mother Mary's speech. The believers were
beginning to assemble. He remembered his watch. He didn't know
if Ringers wore them, but to be safe he took it off and threw it
after the parka.

Time to mingle.

22

Mother Mary Grace stood with her head bowed and her eyes closed, waiting at the back of the platform. She listened to the murmuring of the crowd, five thousand strong, every single one of the faithful who lived inside New Jerusalem and many followers who had driven or flown in from other states to hear the news. The rest of her flock in California would be watching on television, because the speech would be beamed to them on cable. Somewhere near the media stand a cameraman was complaining loudly as he jostled for position. Around her she felt the comforting presence of her Holy Guards as they shielded her from the view of the masses.

"Two minutes, Holy Mother," an adviser's voice said softly in her ear.

She breathed deeply to calm herself, but it was wrong; she could feel it. He wasn't there, not in the secret listening part of her mind, and she knew she couldn't face the crowd, the reporters, without his presence. She sent a silent inquiry, *Are you there?*, but there was only emptiness.

"One minute," the adviser said.

Come to me, she thought. *Come . . .*

"Wait," she said. "I can't . . ."

"Time. You're on."

But she remained unmoving, head bowed, eyes closed. The time had been when she had heard many voices, felt many spirits inside her mind, long ago when she had been only Paula Sue Tulley. No longer. They had all gone away, gone for—how long had it been now, twelve years? Driven out by him, the strong voice, the angry voice, the one. It was he who had given her the idea of founding the Church of True Atonement, who infused her with the power to succeed. He was all she needed now.

Please, she thought, *don't do this to me. Come to me; you know I need you. I need your strength, your power; I need . . .*

And he was there. She felt him instantly, her voice of power. She felt his strength, his constant anger, his contempt for her, for everyone. But she felt something else as well. She opened her eyes in surprise. Petulance. He was sulking, like a child.

What's wrong? she thought, closing her eyes again.

The answer came strongly into her mind. *The baby. Why do you need him? Haven't I always been enough? Haven't I achieved power and wealth for you? Rid yourself of him.*

She felt her adviser's hand on her elbow, trying to move her forward. "Time, Mother."

"Let me go," she commanded and shook her arm free.

You are the one, she thought, *the only one. To you I owe everything. But the child was your idea, and think how much more we can do now that we have him. Now we have only a few thousand at our command. With him we will have millions. He means nothing, only a tool provided by science, a power you've always told me to use.*

He is nothing, came the silent answer. *He is a worm.*

He's a worm, she agreed. *But with him we will rule, you and I. Be my strength and to you only will I pray.*

Yes, came the answer, *you will pray to me. And when he has served his purpose, you will kill him.*

She hesitated and felt him recede from her mind, then in panic agreed. *Yes, I will kill him. He means nothing to me. Please.*

She felt the change in him, not a diminishing of the contempt or the anger; those were always present. But the resistance was gone and in its place the familiar, empowering will that drove her.

"Yes," she whispered, "yes. Thank you."

She opened her eyes and lifted her head, nodded at the man glancing anxiously from his watch to her and back again. He blew out his breath in relief and strode to the battery of microphones. The murmur of the crowd instantly ceased.

"Brothers and sisters in God," he said. His amplified voice bounced off the barracks a hundred yards behind the crowd and returned in a hollow echo. "Ladies and gentlemen of the media, viewers throughout America and the world, welcome to this very special telecast of the Church of True Atonement 'World of Power.'"

Mother Mary took a step forward and waited as the lights found her, lights tinted in warm shades to give life to her pale skin. This was what it was about; this was her purpose, proof that she was special. Her mind seemed to fly out above the crowd, looking back down on her body, as it often did when she spoke in public. She saw herself as others saw her and was not displeased. Tall, a commanding figure, eyes set wide apart, wide mouth, nose a little too thick and long, but strong, a face that looked younger than her forty-two years, the whole impression one of strength and command.

"And now," the announcer said, "I give you our revered leader, the prophet and living saint, Mother Mary Grace."

Vic Lopak stood at the edge of the crowd, keeping his eyes on Michael Walker. He'd spotted him right away, no problem. Walker'd been up on the platform before the speech or sermon or whatever it was, with another stooge, straightening the purple carpet that the broad was standing on now. But Vic had stayed away from him, making sure the guy didn't see him.

He took his eyes off Michael for a minute—he wasn't going anywhere—and out of curiosity watched the woman, Mother Mary or whatever she called herself. She was gazing out at the crowd, ignoring the television cameras, lifting her head to look at . . . something. He turned to look; must be the mountains. Then she brought her attention back to the front row, to a kid, a little girl who was being held up on the shoulders of her old man. The woman stooped and took the girl's head in her hands and kissed the top of it.

The crowd applauded. Vic snorted.

Mother Mary straightened, raised her hands for silence, and got it right away. Now that was power.

She said, "Let the little children come to me and forbid them not." She smiled. "Good people, brothers and sisters in God, keepers of the Book of Life. Thank you for coming. Today I have a very special thing to share with you, for today we are all as little children, watching the dawning of a new day and the ending of the old age of corruption and evil."

The crowd so quiet you could hear a pin drop.

OK, she was good; Vic had to admit that. Not bad-looking, either, from back here, but he'd bet she was older than she said. Good scam. But he was cold and it was time to close old Michael. Vic started to inch his way through the crowd, keeping one ear on what the old broad had to say. Just out of curiosity.

"Two years ago," she said, her words bouncing in quick echo off the buildings, "on this very day, I was walking in my garden by the stream, feeling disconsolate, for in spite of all my work, all of our efforts together, I had been unable to bring much of the world to see the truth of our way, the wisdom of the teachings of the Master Spirits, of Solomon, Socrates, Plato, Magnus Apollo, and the others."

Vic stepped on some guy's toes and muttered, " 'Scuse me; coming through." Smiling, thinking, *Must hurt like hell, cowboy boots on sandals and bare feet.*

"And while I was kneeling there in the garden seeking guidance," Mother Mary said, "God himself descended from heaven through the Holy Spirit and, in a ray of blinding light, spoke to me. So great was the force of that light I was struck dumb and blind and could only listen."

Yeah, she had them now, Vic could see. He glanced at Michael to make sure he hadn't moved. Schmuck was still there, staring up at her like the rest of the sheep.

Mother Mary paused a moment before she continued. "God spoke to me. He said, 'Behold I come as a thief in the night.' He told me the end is at hand. Judgment Day is near. And God informed me of the exact day, a day coming very soon, but he instructed me not to disclose it."

A murmur from the crowd.

Yeah, Vic thought, *the end is near, Michael. Can you feel it?*

"But I can tell you that it will come . . ."—Mother Mary lowered her voice—"this very year."

There were gasps. A shocked silence.

Now she glanced at the television cameras. "I sense there are doubters among us," she said, "doubters, too, watching this holy word on television." She smiled at the cameras and spoke directly to them now. "I do not fault you for that. Many times charlatans have threatened you with the end of the world and nothing has happened. Many predicted the end would come with the dawning of the year 2000. They were false prophets, and you were wise not to believe them."

Vic was making progress—good thing he was tall enough to see over most of these stiffs—but the closer he got to the front, the more packed together the crowd was. He was blocked now by a couple of fat guys in brown robes, big suckers. " 'Scuse me; coming through." But all that got him was a couple of dirty looks and a, "Shhh!" Assholes.

While Mother Mary rattled on about Judgment Day and that kind of shit he waited for his chance, thinking, *Gimme a knife and I'll show these bozos in front of me Judgment Day.*

Uh-oh. Looked like she was winding up; better move.

Mother Mary said, "I only ask you to recall the prophecies of the Bible."

Vic elbowed one guy in the kidney, and he moved over with a grunt of pain. " 'Scuse me," and Vic was through.

Now where was Michael?

"You have only to watch your television news programs to know the end is at hand," Mother Mary said. "The trumpets are sounding in heaven even as I speak."

Yeah, there he was, hadn't moved an inch, dumb shit.

"Prepare for judgment," Mary said, and she was finished. She stepped back from the microphone.

Vic pushed faster now, just a handful of people between him and Michael. *Christ, don't these stiffs ever take showers?* Even with a cold he could smell them.

Mother Mary raised her arms in a brief blessing, turned away, and walked to the far edge of the stage. She started down the steps. What was she gonna do, work the crowd? Looked like it. Yeah, she was heading this way.

Made it. Vic was standing next to Michael, Walker's face turned away as he watched the broad come down the steps. *Hell, let her walk right by us; doesn't matter with this little gadget. No sound, she'll be past, and I'll be outta here before old Walker knows he's dead.*

He grinned; this was gonna be fun.

Michael watched Mother Mary as she descended the steps and started through the crowd. Since he'd been put on report for being in the nursery he hadn't been left alone for a second. A white-robed guard had spent thirty minutes questioning him about how he'd gotten there, what he wanted, why he was alone. Michael stuck to his story: he'd gotten lost after taking Brother Jeremy to the infirmary. The guard, he thought, had finally accepted it. But he let Michael know that one more bad report and he was out of New Jerusalem.

The Holy Guards formed a phalanx around Mother Mary, shoving the crowd back. She frowned and said something and the guards fell behind her a few steps. She had a power about her; he had to admit that.

She worked her way in his direction, holding out her hands, letting the faithful touch her, putting her hands on a few of the favored. Cult members bowed their heads as she passed them, not looking directly at her. The crowd parted in front of her like the Red Sea, then closed in again behind.

On his left Brother Jeremy bowed his head, elbowing Michael to do the same. Michael looked at the ground, waiting for Mother Mary to pass, trying to think how he could get a few minutes alone, looking at his sandals, wondering if he'd misinterpreted Yates's note, *maybe the baby isn't even here; maybe he's still in California,* looking at Brother Jeremy's dirty toes sticking out of his cast on his left, then at the cowboy boots of the Ringer on his right . . .

Cowboy boots?

The man's hand came out of the pocket of his robe.

Mother Mary was ten feet away now.

The man's hand a blur of motion, something in it.

Arm!

Michael threw his shoulder into the assassin. A tiny glint of silver flashed past his face. Someone to his left yelped a startled, "Ow!"

He thrust his hand, fingers stiff, into the man's windpipe, and the man gagged and stumbled backward, eyes widening in surprise as Michael kicked his legs from under him.

On the ground now, the man tried to roll away, getting tangled in a crowd of legs. Then the guards were there.

Two guards seized Michael, while two more grabbed the man and jerked him upright as he gasped for breath, holding him in an iron grip. More white-robed guards surrounded them and aimed assault rifles at both of them. Where had the guns come from, Michael wondered, under their robes?

Holding his throat, the assassin croaked, "This brother attacked me for no reason."

Mother Mary, close enough to touch, glared at them. "How dare you cause a disturbance at my audience."

Michael glanced directly at her for the first time, then flinched. It was like being struck. Her eyes, he'd never seen any like them. They were green, wide-set, hooded. And they were incredibly hard and cold. He'd seen photos of Gandhi and of Buddhist monks and been impressed by the kindness and patience in their eyes. This woman's eyes were strong and powerful and totally devoid of kindness. They looked like her soul was missing.

Shaken, Michael lowered his gaze. "He was going to attack you, Holy Mother."

"That's a lie," the assassin rasped. He pointed at the silver metal thing on the ground. "I saw this in that brother's hand and took it away. It's a weapon. It opens up."

A guard reached down and snatched it.

"How would he know that," Michael said, "unless it belonged to him?"

Someone shrieked, "Brother Joel is dead!"

Michael turned. A few feet away, a cult member was lying faceup on the ground, eyes open as if in wonder. From his neck protruded a needle.

"The needle came from that silver thing, Holy Mother," Michael said. "He was aiming for you."

"Matthew is right," Brother Jeremy said. "I saw that thing of Satan in this man's hand when they were fighting. I don't recognize him; he's not one of us."

Mother Mary glanced at her dead follower, then looked at the assassin, studying him. After a moment she nodded. The guards pinned the man's arms to his side and hustled him away.

Michael rubbed his shoulder, chagrined at drawing attention to himself. He took a step back; maybe he could melt back into the crowd and disappear.

He looked up to find her watching him again.

"He saved Holy Mother," a voice behind him said. Brother Jeremy caught him in a bear hug and lifted him off his feet. Bad breath and body odor. Michael winced. "He saved her life."

There were murmurs of assent; then he found himself surrounded by back-pounding, hugging Ringers, congratulating him, thanking him.

Mother Mary was in front of him, still watching him, a hawk searching for movements in the grass. "What is your name, novitiate?"

He looked away from those evil eyes. "Matthew, Holy Mother."

"Were you hurt?"

"No, Holy Mother."

She nodded. To a guard, she said, "Take Brother Joel to the infirmary," and she turned away, striding quickly toward her limousine.

23

When Nestor Pruitt called from Oklahoma City, Annie Soares was at her desk in Atlanta, rubbing her eyes and wondering what she'd gotten into. What she thought would be a cursory review of the recent major disease outbreaks in the United States had slid imperceptibly into substantive research, pulling her against her will into the mystery and urgency of what was happening, although she gave Nestor plain English updates every day.

Nestor sounded more worried than she'd ever heard him. "We got us a situation out in New Mexico," he said. "I need you to get on out there. I'd go myself, but I'm going to have to oversee evacuation of some coastal areas in Louisiana and Texas 'cause of rotten fish floating ashore."

"What's happening in New Mexico?"

"We don't know. Two hunnert and thirty-three people dropped dead in twenty-four hours, place called Indian Springs. That's one hunnert percent mortality."

He must have his facts wrong. "Are you sure about the numbers?"

"I'm sure."

"All in one location?"

"So far."

"No disease is a hundred percent lethal. How about chemicals?"

"Could be anything at this point. New Mexico Department of Health is on it. CDC's sent a biological strike force. But I need some eyes and ears of my own out there."

"All right."

"Today, Annie. Look around; do whatever you think. I'm giving you the full authority of the task force. You're my representative."

She sighed, thinking of Nicky's play-off game this weekend. "I'll get there as soon as I can."

●●●

Friday, January 12, 8:51 A.M.

As she drove south on Highway 64 from Colorado Springs, where she'd rented the car, toward Indian Springs, New Mexico, Annie looked around. She was an ocean person, but she could see how people could get attached to this kind of place. The sky was so . . . huge and empty. To the south and east stretched miles of sagebrush prairie. To the west rose the blue-shadowed Sangre de Cristo Mountains.

Two miles outside Indian Springs Annie found the road barricaded. Nailed to the barricade was a red circle with three crab claws facing outward, the biohazard symbol. Beside the highway a double-wide mobile home had been set up, with several tents next to it and an ambulance and a dozen cars parked in front of it.

She slowed and pulled off the road in front of the mobile home as a nervous-looking highway patrolman approached.

"Highway Sixty-four is closed beyond this point, ma'am."

"I know. I'm supposed to meet someone here, a . . ." She checked her notes. "Raymond Miles. Of the New Mexico Department of Health?"

"He'd be in the trailer, I imagine."

She nodded and got out, hoping the CDC team had set up the

command center far enough away from the town, far enough away from whatever agent had destroyed it. She climbed the wooden steps, thankful the press hadn't learned about the disaster yet— she had no answers for them. Inside the mobile home, voices were arguing. Annie opened the door and stepped in.

The living room had been turned into an office, with a half-dozen desks cluttered by computers, phones, and fax machines. Most of the desks were deserted, but seven or eight men sat around the table in the adjoining kitchen in heated discussion.

"Excuse me." She raised her voice. "I'm Dr. Annie Soares. Is there a Raymond Miles here?"

A man about forty at the end of the table lifted his head and looked her over, then stood with a smile that involved his whole round face and stuck out his hand. He was the only Native American in the room and the only man smoking. "I'm Raymond Miles," he said. "You another CDC epidemiologist?"

"No. I'm here representing the federal task force, on loan from Florida DNR."

The other scientists exchanged glances, and one of them rolled his eyes.

"Well, the more the merrier," Raymond Miles said.

"Somebody mind filling me in?"

"Sure." Raymond made quick introductions of the men around the table, most of whom were part of the CDC strike force and most of whose names Annie instantly forgot.

"Let's see," Raymond said. "Town's been cordoned off. We're treatin' it as a level-four hot zone. Patients have been triple-bagged and removed for cremation. We're takin' air samples for aerosols and we were just making a list of possible causes when you came in. Tryin' to narrow things down a little."

He grabbed a chair from one of the desks and rolled it into the kitchen, inserting it in the circle around the table. "Have a seat."

"Thanks; I need to stand after driving this long. Why did you choose two miles as the safe radius?"

"Best guess," Raymond said with a wry smile. He had wide-set brown eyes, shy eyes that glanced at her and danced away. "Since we're dealing with an unknown agent, we really don't know how far away we have to get to be safe. But the wind direction's in our favor here and our air samples don't show any evidence of aerosols. Yet."

She shook her head at an offered cup of coffee. "What have you found out so far?"

One of the scientists, who wore an Argyle sweater stretched over a basketball paunch, checked a notepad in front of him. "Possibles include an unknown chemical toxin—we're running a computer search now of toxins that could cause respiratory failure—a new virulent flu strain, hantavirus, Bolivian hemorrhagic fever, anthrax, and Ebola. But it doesn't seem an exact fit for any of them."

"Were the bodies autopsied?" Annie said.

"Let's call them patients," the scientist said. J. P. something, Annie thought. Or was it P. J.? He couldn't be more than twenty-eight. "And yes, all patients are under autopsy orders. Not all the findings are in, though."

"What about the findings you do have?"

"Lungs filled with blood and fluid," Raymond said. "Tissue weighed three times what it should have. Spleen and liver destroyed, almost liquefied. No evidence of common bacteria in blood or tissue samples. That's why we ruled out pneumonic plague."

"What were the symptoms?"

J. P.—she thought that was it—exchanged glances with another scientist. "Extreme," he said.

"Well, there were no survivors to tell us," Raymond said, "but lucky for us the doctor who died there left some notes. Problem started with symptoms like flu: fever, muscle, and headache, and progressed extremely quickly to irritation of the lungs and cough-ing. That'd be from the blood leakin' into the lungs as the capillary network was destroyed. Death from hypoxia a few hours after on-set. Lungs couldn't absorb oxygen."

Annie thought a moment. "We can probably eliminate chem-icals as a cause, right? Not many of them produce fevers. And U.S. hantavirus doesn't cause bleeding, just lung edema."

"True," Raymond said. "But the symptoms show some hanta-virus similarities. And we've had outbreaks in the region before—the Sin Nombre strain in the Four Corners area in '93 and '97. But those produced only fifty percent lethality. Whatever this is produces a hundred percent."

"Let's just say in excess of ninety-nine percent," J. P. said. "No virus is one hundred percent lethal. There just wasn't a large-enough population to test it."

"You took blood and tissue samples from all the patients?"

"Every damn one of 'em," Raymond said. "They're on their way to Atlanta."

"Have you begun trapping rodents?"

He nodded. "We've got people setting aluminum live traps in a five-mile radius around Indian Springs. Deer mice, rats, chip-munks, skunks, prairie dogs, anything we can catch."

Annie shook her head. "I've never heard of a disease spreading that quickly through a town. Even the most contagious disease needs contact with people. And if most of the town residents were in separate houses or stores, it should have taken days or even weeks to spread."

"Almost all the adults were in the café," Raymond said. "Some sort of town meeting. The kids were in school. That's where the second cluster was."

She thought a moment. "I'd like to take a look around town."

"What for?" J. P. said. "The patients have been removed. What do you expect to find?"

"I'm not sure. Whatever there is to find."

He snorted. "You won't find anything we haven't. Are you checked out on Racals?"

"Yes." She didn't mention she'd only used the biological safety suits in training. She'd never worn one in a level-four hot zone.

J. P. shrugged. "Your funeral."

Raymond looked at her thoughtfully. "I'll go with you."

In the tent that served as the staging area, Annie stripped naked and then pulled on a green surgical scrub suit. When she was dressed she shouted, "OK."

Raymond Miles lifted the tent flap and came in. She put on rubber gloves and held her arms out straight while he taped them to her sleeves, then taped her socks to her pants. His fingers were long and brown, and he wore no rings. "You married?" he asked, not looking at her.

"Divorced. Why?"

"No reason." He got up.

She laid the bright orange Racal field biological suit on the floor of tent and stepped into it.

"Doctor's notes say the first symptoms showed up around ten-thirty in the morning," he said.

"OK." She pulled the suit up over her shoulders, then zipped up the airtight zipper.

"Last call for help came from the druggist. Around five-forty P.M." He handed her a helmet with a soft plastic faceplate. "Whatever it is not only moves quick; it kills fast as hell."

She settled the helmet over her head, fought down an instant of panic when she couldn't breathe, then plugged her air hose into the suit. Air rushed into her helmet, and the suit puffed up. She left the tent while Raymond put on his surgical suit, and then she came back and helped him tape his cuffs and gloves and climb into his Racal. For a moment they stood looking at each other. Then Raymond picked up a radio and motioned her to do the same. "You have six hours of battery life," he said. "Whatever you do, don't puncture your suit."

As she and Raymond Miles drove slowly down Main Street of Indian Springs, Annie could almost believe that no danger lurked here. Everything looked so normal, a southwestern town on a slow day: cars and pickup trucks still parked along the curb; a mongrel dog lifting its leg against a parking meter, then trotting across the street.

She pointed to the dog, and Raymond nodded. "It didn't affect the animals," he said. "Only humans."

He parked the state van in front of the drugstore, and Annie got out, moving slowly, careful not to snag her suit. She looked around. It didn't feel normal, though. The town already felt like a ghost town, exuding a sense of desolation that went beyond the emptiness of the streets. She thought of Nicky and Zach. What would happen to them if she died? Ronald would take them, she supposed, but she knew her ex-husband would neglect them. Then she wondered if she was neglecting them herself. She put the thought out of her mind.

Raymond came around the rear of the van and spoke into his handheld radio. Annie lifted hers to her ear and listened to make out the words over the rush of air inside her helmet.

"Lookin' for anything in particular?" he said.

She shook her head. She didn't know what she was looking for. She'd read the reports, studied what data there was. They told her little. She had the feeling that the answer to what had killed these people would be here in town.

"According to the doctor's notes, the first people with symptoms were in the café," Raymond said. "Why don't we start there?"

They walked down the sidewalk. On the glass door of the café hung an ancient green-and-white Kool Cigarettes sign with the name DOLORES'S.

Annie had the eerie feeling she was being watched. She glanced around but saw nothing. A drop of something fell past her face-plate. She looked up to see a flock of sparrows perched on the edge of the roof.

The café door wasn't locked. Raymond opened it and they stepped in. Along the right wall were four wooden booths. Along the left wall ran a row of red plastic stools fronting a counter with dirty dishes still sitting on it. A plate of bacon and eggs had been left half-eaten.

"Food's been analyzed," Raymond's voice crackled. "Nothing unusual in it."

Down the counter a cup of coffee lay on its side, a brown stain, now dried, running across the counter and onto the floor. "Coffee, too," he said. "Negative."

Annie glanced around. Why here? Why did it break out in the café first? Had someone come to the meeting already infected? If so, where had he or she been exposed?

Annie went through the dining room into the kitchen. A dozen eggs sat on the wooden chopping block. The shelves were full of canned food and condiments. "That stuff been tested?"

"We're workin' on it. Nothin' so far."

She stepped out the back door and stood in the alley. A gray cat slunk around the side of a garbage can and disappeared. She lifted the lid of the can. Empty.

"We collected it and tested it," Raymond said. "Nothin' you wouldn't expect to find."

The CDC and the New Mexico Department of Health had been thorough, she had to admit. But there was something here, damn it; there must be. Frustrated, she walked down the alley and back to Main Street.

They passed a supermarket and she stopped at the door to look in. The automatic doors jumped open and she stumbled back in surprise. Then, feeling sheepish, she took a deep breath of canned air and walked in.

Fluorescent lights still bathed the aisles in white, lighting row upon row of boxed and canned food no one would ever eat. Had it been something in here? Maybe the cause was lurking in the meat counter. Anthrax? Samples had been taken. They were still being analyzed, Raymond told her, and the results would be known within a day or two. But it didn't feel likely, that line of search. The symptoms didn't sound like anthrax. Baffled, she followed him outside.

From the supermarket he drove her to the school, an old two-story building of red brick. A flag still fluttered from the aluminum pole.

"According to the doctor's notes," Raymond said, "the first kids who got sick were out on the playground for recess."

They walked behind the school to the fenced playground. A breeze caught the swings and stirred them, creaking the chains as if the ghosts of the children who had played here were returning. Annie watched the swings, thinking of her own sons.

"It could have drifted down from the café," Raymond said.

She looked at the flag to gauge the direction of the breeze. "Right now we're upwind of the café," she said. "Was the breeze from the same direction that day?"

"Good question. I'll check and see."

They went inside the school, walking through each room. She saw no clues to the cause of the disaster, but everywhere were signs that the place had been vacated quickly. Blackboards demonstrated half-finished lessons. Books and papers lay scattered on desks and the floor. In a few places dried stains told her where a student had vomited or bled. She had thought she was hardened to disease and death, but the horror of what had happened here stunned her. It seemed to eat away the fiber between her thoughts, and they drifted and collided, unconnected, as she stood gaping.

Raymond touched her arm and pointed to the exit.

From the school he took her to the bakery, then to the three adjacent stores, and finally to the doctor's office. From the ransacked look of it, the CDC team had gone through it thoroughly.

Raymond tapped his wrist. "Five hours. Time to leave."

Annie stood in the reception room, biting her lip in frustration. *Talk to me. What happened here?*

The only response was silence.

"Time to go," Raymond said again.

She sighed. The answer might be here, but she wasn't going to find it today. Reluctantly she nodded and followed him back to the van.

As she got in, she felt a tug on the back of her suit and looked around to see it caught on the sharp edge of the door latch. She backed out, a shock of fear sweeping through her. Even a pinhole would be enough to expose her to the invisible killer that lived in this town. She twisted around but couldn't tell if the suit had been punctured.

"Raymond!"

He came running around the van. "Hold still. Turn around." He squatted and peered at the seat of her suit. "Can't see anything. I'm going to rub my hand over it. Don't take it personally." She felt his gloved fingers probing gently at her right buttock. After a moment he stood, his face worried inside his helmet.

"We'd better get you back. We've got an isolation chamber set up at the command center."

He made a U-turn and raced back the way they had come. As they tore past the CITY LIMITS sign, panic threatened to overwhelm her. Was that a cold spot she felt on her buttock? She forced herself to take deep, slow breaths, but her mind spun, flooding her brain with incongruous thoughts. She remembered the lights in the su-

permarket and wished she had turned them off. A thought came
to her, something she'd read in a science fiction story somewhere,
and she shivered. *Will the last person on earth please turn off the
lights?*

24

In the decontamination shower, Annie Soares pulled a chain dangling from the ceiling. A spray of water hit her suit, washing away the dust and contaminated particles. When it stopped, jets of Envirochem squirted from the nozzles that surrounded her.

She waited while the chemical bath washed over her. *One minute.* Why hadn't she been more careful? One careless second. Why hadn't she looked? *Two minutes.* If she'd been infected, she'd never leave the isolation chamber alive. Nicky and Zach would never see her again. *Three minutes.* She had no business in this kind of work. Who'd take care of them? Who'd tell Carmela? *Four minutes.* Damn it! Damn it! Damn it!

The jets turned to water again, rinsing the Envirochem from her suit. When at last the shower shut off, she ran into the isolation chamber where Raymond waited in his cleaned Racal. Fighting back the urge to throw up, she stripped off her suit, then watched as he inflated it with water from a pressure hose. *Please, please, please, no leaks.*

Lying front down on the floor, the suit filled, then grew fat and tight. She knelt and peered at the fabric. She couldn't see any moisture.

Raymond bent over and ran his hand over the fabric, then examined his glove. He grinned.

Annie fainted.

The next day she drove from New Mexico to Colorado Springs, then took the red-eye to Atlanta. She was reluctant to leave Indian Springs; she still sensed the answer lay somewhere in the town. But she was glad to be leaving, too. She told herself it wasn't fear. How could she find the cause when she didn't even know what she was to look for? By now the CDC would be analyzing tissue and blood samples, and logic told her she could learn more in Atlanta.

When her plane landed, she checked into her motel for a few hours' sleep. At six-thirty her alarm rang and she stumbled into the shower to stand comatose under the cold water. When she was finally awake she called home.

A sleepy Carmela answered. Zach wasn't home—he'd gone to a party and hadn't gotten back yet—did she want to speak to Nicky?

"Please. Why didn't you tell Zach to be home at a decent hour?"

"I did, missus. That boy, I can't do nothing with him."

Annie bit back the anger she felt, knowing it was really directed at herself. It wasn't her housekeeper's responsibility to parent her children; it was her own.

When her ten-year-old son came on the line she said, "Hi, honey. Got a game today?"

He yawned. "Mom, it's Sunday. It was yesterday."

"Oh. I'm sorry, Nicky. I've been so busy I've lost track of time."

"It's OK."

"You getting along all right? You need anything?"

"No."

"Sorry I woke you, sweetie. I'll let you go. I just wanted to hear your voice. Where did Zach go, do you know?"

"He didn't say. When are you coming home?"

"I'm not sure. Soon, I hope."

She told him she loved him and hung up, feeling like a failure.

Arnold Gehring, director of the CDC, looked haggard and over-worked and less than happy to see her. "Oh, right. Dr. Soares from the task force."

"I just got back from New Mexico," she said. "The Indian Springs outbreak. I'd like a BSL-four lab and a couple of research assistants to look at the tissue and blood samples they sent."

"No, I can't give you one. We're already working on it, anyway."

Taken aback, she asked, "What's your plan of attack?"

"For starters, a broad screen of autopsy specimens with an RT-PCR assay."

"That's fine, but it wouldn't hurt to have another person help-ing."

"It *would* hurt," he said. "We're stretched thin already, resource-wise. We can't spare an extra lab."

"Can I at least observe?"

"Frankly, I'd just as soon you didn't get in the way. Go file your reports, or whatever it is you do, and let my people work in peace. If it's hantavirus, we should know within a day or two, and you'll get a full report."

Furious, she stalked to the elevator and rode it down to her basement cubicle. She should be home with her family, instead of hanging around someplace she wasn't wanted, working for a red-neck Bible-thumper. She took a deep breath and let it out slowly. No, that wasn't fair. Nestor was all right. He wasn't as dumb as he pretended to be, and at least he was trying. But he wasn't getting a lot of cooperation from the CDC.

Four days later she still hadn't heard anything from Gehring about the New Mexico investigation. Impatient, she interrupted work on her cytomegalovirus report to track down one of the men working on the Indian Springs outbreak, an older man by the name of Bertinelli, whom she knew slightly from conferences. He was leaving for the day but was willing to stop and talk. What he told her wasn't encouraging.

They knew they were dealing with a virus but little more. It attacked only humans. Not monkeys, not mice, not any other mammal. It resembled hantavirus to some extent but didn't match any known strain. They didn't know what it was except that it was something totally new. And totally deadly. Many of the internal organs of its victims were almost liquefied, the result of the virus trying to turn the human body into a copy of itself. She listened in growing apprehension as he described their search.

"The only good thing about it," Bertinelli said, "if *good* is the word, is that it kills its hosts so quickly it doesn't have time to spread very far. That's why the outbreak didn't reach beyond Indian Springs, New Mexico. But let it break out in New York . . ."

Disturbed, she went back to her office. She picked up the phone and punched in the number of the Indian Springs command center. When a man's voice answered, she asked for Raymond Miles, hoping he hadn't gone home.

He hadn't. When he came on the line, he said, "Hey, Florida, I was just thinkin' to call you."

"Oh? What's up, Raymond?"

"I finally got a chance to check on that weather information you asked about. According to the weather service, the winds in Indian Springs the day of the outbreak were light and they were from the southwest."

"Southwest? Am I wrong or would that make the school upwind from the café?"

"You're not wrong."

"It doesn't make sense, Raymond. An airborne virus doesn't spread upwind, certainly not that quickly. And why did it just happen to break out in the two places in town it would do the most damage?"

"Doesn't sound like a coincidence, does it? So what have you found out about it?"

"They've isolated it, but they can't identify it. It's a virus, no question, but if it's hantavirus, it's like nothing that ever existed before. It's not Sin Nombre. It's not any known strain. They've done a polymerase chain reaction search, screened it against the viruses in the rodents you sent. No matches. The DNA bands contain hantaviruslike sequences, but they differ from any of the known hantaviruses by at least thirty percent."

"They run antibody tests?"

"Yeah, they did. Blood from patients who died in Indian Springs cross-reacts in test tubes with antibodies against hantavirus. But they've injected patient blood into mice. The mice didn't develop antibodies."

"They didn't? That's strange."

"It gets stranger, Raymond. They used PCR to screen it against every damn virus archived in the Genbank in Los Alamos. No matches. Nothing even close."

"Well, viruses mutate," he said. "We know that. They mutate pretty often, really."

"But that much? Besides, if a local strain mutated, we should find a match in the area. You catch any more mice?"

"Not many. They're down this year, deer mice especially."

"Raymond, you remember those Sin Nombre outbreaks in '93 and '97? What was the weather like those years?"

"I don't know. I was at Dartmouth in '93. In '97 I was at UCLA doing my internship. But I know what you're thinking. I'll find out."

"Thanks."

"I'm beginning to feel like a weatherman." He laughed and hung up.

———

At ten minutes to eight the next morning he called back. "I phoned a friend in the Indian Health Service over on the Navajo rez, asked him about '93. Real wet year, lots of piñon nuts, record numbers of mice. The '97 outbreak was around Taos, so I drove over there last night, talked to the Taos Pueblo elders. They say they had more snow that year than any in the last fifty."

"Let me guess. Record numbers of mice."

"You got it."

"Raymond, we've known about hantaviruses since the Korean War. There've been outbreaks in New York, in Sweden, France, China, Russia—a lot of places—but all of them came after some environmental factor triggered an explosion of rodents."

"Makes sense, since they carry it."

"Exactly. But there's no reason it should have broken out in Indian Springs. Conditions aren't right. That area's been in a drought, very few rodents. So where did it come from?"

"Somebody brought it in? Mice in a grain truck, maybe."

"Doesn't sound plausible. You don't believe that, either, do you?"

"No. Doesn't explain travelin' upwind. Or the speed of infection."

There was silence on the line. Finally, Annie said, "Are you thinking what I'm thinking?"

"I'm thinkin' about takin' the weekend off to go fishing. What are you thinkin'?"

"That someone infected that town deliberately."

"That's what I was afraid of. You mean terrorism?"

"What else would you call it? But if we're right, there has to be some evidence of it, doesn't there?"

"Well, they *would* have to carry the virus in something," Raymond said thoughtfully. "And whoever released it wouldn't do it while he was hanging around, so there must have been some way to delay the release."

"Raymond, I'm stuck here, or I'd come back and go through the town again. I hate to ask it, but would you be willing to go in there once more and look around?"

There was a pause; then he said, "I can do that. But it's gonna cost you."

"What do you want?"

"To see you again, Florida."

She found herself grinning. "I'll see what I can do. And, Raymond . . . keep your suit on."

25

When the two white-robed guards sauntered in, Michael was on his hands and knees scrubbing the latrine floor with Brother Jeremy, who hadn't stopped babbling about the Final Days since Mother Mary's speech. Michael was thinking about the Arm assassin. How had he known he was here? Had he traced him to Sweetwater? If so, then Darby's life could be in danger, too. He needed to warn her, somehow.

He saw the guards and his heart lurched.

"Which one of you is Matthew?" one of them said. The speaker's hair had been shaved, his scalp oiled. Michael figured he'd go at least six-three, two-forty, with the other not much smaller. No way could he take them.

The guard was looking at Brother Jeremy, whose mouth was frozen open in midbabble. Jeremy pointed to Michael.

"I'm Matthew Cooper."

The guard turned to him with the look of a jackal lifting its yellow eyes from meat. "Come with us."

"What did I do?"

Instead of answering, he just stared.

Michael looked at Jeremy, who looked away. Michael got to his feet, and they escorted him out of the barracks. "Where am I going?"

"Don't ask questions," the bald guard said. "Get in back." He pointed to a Jeep Wagoneer.

He did what he was told.

The Jeep bounced over a washboard gravel road that took them deeper into the ranch, into an area where he'd never been. He wondered how they'd found out about him. They were probably taking him into the backcountry to kill him, somewhere his body would never be found. Then he told himself he was being silly. Even a cult like the Ringers wouldn't murder someone just because he was trying to spy on them, would they? Except that they'd tried to murder his sister. And she wasn't doing anything to them.

On both sides the mountains drew close, their fir-covered slopes disappearing above him into low white clouds. They climbed into a narrow canyon. To Michael it looked like a grave without a lid.

The road was little more than a boulder-strewn trail as it plunged through the canyon, then switchbacked up one side of the mountain. Even this high, only a few patches of dirty snow clung to the back sides of boulders or hid in the shade of Douglas firs.

Four or five miles later, the mountain fell back on one side, making a circular plateau, and the road turned onto it. They came to a closed gate, with a purple guardhouse beside it and a chain-link fence running away from it in both directions, enclosing the entire plateau. The fence was topped with razor wire.

A guard carrying a clipboard walked up to the window and inspected the identification card handed to him by the driver. Then he bent down and peered at Michael in the back. "Your name?"

"Matthew." Michael eyed the bulge under the guard's robe, about the size of a machine pistol.

"Matthew what?"

"Cooper."

The guard checked his clipboard, then pressed a remote control. The gate slid open.

They drove past the gatehouse through an open field as flat as a pool table, toward a cluster of buildings. Behind the buildings the mountain rose upward again, forming an almost vertical wall capped by clouds. The other three sides dropped off into the valley far below. In the center of the field, two communication towers jutted skyward, their red lights blinking.

This had to be Heaven's Door, Michael thought. Mother Mary's stronghold. The communication towers spoke of a sophistication unknown to the lower ranch.

The Jeep headed for the largest building, an A-frame mansion made of logs, with wings jutting out from both sides. It hugged the base of the mountain, its huge windows a violent red in the rays of the morning sun. So this was where she spent her money. Almost homey-looking, with a thread of smoke rising from the chimney. Except for the communication towers. And the low concrete structures flanking the mansion, almost like bunkers. No, exactly like bunkers.

They drove under the porte-cochere of the mansion and stopped. The two guards got out and opened the door for him, and he climbed out. The air was cold and clean and thin, smelling of pines, and he took a deep breath to steady himself.

Flanked by the guards he walked up the wide steps. Another white-robed guard stood at attention in front of the massive door, which was hand-carved with a sword piercing a cross. Staring at Michael, the guard reached behind him and opened the door, and, at a gesture from his escorts, Michael walked through.

He stepped into an immense room with a cathedral ceiling. A massive moss-rock fireplace dominated the far wall. Flanking it were life-size oil portraits of Jesus Christ on the left side and Mother Mary Grace on the right.

"This way." The bald guard turned left and led the way into one of the wings, while the other guard fell in behind Michael. Their footsteps sounded loud in the stillness of the hall, and Michael found himself falling into step with the measured tread of the guards. He broke stride and was rewarded with a scowl from baldy. At a closed door they stopped and the guard knocked twice.

A voice inside said, "Come."

The room could have been any office in any office building, with a computer, fax machine, and photocopier on a table against the wall. At a desk in the center sat Salway, the tiny man who'd lectured them on suffering. In his business suit he looked like a little boy playing executive.

He nodded at the guards, and they backed out, closing the door behind them.

Salway gazed at Michael a moment. His eyes reminded Michael of a transparent fish he'd seen in an aquarium once, clear and filmy with red streaks running through them. He said, "Matthew Cooper, is it?"

"Yes, Brother Salway."

"Just Salway, please. Welcome to Heaven's Door." His look grew quizzical. "Haven't I seen you before?"

"I don't think so, sir."

"Mm. Perhaps it will come to me. That was an excellent thing you did the other day."

"Thank you, sir. I just happened to be in the right place."

"Fortunately for us." He studied Michael. "The man you captured has said all kinds of interesting things about you. Can you guess what any of them are?"

Oh, shit. They did know. "No, sir, I can't," he managed, his voice cracking.

"The man—his name is Lopak, by the way—says you're a government assassin; can you imagine that? And that he was trying to kill *you*, not Holy Mother."

Michael tried to look astonished. "Me, Brother? An assassin? I couldn't do anything like that. And I'm not important enough for anyone to kill."

"I was skeptical of his story, myself. You don't seem the type, if you'll pardon me. And under further . . . interrogation, Mr. Lopak admitted his true purpose here. As we suspected, he was sent by the Vatican to eliminate Holy Mother as a rival."

Michael stared at him, caught between weak-kneed terror and astonishment at their paranoia. The Vatican? Then he realized what they must have done to Lopak. If he hadn't been certain before that these people were the ones who had shot Ursula, he was now. He almost felt sorry for the Arm assassin. Michael had witnessed torture in Iraq, and he could imagine what the man had undergone. A person in that kind of pain would say anything at all to please his captors.

"Mr. Lopak said your Satanic name was Walker. Is that true?"

"No, sir. My name is Matthew Cooper."

"Yes, so your record says. Originally from Duluth, Minnesota, I believe?"

"Yes."

"Where did you learn to handle yourself like that?" Salway said.

"In the army, sir."

"Can you handle weapons as well?"

"I, uh, received some weapons training."

"Would you be willing to kill a human being if Mother Mary asked you to? Not that she would, of course."

Michael hesitated. "May I ask why, sir? I thought killing was wrong."

Salway frowned. "Who told you that?"

"I've always heard—"

"You've heard what Satanic society wants you to hear." Salway slid off his chair and came around the desk. The top of his head barely reached Michael's chest. "Killing *is* wrong, Matthew, as a general premise. However, if you complete your training with us, you'll learn that there are certain situations in which the Bible allows killing. I'm speaking theoretically, of course. The situation has yet to arise."

"Oh."

"We live at a crucial time, Matthew. The most exciting time in history. And we, you and I, have an opportunity to serve God as no man has ever done before. Do you understand?" Salway's soft voice seemed to cling to Michael's skin like sweat.

"I think so."

"The world is full of evil," Salway said, smiling. "Evil which works through fanatics such as that man who tried to deprive us of a living saint. You have a quick mind and good reflexes. We need people like you on the front line. Are you willing to stay here and complete your training?"

To kill people? Here we go again. "I guess so, sir."

"Why do you hesitate? You should be honored Holy Mother has chosen you."

"I am honored, sir. It's . . . it's my own ability I doubt."

"Let us be the judges of that." He went back behind his desk. "Of course, we'll have to check this Lopak's story. I hope you're not lying to us. Holy Mother will be very disappointed."

"No, sir, I'm not." His heart felt like something punching its way out of a box. With their resources they would learn the truth; they had to. How long did he have before he shared Lopak's fate?

"In the meantime," Salway said with a smile, "I hope you won't mind being our guest here at Heaven's Door."

"Not at all, sir."

"Naturally we'll have to keep you confined, for security reasons, until our investigation of your background is complete. But the cell will be quite comfortable and the food excellent. We do appreciate your service to Mother Mary." He rang a bell on his desk, and the guard with the shaved head opened the door. "Show Mr. Cooper to the, ah, guest quarters."

With a malevolent grin, the guard grasped Michael by the arm and led him out.

•••

Thursday, January 18, 5:56 P.M.

In his sparsely furnished efficiency apartment in northwest Washington, D.C., James Walker pulled a chair away from the kitchen table, turned it around, and sat with his arms across the back, staring moodily at nothing. He wasn't often depressed, but tonight he was. Michael had disappeared and Lopak hadn't phoned in since he'd reported killing the rancher. James had to consider the possibility Lopak was either in jail or dead.

What depressed him most, however, was his sense that his supervisor had some plan for James that he didn't know about. He could feel it. When he'd asked him about it, James had been told, "Remember the rule, James: Arm functions on a need to know."

He understood the reason he couldn't know everything; it was the same reason he didn't tell his closers who they worked for: they were exposed, and the less they knew, the safer for the group. Still, he felt isolated, on the fringes of the cause. What made it worse was the fact that his part of the effort was not going well.

He shook his head. Hard to believe, two experienced men screwing up a simple closing like Michael. Things were getting out of hand. And his supervisor had questioned an entry on his last balance sheet, one that involved money James had shifted from another account to finance the search for his brother. He'd explained it as a mistake, and he thought his supervisor had bought it, but the man was alert now. There couldn't be another such mistake. It was time to take matters into his own hands, to end the problem now. If you wanted something done right, do it yourself.

He thought a moment. He doubted Lopak was in jail; the man was too good to get caught killing a stupid rancher. It was possible he'd met up with Michael and that somehow his brother had killed him. Hard to believe, though. In any case, Lopak's last location was Montana. That would be the place to look.

He sighed, mentally checking his calendar. Nothing for the next three days that Margaret couldn't cover for him. There was that double closing next week, but he'd be back in time to make the advance deposit. He stood and went to the phone.

No airline flew into Sweetwater, Montana, but several of them flew into Bozeman, sixty miles away. He made a reservation on Northwest for a 7:30 flight.

26

Annie Soares flew to Oklahoma City to see Nestor Pruitt, even though it was Saturday, because the feeling of urgency wouldn't let her wait. From the airport she took a cab to the task force building on Shartel, where a guard told her Nestor had left for the day to play softball, but she might be able to catch him at Lincoln Park if she hurried.

When she got to the softball complex, she found games being played on three different fields and realized she'd forgotten to ask the guard which team was Nestor's. At one field, Capitol Employees were playing Avis, but neither sounded like her boss's kind of team.

She walked over to a set of aluminum bleachers where a scattering of wives and children were making encouraging noises. On the field the Slugging Angels of the United Baptist Church—that had to be Nestor's—were batting against a team called St. Anthony's. The game made her think of Nicky—he'd be playing soccer this morning—and guilt washed over her. She should be watching his game, not this one. She'd call him this afternoon and see how he had done.

As she carried her briefcase to the backstop screen, the man at the plate hit a slow grounder toward the third baseman. Easy out at first.

Nestor got up from the bench and grabbed a bat. "That's all right, Jimmie!" he shouted. "Way to hustle!"

He strode toward home plate, swinging the bat. Unlike the custom-tailored suits Annie had seen him in, the uniform did little to hide his potbelly and bandy legs. She smiled.

"Mr. Pruitt," she called. "I need to talk to you when you're done."

He stopped, turned, and squinted in her direction, shading his eyes with his hands. "Who's that?"

"Annie Soares."

A worried look on his face, he trotted toward the screen. "Annie? By gol', what are you doing here?"

"I need to talk to you."

"Daggone it, can't it wait? This is my first day off in a month."

"It's very important, Mr. Pruitt."

"Well . . . OK. I'll get someone to play for me."

"Go ahead and bat," she said. "It'll wait that long."

He nodded, turned, and hurried to the plate.

The St. Anthony's pitcher fired an underhanded screamer that Nestor started to swing at; then tried to hold back. Strike one.

"That was outside, daggone it. Outside."

The second pitch was definitely outside and Nestor took it for a ball.

On the third pitch he ripped a swing that would have sent the ball over the fence if he had gotten much of it. Instead he popped a high fly into right field. The fielder caught it, and Nestor, rounding first, turned and trotted off the field.

Annie walked over to meet him, away from the listening ears in the bleachers.

He came trotting up to her. "Now what's this all about?"

"I need to ask you something. I faxed you a report on the New Mexico outbreak, did you get it?"

He pulled off his cap and wiped his forehead with a sleeve. "Yeah, that hantavirus thing."

"Not exactly. It's a virus, yes, but it's not hantavirus, at least none we've ever seen."

"Well, that doesn't surprise me, Annie, way things are going. Wasn't it you told me viruses are mutating every day?"

"That's true," she said. "And this one may have mutated from another strain of hantavirus. But it didn't mutate around Indian Springs, New Mexico. There are no genetic matches to any of the local virus strains."

"Yeah? What's that mean?"

"I think this virus was carried in from somewhere else."

He shrugged. "It's possible. Happens all the time. Any tourist passing through—"

"I don't think so. No tourists died in Indian Springs. And if one had left town infected, he'd be dead by now. We'd have had a report. Mr. Pruitt, there were two virus outbreaks in that town on the same day. The first was at the café; the second was at the school. But the wind wasn't right for it to happen that way. The school was upwind from the café."

His raised eyebrows told her he understood the direction she was going. As she'd thought, he wasn't as dumb as he pretended to be. "You saying this virus outbreak might have been intentional? Somebody brought it in on purpose?"

"There's a good possibility of that, yes."

A cheer rose from the spectators. The batter had gotten a hit and was sliding into second. Nestor ignored the game now, frowning at her. "So you're talking terrorism."

She nodded. "I think you should bring the FBI into it."

"But why would anyone attack a little bitty place in New Mexico? It doesn't make any sense."

"I don't know," she admitted.

He turned and gazed off across the field, slapping his baseball cap absently on his thigh. He wasn't looking at the game. "Annie," he said after a moment, "my credibility with the other agencies is pretty thin already. The FBI is gonna want something more concrete than a little wind. You got anything more solid?"

"No," she said. "Not yet."

He murmured something she didn't catch, and she leaned closer. "What?"

Nestor turned back to her. "I said, it's in the Book of Revelation. My church believes we're in the last days, and they interpret the Bible to mean that when the last days come, God will pour out the vials of his wrath on earth. My fellow parishioners believe that's what we're seeing, this pattern, with all these new diseases and calamities. The wrath of God."

"It wasn't the wrath of God in Indian Springs, Mr. Pruitt," she said. "It was the wrath of some terrorist organization."

"I tend to agree with you." He settled his baseball cap back on his head and tugged it down. "All right, if you're convinced we need the FBI in this, I'll call them. But I can't guarantee they'll listen to me."

"All I ask is that you try, Mr. Pruitt."

He nodded and trotted away.

27

What Salway called the guest quarters was an old bunkhouse made of thick logs, with two doors, each opening into a separate cell. Through the small barred window in the door of Michael's cell he could see the mansion and, behind it, what he'd been told was Holy Mother's personal helicopter, a JetRanger 3. Through a window in the south wall, also barred, he could see nothing but rocks and old mine tailings as the mountain rose steeply behind him. The cell was spartan, with only a metal bunk and a toilet, but it was clean, and the vegetarian food tasted better than the stuff he'd been eating at the lower ranch. For an hour a day he was allowed out of his cell to exercise, although it was under supervision and the areas in which he could walk were restricted. When he told the guards he liked to jog, they even provided him with brown sweatpants, sweatshirt, and canvas shoes.

His guards during the exercise periods alternated between the bald goon who'd brought him here, whose name was Brother Saul, and a black former welterweight boxer, whom Michael thought he recognized but who refused to reveal his Satanic name. He called himself Brother Micah. Although Micah treated Michael almost as a hero, Saul let him know he wasn't fooled. He knew Michael was a spy, he said, and told him he hated baby-sitting a spy. He looked forward to doing to Michael what he'd already done to Lopak.

Michael didn't know what that was, but he could guess. Still, he had to find a way to shake his escort and look around.

On the third day as he was let out of his cell to exercise, he told Saul, "You don't have to baby-sit me. Go ahead without me. I can find my way back here."

"You're not funny," Saul said. His scalp glistened in the sunlight.

"How long you been out of the marines, Sergeant Brother?"

He stared at Michael suspiciously. "How'd you know that?"

"Just a guess. You don't look in great shape to me, though. You want to race?"

"No. You think I don't know what you're up to?"

"What am I up to?"

"You're a Satanic faggot spy."

"I'm just a seeker of truth, like you." He began to jog.

"When the judgment comes," Saul said, "and that'll be real soon now, you'll be seeking the truth in hell." He broke into a trot to keep up with Michael.

"Not as long as I follow Holy Mother," Michael said. "Is that trail all right to take?" He pointed to a well-worn path that disappeared into the trees.

"You can't do that loop in one hour."

"How long is it?"

"Ten clicks."

"No problem. But you may not be able to keep up." He set off down the path, Saul behind him.

He hoped the trail would follow the perimeter of the compound, so that he could examine the concertina wire fence and any other security measures the cult had installed. But instead it cut a winding swath through a thick stand of lodgepole pines and he saw nothing but trees.

Forty minutes later, his sweatshirt soaked from exertion in spite of the cool temperature, he slowed. Saul, smirking, moved ahead of him. "Not so tough now, are we?"

Ahead, the path lifted over a hill and Saul disappeared from view.

Discouraged, Michael sagged onto a boulder to catch his breath. Not only hadn't he learned any more about the cult's security, he still didn't know if Ursula's baby was even here. He shook his head. It might not matter anyway. A day or two more and Salway would know he was a fake. And then . . .

A noise came from the woods to his right, a sound like a whimper. He slowed his breathing a moment to listen. Nothing. Must have imagined it.

But as he forced himself to his feet, it came again, the sound of a frightened child. Ursula's? No, it sounded older than that. He stepped off the trail and made his way through the pines toward where he'd heard the whimper. He stopped to listen, but he heard nothing now except his own breathing.

It wasn't this far, he thought. *I must have missed it.* He turned, climbed a low rise, and stepped into a clearing.

In the center of the clearing a pit had been dug, dirt piled up beside it. Michael trotted to the edge and looked down.

At the bottom, ten feet down, a girl of about four lay curled in the fetal position, her thumb in her mouth, her eyes closed. She wore a green robe, ragged and smeared with dirt.

What the hell? He leaned over, his hands on his knees. "Are you all right?"

The girl whimpered but didn't answer.

Michael looked for a way down into the pit but saw none. "Can you hear me? Did you fall in? Are you hurt?"

He glanced around for someone, wondering how the girl got here. The nursery was on the lower ranch. Where were her caretakers?

She sat up slowly and looked up at him, shielding her eyes with small, grubby hands. "Can I get out now?"

A voice behind Michael said, "What the hell you doing?"

He wheeled to see Brother Saul.

"You got a problem here?" Saul said. "Why'd you leave the trail?" He was jogging in place, not even breathing hard.

"I stopped to rest a minute and I heard this girl. What's she doing down there? Help me get her out."

"That kid's none of your freaking business."

"Are you kidding me? She could die down there."

Michael scarcely saw Saul's foot as it kicked him in the stomach, doubling him over. Another kick exploded against his head and he found himself on his hands and knees at the edge of the pit, his ears ringing.

"First thing you learn, you don't ask questions. You do what you're told, got it?"

Michael backed into a crouch, wiping his bloody nose with his hand. Just one good punch; it'd be worth getting pounded.

Saul grinned at him, beckoning him.

The baby, Michael. The baby. Don't screw it up now. He spit blood and put his hands up. "You're right, Brother Saul. I'm sorry. I lost my head." He stood, gingerly feeling his stomach.

Brother Saul sneered. "You're a faggot."

"Yes, sir. We've established that."

"Get your butt moving, you hear."

"May I ask a question, Brother?"

"No."

"Why is that little girl down there?"

"I told you it's none of your freaking business. But just so you know what happens to people who disobey, that kid's being punished."

"A four-year-old girl?"

"Satan don't give a rip how old you are. We've got to keep him from taking over these little people. Now this kid here only got a warning. She just spent a night out here, that's all, so the demons could scare her. Make her mind. Her watchers'll be up from the ranch anytime to get her. Now get moving, maggot, or you'll be dancing with the wolf, you hear me?"

Michael glanced down into the pit. The little girl had lain down and curled into a ball again. His fists clenched in helpless anger.

"Move!"

He limped into a trot, Brother Saul at his heels shouting threats. Michael wondered what dancing with the wolf meant. Somehow he didn't think it meant watching an old Kevin Costner movie. He forced his legs into a faster trot.

• • •

Saturday, January 20, 7:30 p.m.

On the flight back to Atlanta, Annie had to admit that Nestor had a point. Why would a terrorist destroy a small town in New Mexico? Even terrorists had a motive for what they did, and this action made no sense. If they were using a virus as a weapon, why not release it in a city like Los Angeles?

She thought about what her boss had said, that the people in his church believed it was God who was at work here, not terrorists. That the New Mexico outbreak was just a part of the overall pattern, the beginning of the end of days.

Was there a pattern here? Something Nestor had said niggled at the back of her consciousness.

A pattern, something about a pattern.

In the Book of Revelation!

When the plane landed, she hurried into an airport gift shop and bought a Bible. She gave her cabdriver the address of the Centers for Disease Control on Clifton Road, then settled back to read her new Bible on the way. When she got there, she went to the coffee room, poured herself a cup of hot water, and went back to her office. Then she dug her box of chamomile tea from her purse and booted up her computer.

When the last of the Saturday afternoon workers left, she hardly noticed.

She worked through the night, occasionally getting up from her computer to check passages from the Bible, finally catching a few hours' sleep on a cold Naugahyde couch in the coffee room. She worked through Sunday, surrendering at last to fatigue and catching a cab to her motel for a shower and a little sleep.

The next morning a secretary intercepted her on her way into her office. "You had a call about an hour ago from a Raymond Miles in New Mexico. He says it's important."

Fatigue forgotten, she dialed the New Mexico command center at Indian Springs.

"Sorry, he's not here," said a male voice on the other end.

"Do you know where I can reach him?"

"Try the Colfax County sheriff's office." He gave her the number.

Annie dialed the number, hoping Raymond was not in some kind of trouble. But the dispatcher who answered said, "Yeah, I think he's around somewhere. Hang on a minute."

A moment later Raymond said, "Hello?"

Her spirits lifted at the sound of his voice. "Annie Soares, Raymond. What's up?"

"Hey, Florida. Well, I talked a couple of friends of mine in the sheriff's office into going back to Indian Springs with me. We spent all day yesterday looking through the place. Had to promise I'd take 'em to my secret fishing lake up in the Sangres. But . . . it might have been worth it."

"What did you find?"

"Not sure. Maybe nothing. Or it could be a little piece of an explosives detonator. We can't be positive yet; we're keeping it sealed. Found it in the café, surrounded by traces of what looks like powdered glass or plastic."

"Glass? As in exploding flask?"

"Flask, maybe, or vial, something like that. Or it could just be a broken bottle. But we found a trace of the same powder at the school playground."

"What do your deputy friends think it is?"

"Well, they're of a suspicious bent. Always inclined to believe the worst."

"What do you think?"

"My guess is that the virus was carried in a small laboratory flask and rigged with a detonator set with some kind of timer. When it exploded, it would spray the virus all over the place."

"Dear God. That's so cold-blooded."

"Not someone you'd want for a next-door neighbor."

"So what are you going to do with what you've found?" she said.

"Well, as soon as we're satisfied there's no creepy-crawlies on it we'll send it to the FBI. Ask them to put a rush on it."

"Raymond, good work. Thanks. I owe you."

"And I intend to collect. You owe me a date."

"Deal."

Smiling, she severed the connection, then dialed Nestor Pruitt's number in Oklahoma City. When his secretary put him on, Annie explained what Raymond Miles had found. She hung up and gazed at her computer printouts, shaking her head. A vial. Nestor Pruitt was right after all. The vials of wrath were loose on earth.

● ● ●

Sunday, January 21, 1:30 P.M.

While Michael waited for his exercise period, he stared moodily out the tiny window in the door of his cell. Time was running out and he was no closer to finding Ursula's baby. He doubted he'd ever see Darby again. He found himself wishing he hadn't tried to be a hero; he'd done no good for anyone. But he knew he couldn't have lived with himself if he hadn't made the attempt.

He examined the cell for some way to escape. The window could be opened, but the bars on it were too close together to squeeze through. He thought about breaking a pane of glass and using it to cut through the logs but abandoned the idea as unrealistic. It would take days. He could, however, use a shard of glass as a weapon when the time came. They wouldn't kill him without a fight.

Staring out the window, he watched the activity at the mansion. Cars and Jeeps arrived and left, mostly driven by men in crimson robes with purple trim. He wasn't certain about their place in the cult hierarchy, but they seemed to have more rank than the guards, and other cult members appeared to be afraid of them. There weren't very many of them—he'd seen only six or seven—and unlike the guards, they came and went freely. Most of them were here today. From the increased activity Michael sensed that something important was happening.

A black man in a white robe approached from the direction of the mansion, whistling. Brother Micah, the ex-boxer. "Afternoon, Matthew," he said cheerfully as he opened the door. "You ready for a little walk?"

"Sure. Say, Brother, who are those guys in the red robes? Are they special?"

Micah glanced over his shoulder, and Michael thought he saw a glint of fear in his eyes. "They're Holy Mother's personal servants, man. Her Avenging Angels."

"What's going on?"

"Just church business. Where you want to go today?"

"I don't suppose I could have a tour of the mansion?"

Brother Micah chuckled. "No, sorry. But after you're cleared,

I'll give you my own personal tour, Brother. You're not high-priority, but it shouldn't be too long now. Salway says he should hear anytime."

Michael felt sick.

"You all right?" Micah said.

"Yeah. Fine. How about if we just walk around the grounds here, then?"

"No problem."

Michael set off toward the mansion, hoping to get close enough to at least look in the windows. The Ringer fell in beside him. *Come on, Michael; come up with a plan. Anything.* "You married?" he asked.

"Was, once."

"Kids?"

"Curious today, huh, Matthew? Yeah, I had three. Wife in my Satanic life took 'em when she walked out on me. Went to Chicago with that . . . Never mind. That's over."

"Are there any kids up here? I thought I heard a baby cry the other day." It was worth a try.

Micah glanced at him. "There's such a thing as being too curious, man. Hear what I'm saying?"

"Yeah."

They walked on without speaking. As they neared the mansion, Brother Micah steered him to the right, circling behind it but keeping him too far away to see anything inside. The JetRanger was gone. Beyond the helicopter pad the mountain rose steeply. An ancient road wound up the slope toward several holes cut into the mountainside. All but one looked old, their entrances covered by decaying boards.

"Mines?" he said.

"Yeah," Micah said. "This place used to be a mining camp, I guess. Silver. Or maybe gold; I don't know."

"That one looks like it's still being worked." He pointed to the mine entrance nearest the mansion. The rock had been blasted away and a steel door placed over the entrance.

"Not for silver, it ain't," Brother Micah said. "That's a judgment shelter."

"What's that?"

"When the final day comes, man, and the wrath of God descends on the world, those who are written in the Book of Life will be sheltered in the rock from all harm. That's Holy Mother's own shelter. Someday those other mine shafts'll be turned into judgment shelters for the followers down on the ranch."

"When is this Judgment Day, Brother Micah?"

"Mother knows," he said. "When the time comes, she'll tell us."

They circled the mansion, then walked toward the half-dozen cabins clustered on the east side of the meadow. As they passed one of them, the front door opened. Michael glanced around. A white-robed guard was backing out the doorway, pulling something. Michael slowed.

When he was out of the house, the guard turned and Michael saw what he was pulling. A woman in a wheelchair.

The guard turned the wheelchair until the woman's face was plainly visible.

Jocelyn Yates.

Yates glanced up and Michael quickly turned his face away. Had she recognized him? He walked past, his heart hammering against his ribs. He was certain it was the woman he'd talked to in California. Was she a cult member, or was she a prisoner like him?

After they'd gone a few hundred feet, he said as casually as he could, "Who was that woman, Brother? I noticed she wasn't wearing a church robe. Is she a sister?"

"What woman?" Micah said.

"The one in the wheelchair."

"I didn't see any woman."

"Right back there. The one—"

"I didn't see any woman," Brother Micah snapped. He stopped and stared at Michael. "You didn't, either, understand me?" He shook his head. "Man keep asking questions about things that don't concern him, he's liable to make people think he really is a spy."

"Sorry," Michael said. "I was just making conversation."

"Yeah? Well, I think maybe it'd be better if we made conversation back in your room, you know? I think you've had enough exercise for today."

He grabbed Michael's arm and led him back toward his cell.

28

FBI Special Agent Willard Perkins sat on the edge of his desk and reread the faxed report he'd just taken from the machine. It was from the assistant director, top priority, and it instructed him to send the information along to Nestor Pruitt.

Perkins thought about taking a copy up to Pruitt's ninth-floor office personally, then decided to call him instead. He preferred to deal with the man by phone whenever possible.

As he picked up the receiver he wondered again if Pruitt was as dumb as he seemed. He suspected not, that it was a well-polished good-old-boy act. Still, he had a hard time liking him, partly because Pruitt kept asking him where he'd played basketball in college. Willard had never played any kind of sport; he'd gone to Georgetown Law School on an academic scholarship. But Nestor Pruitt couldn't seem to get it through his head that a six-foot-five black man had never played basketball.

He punched in Pruitt's extension, telling himself he was lucky to be here. FBI liaison to the task force was easy duty. But he hated it. He wanted action, not paper shuffling, and he'd filed for a transfer back to the Special Operations and Research Unit, his former assignment for ten years. But the Bureau, trying to deflect criticism for still having too few African-American agents, was keeping him in a high-visibility position. Fine; he could handle it until his transfer came through. But he could think of a hundred people he'd rather deal with than Nestor Pruitt.

"Mr. Pruitt's office," a young woman's honey drawl said.

"Cyndee, Willard Perkins. I need to speak to Nestor, please."

A moment later Nestor's voice said, "Willard, how are you, son?"

"Fine, sir. We just got a progress report on those materials from New Mexico. I thought you should know."

"Materials?"

"Yes, sir. The fragments of powdered material that were found in the café." Willard checked the letter. "The lab found traces of diazodinitrophenol."

"Di what?"

"It's an initiator, used in conjunction with PETN. As an explosives detonator. The minute quantity would indicate it was a pretty small charge."

"An explosive. So what did it blow up?"

"Probably the flask or vial, sir. We've traced the shard to an explosives company in Cleveland, name of Emtech Explosives. The company is legitimate."

"Uh-huh."

"We also secured a list of customers who bought this type of device from Emtech within the last two years. A hundred and ninety-six of them, to be exact."

"Good man."

"We've run a check on all of them," Willard said.

"Yeah?" Nestor said. "Aren't computers wonderful?"

"Yes, sir. Most of the customers have legitimate reasons for buying the detonators. But after eliminating those, we're still left with four buyers whose motives may be suspect."

"Who are they?"

"Let's see, one company with organized crime connections and a couple we know are involved in illegal arms trafficking. Oh, and one we just want more information on, not really a suspect. Some fertility clinic in California."

"How long will it take for you to run 'em to ground?" Nestor said.

"A couple of days. By the way, the powdered material turned out to be plastic."

"Plastic?"

"Right."

"What kind of plastic?"

"Polyethylene terephthalate."

"Poly . . . Spell that, will you? I'm trying to write this down."

Willard did.

"What is that?"

"It's a very common type of plastic. Used for a lot of things, including laboratory flasks."

"Could they keep viruses in them?"

"I believe so, sir."

"OK. That it?"

"That's all, yes, sir. I'll fax you a copy."

"Good. Well, keep up the good work, son. Let me know you get anything else." The line went dead.

•••

Monday, January 22, 1:10 P.M.

Annie Soares lugged her expandable briefcase crammed with computer printouts into Nestor Pruitt's office.

Nestor was expecting her. "Cyndee, honey," he said, "get Annie and me a cup of coffee, will you?"

"None for me, thanks," Annie said, "but I'll take herbal tea if you have some."

"Have a seat, have a seat," Nestor said.

"I've just read a copy of that FBI report," she said. She hadn't slept much in a week, and the exhaustion added to her level of tension made her abrupt.

"Yeah." Nestor frowned. "I've got a copy right here. We're talking terrorism, all right."

Cyndee came in carrying two steaming cups and set one in front of each of them.

"The problem is," Annie said as Cyndee left, "the terrorism goes way beyond Indian Springs, New Mexico. It extends worldwide."

Nestor looked startled. "What makes you think that?"

"Something you said at the softball field. About Revelation and the recent disasters being God's will."

He studied her to see if she was making fun of him. "That's what a lot of folks believe," he said.

"Well, it got me thinking. There's a passage in there about vials. The powdered glass they found in Indian Springs was from a laboratory flask. Raymond Miles called it a vial. It's the pattern. Do you have a Bible handy, Mr. Pruitt?"

He turned and pulled open a credenza drawer and took out a well-worn black leather Bible.

"Turn to Revelation, chapter sixteen, please."

"I didn't realize you were familiar with the Good Book, Annie."

She didn't tell him she'd just bought her first one. "Would you read it, please?"

He wet his index finger and flipped the pages. "Here it is." He cleared his throat. " 'And I heard a great voice out of the temple saying to the seven angels, Go your ways, and pour out the vials of the wrath of God upon the earth. And the first went, and poured out his vial upon the earth; and there fell a noisome and grievous sore upon the men who had the mark of the beast—' "

"Sores, Nestor. Welts. The anthrax outbreak. Go on."

He paused, then read on. " 'And the second angel poured out

his vial upon the sea; and it became as the blood of a dead man; and every living soul died in the sea.' "

"Does that sound like a red tide to you?" she said.

He looked at her. "I never thought of that, but it might be."

"Those algae blooms are not the work of God, Nestor. You remember at the fish-kill conference, I had reservations about their conclusion of natural causes? Something about the pattern, but I couldn't put my finger on it? Well, last week I looked at the Gulf bloom and the other kills. All red tides, true. But what caused the algae to bloom in the first place? It wasn't the time of year for red tide in the Gulf. And it's not very likely all these species would bloom in all these different places at exactly the same time."

She dug into her briefcase and pulled out a sheaf of papers. "Here are the results of tissue samples from all the fish kills. The same categories of pollutants are present in all of them, but with one exception, the quantities vary from area to area. You'd expect that—different countries, different pollution. That one exception is arsenic. The levels are remarkably consistent in every area where fish have died."

Nestor stared at her. "Arsenic?"

She nodded. "It's almost as if the amount added to the water was measured. By someone who knew what they were doing." She handed him a printout.

"You're saying somebody poisoned the fish?" He studied the paper. "Is that the arsenic? It doesn't look like a lot."

"By itself, no. If arsenic were the only pollutant found in the fish, it wouldn't have killed them. But their systems are already loaded with pollutants. The arsenic may have killed some by being the straw that broke the camel's back. But that's not my point."

She handed him another printout. "Experiments show arsenic stimulates rapid growth in several species of algae, including the ones responsible for these die-offs. It makes them bloom, Nestor.

Someone deliberately dumped arsenic in the coastal waters to create red tides."

He shook his head. "A month ago, I would have said you were crazy, Annie. But now..."

"Read the next verse," she said.

He looked down at his Bible. " 'And the third angel poured out his vial upon the rivers and fountains of waters and they became blood.' "

"Blood," she said. "Literally blood. In the rivers and springs. The source of the contamination of the water supplies of Boston, New York, and five other cities. Someone dumped contaminated blood in the rivers that supply their drinking water. The hepatitis B that thousands of people contracted in those cities is resistant to chlorine. And it's contracted from contaminated blood."

"Contaminated blood," he breathed.

"Go on."

He cleared his throat again. " 'And the fourth angel poured out his vial...' Oh, Lord. '...and men were scorched with great heat.' "

"The forest fires," she said. "Most of the major fires have been arson."

Nestor's voice shook. " 'And the fifth angel poured his vial on the seat of the beast; and his kingdom was full of darkness and they gnawed their tongues for pain.' " He thought a moment, then looked up. "Spiritual darkness, maybe? This country's in a bad way."

"No," she said. "Whoever's doing this thinks more literally than that. It means blindness. Cytomegalovirus. The virus causes blindness and it's broken into the general population. It's mutated. It was engineered to mutate."

"Holy God, you might be right."

"Read on."

"Let's see; next the River Euphrates dries up. Well, they wouldn't have to do much there, would they? Most of the rivers in this country are pretty dry, and *Time* magazine says the drought in the Middle East is worse than it is here."

"Right. Read the verse about the last vial, Nestor."

He read, " 'And the seventh angel poured out his vial into the air, and there came a great voice out of the temple of heaven, from the throne, saying it is done.' " He looked up, his eyes wide. "It's God's punishment on Babylon, the wicked city."

She nodded. "It's the New Mexico virus. It travels through the air."

"But that little town in New Mexico couldn't have been Babylon, Annie. The Bible's talking about a great city."

"True. But if they genetically engineered a new virus, they'd want to test it, wouldn't they? A very small change in the structure of a virus can change its effect on humans. Ebola Zaire, for example, is ninety percent lethal to humans, while Ebola Reston, which is almost identical, doesn't kill humans at all. New Mexico was a test to see if their new virus worked."

"Wouldn't they have had to test the cytomegalovirus, too?"

"Maybe they did."

"But where do they plan to use this New Mexico virus for real?"

She sighed. "That I don't know. It could be Washington. It could be New York or Los Angeles. Whatever city they believe is the Great Babylon. But I think it's going to happen soon. Nestor, we're dealing with a group of religious fanatics. Tell the FBI that one of their suspects must have a religious connection. They've got to find it."

He picked up the phone and punched in some numbers. "Willard? Nestor Pruitt. Come on up here, son. And hurry."

29

Michael woke abruptly to overhead lights glaring in his eyes.

"Rise and shine, maggot," Saul's voice grated. He sounded excited. "Special treat tonight."

Confused, Michael sat up and glanced out the window. He saw only darkness. "What time is it?"

"Night. Now snap it up."

A chill washed through him as he got out of bed and threw on his robe and sandals. Salway had gotten his report. This was the end. "Where are you taking me?"

"To a little ceremony. Now shut up and get moving."

Saul pushed him out the door into the cold darkness of a high mountain night. A hundred yards away a ring of orange mercury vapor lights lit up Mother Mary's mansion. The other buildings were only faintly etched by the white light of a waning moon rising over the plateau.

The beam of Saul's flashlight poked the ground ahead of him. "That way."

They walked along a Jeep road. Ahead and behind him, Michael saw other bobbing lights making their way in the same direction.

"You're going to find out what happens to enemies of the Church of True Atonement," Saul said.

Michael nerved himself to make a break. The darkness favored him. If he could get a jump on Saul, just two or three steps, he might make the woods.

As if reading his thoughts, the guard seized Michael's arm in an iron grip. "Wouldn't want you to miss the fun."

Around them, trees rose up on both sides, darker shadows in the gloom. Saul jerked him to the left. "Over here."

Through the trees ahead he caught glimpses of a fire. A few minutes later they stepped into a clearing, in the middle of which a bonfire blazed, sending sparks skyward. Near the fire grew a lone fir tree. Saul pulled him toward it. The other people there, mostly Holy Guards, formed a rough circle around the fire and the tree.

"What have I done?" Michael said.

Saul laughed. "Oh, so you think this is for you. Guilty conscience, maggot?" He leaned closer and lowered his voice. "Not yet. This is your friend's party. I just wanted to give you a taste of what's in store for you when we find out you've been lying to us."

Car lights flashed. Michael glanced around as a Jeep Wagoneer drove through the circle. Two men in purple-trimmed crimson robes got out.

"What's happening?"

"Shut up and watch."

The men opened the back doors of the Wagoneer and reached inside. Michael heard a low growl. From the cargo hold they hauled a large cage and, grunting, lowered it to the ground. Inside was a dog, a big one, lying helpless on the cage floor, his legs trussed and bound with duct tape and his mouth muzzled.

One of the Avenging Angels opened the cage door, seized the dog by the scruff of the neck, and dragged him out onto the ground. The dog growled again but seemed to realize he was helpless and didn't move.

The dog was huge. In fact . . . Michael looked closer. That was no dog. It was a wolf, 140 pounds at least, a beautiful animal, gray and brown with a white underbelly.

The Angels slipped a rope around the wolf's haunches and dragged him toward the tree as the guards jumped out of the way. When they reached the tree, one of the Angels threw the rope over a limb and they both pulled, dragging the wolf into the air upside down, whining and yelping.

Michael watched in disbelief and outrage.

The two men taunted the bound wolf, making growling noises and feinting at it. Then, laughing, they turned and went back to the Wagoneer.

A moment later they came back leading a man between them. He was naked, his body covered with bruises and burns. His arms and hands were bound with duct tape, and his face was so purple and swollen it took Michael a few moments to recognize him as Lopak, the Arm assassin.

One of the Angels slipped a coil of rope from his shoulder and worked a loop of it under Lopak's feet while the other held him. "Strike Satan," the Angel with the rope said, and jerked Lopak's feet out from under him. His head hit the ground with a *thunk*.

The other Angel laughed. "Strike Satan."

They dragged Lopak to the tree.

One of the men threw the rope over the limb, and together they hauled Lopak up next to the wolf. He knew what was coming now, and his eyes went wide with fear.

An Angel pulled a long knife from his robe, and Michael wanted to take it away and use it on him. The man slashed the blade across the wolf's flank, and the animal struggled in rage and pain. Blood dripped from his fur.

They cut the tape away from the wolf's hind feet, then quickly slit the tape around the front feet and jumped back as the wolf clawed at them. One of them seized a leather thong attached to the muzzle and jerked. The muzzle fell off.

The wolf, maddened with pain, turned on the only human he could reach. Bared teeth flashed into Lopak's throat and blood spurted. Lopak shrieked. The wolf snapped again, his jaws closing on the assassin's neck, claws raking his body, his testicles, drawing blood from a dozen wounds. Lopak shrieked again, the noise turning into a wailing gurgle.

Sickened, Michael looked away. In his eagerness to see the torture, Saul had moved forward, and the other guards had also unconsciously tightened the circle, cheering on the wolf and the Avenging Angels. For a moment Michael was behind them, unwatched.

He backed quietly away. No one noticed.

He kept backing. When he reached the shadows of the trees, he turned and ran.

The forest shut out the light from the fire, but enough moonlight filtered through the trees to outline the road, and he ran along it. What now? He still didn't know where Ursula's baby was or even if the child was here. But there was one person who would know. It was a risk. She might turn him in, but he had nowhere else to go.

He headed for Jocelyn Yates's cabin.

Her windows were dark. If this was really her cabin. He'd only seen her coming out of it once. He paused at the door to catch his breath, then knocked.

Nothing happened.

He knocked again louder, glancing over his shoulder.

Inside, a light came on. After a moment a woman's voice said, "Who's there?"

"It's Michael Walker. I need help. Can I come in?"

"No. Go away."

"Please. You're my only chance."

There was silence. Then the voice said, without color or emotion, "The door's not locked."

He opened it and stepped in, blinking in the light, and closed the door behind him.

The cabin had one large room. To his right a bookcase crammed with books stood against the wall, and in front of it was a table overflowing with papers. A narrow high-railed bed occupied the left wall, a wheelchair next to it. Jocelyn Yates was sitting upright in the bed, propped up by pillows. From her neck a pair of glasses hung by a gold chain. Her long gray hair was disheveled, but she made no attempt to smooth it.

As he entered, she glanced at him without interest. Her expression was listless, as if she'd been drugged.

"I'm sorry to wake you."

"You didn't wake me. I don't sleep much these nights." She didn't sound drugged, he thought. She sounded like a woman who had given up and was waiting to die.

"You remember me?"

"Of course. I saw you here two days ago."

"Thanks for not turning me in."

She gave a slight shrug. "It's of no importance."

"It is to me. I need your help."

"You shouldn't be here."

"You left me a note in California that implied the Ringers had kidnapped my sister's baby. What did you expect me to do? I have to get him out. Where is he?"

"You can't escape. You'll only endanger the baby."

"So he is here?"

Yates said nothing.

He walked over to her bed. "Who are you? Are you a member of the Ringers?"

She shook her head. "I'm a prisoner, as you are." She noticed his skepticism and added, "Oh, they don't need to lock me up. How would I escape?"

"Why did they do it? What do these people want with Ursula's baby? She had nothing to do with them, did she?"

"Please don't ask me any more. I'm not supposed to talk to

anyone. There are things worse than death, Mr. Walker, and I'm not a brave woman. Please leave."

"Tell me where the baby is, first."

She shook her head. "I can't."

He sat on the bed.

She glanced nervously at the door. "If they find us together . . ."

"I'm not leaving until I know."

"I don't want him hurt."

"I don't intend to hurt him."

"They'll shoot you, and if the baby's with you, he may get hurt as well."

"Where is he?"

Yates bit her lip but said nothing.

Michael folded his arms. "If they catch me here with you, they'll want to know what you told me. And their methods of finding out are nasty. I'm willing to stay right here until they come." It was a bluff. By now, Saul would have discovered his absence and the search would be on. He couldn't afford to wait much longer.

Her eyes widened in fear and she began wringing her hands. The fingernails were bitten down to blood. "The child isn't Ursula's," she whispered. "You have no claim to him."

"You're wrong. I saw her give birth to him."

She shook her head impatiently. "The embryo was supposed to be implanted in Paula Sue Tulley. Mother Mary. There was a . . . mistake. Your sister received the embryo intended for Tulley."

"And for that they tried to kill her? It wasn't my sister's fault."

"No, but she could have ruined their plans."

"What plans? What's going on?"

"The child is safe and well."

Anger and frustration boiled over and Michael erupted. "Safe?" he shouted. "Are you serious? Do you know what this little group of psychos is doing right now? They're watching a man being torn apart by a wild animal. And they're cheering. That's how safe the kid is. You know damn well what kind of people these are. Why are you helping them?"

Yates went deathly pale. After a moment she said, "I know what they are, yes. But I didn't know when I got involved; please believe me. There's nothing I can do, now." She looked up at him. "I've committed a mortal sin, Mr. Walker. I was raised a Catholic, but I outgrew it, or so I thought. Now I know I'm lost. When the Devil buys your soul, the sale is final."

"The hell it is. You've still got a soul, lady. You're not one of them. Just tell me where the kid is and I'll leave you alone."

She said nothing.

He said, his voice softer, "You know what else I saw on one of my walks, Dr. Yates? A pit dug into the ground. Ten feet deep. You know who was in it? A little girl. She couldn't be more than four. She was being punished. That's how they treat children. Sooner or later, Ursula's baby is going to do something that breaks one of their rules, and the same thing, or something worse, will happen to him. Is that what you want?"

She shook her head, weeping silently now.

"This is his only chance. Please tell me where he is."

Gasping, she said, "In the west wing of the mansion. There's a door at the end of that wing, but it's always locked. And the front door is guarded. There's a guard at the baby's door, too. Please, don't try it; you'll only—"

But Michael was out the door and running for the mansion.

Within ten steps he knew he'd never make it. Searchlights stabbed back and forth across the field. Guards milled under the mercury vapor lights in front of the mansion. A half-mile in the opposite direction, floodlights had been turned on at the gate. He dodged an oval of light that swung past him, and ran across the meadow. If they didn't know he'd been to Yates's cabin there might still be a faint hope, even if they caught him. But as he neared the buildings on the other side of the field, he was pinned by the excruciating brightness of a searchlight.

"Stop or you're dead!" a voice shouted through a bullhorn.

He stopped and raised his hands.

A moment later, Saul ran up to him, an assault rifle aimed at him. "Bad choice."

"I wasn't trying to escape," Michael said as calmly as he could. "I didn't want to watch so I went for a walk."

"In the dark?"

"The company was better."

The butt of Saul's rifle struck him in the stomach and he doubled over. Two pairs of hands seized him and hustled him toward his cell.

"We'll see what Holy Mother says when I tell her you tried to escape." Saul pushed him into the room, sending him sprawling onto the floor. "There isn't much left of your friend Lopak." He grinned as he backed out, covering him with the rifle. "But the wolf is still alive."

30

Tuesday, January 23, 9:05 A.M.

Mother Mary Grace stood at the floor-to-ceiling window of her private office and gazed down at the river cutting a silver track through the rock walls of the canyon far below. Her river. Her world, for she would rule it, oh, yes, after the judgment. She was the Chosen One. She, Paula Sue Tully from Smith Corners, Arkansas, was special.

But in a far, small place in her mind a tiny voice that was not her voice of power was trying to break through to spread doubt, trying to confuse her. *You're not the Chosen One,* it said. *In fact, you're nothing very special at all. And your voice of power is not God; it's only a delusion.*

"Stop it!" she shrieked suddenly. She covered her ears with her hands. "I am the Chosen."

On the ragged edge of control she took deep breaths, breaths that threatened to become panting. "Stop; stop," she whispered. "All right now, it's all right; don't listen to it."

And there, she had done it; the doubting voice was silent. She turned back to the window.

Two sharp raps sounded and the door opened.

She wheeled, furious at the interruption. But it was only Salway, only little Salway. It always surprised her, the way she expected someone of normal height to come through the door and would see nothing until she lowered her eyes a foot and found the top of his graying head. She exhaled her fury in a gusty breath. "What is it?"

He bowed apologetically. "I thought you'd like to know. The Agent of Judgment has been successfully moved from Genflex. We're storing it in the judgment shelter."

See? she told the small, nagging voice. *You need more proof that I'm the Chosen One?* She favored Salway with a smile. "You and the scientists have done well."

"One small thing, Holy Mother. I would suggest we advance Operation Babylon."

"Advance it? Why?"

He cleared his throat. "The FBI is investigating. They searched the building. I don't think they'll be able to trace ownership to us, but to be safe—"

"FBI?" Rage flooded through her. "How dare they! Satan's work! How did they find out?"

Salway flinched. "I don't know. Somehow they've linked the laboratory to New Mexico."

As quickly as it had come, the rage left her and calm washed over her again. It was all right; the FBI was too late. God was guiding her. There was nothing they, or any other Satanic force, could do to stop her now. "How soon can the Avenging Angels be ready?"

"We can have it transported and in place within forty-eight hours."

She nodded. "Then transport it. Babylon will fall Thursday. And call the media. NBC, CBS, ABC, CNN. I want them all. The day after the city becomes a rotting corpse, I'll tell the world about the child."

He bowed.

"And double the security. Red alert." She watched him leave, shutting the door quietly behind him. She wished the moral authority of her announcement would be enough to control America, but she knew it wouldn't be. America was a godless, secular, materialistic culture, and without proof its people wouldn't believe that God had appointed her to bring about the apocalypse. Unfortunately, she would have to use the Agent of Judgment, the terror, to show them she was the Chosen One.

The end of the world. She shook her head. Why did that idea terrify people so much? Wouldn't they all die sooner or later anyway? Their own death or the end of the world, it amounted to the same thing, for them.

Smiling a little sadly, she turned back to the window.

•••

Tuesday, January 23, 10:20 A.M.

Over the intercom in Nestor Pruitt's office Cyndee's voice said, "Mr. Perkins of the FBI on line three."

Nestor picked up the receiver. "What do you have for me, Willard?"

"I've got the results of the raid on the laboratory in California, Mr. Pruitt. Our agents found an empty building. But we went through it very thoroughly. There seem to have been two different operations in that place."

"Two?"

"Well, the front of it was apparently used as the fertility clinic. The name is still on the door—Genflex. But most of the building seems to have been used for something else."

"Like what?"

"Not sure. The place was stripped, all the furniture and fixtures removed. But there were a dozen or so rooms that could have been used as laboratories; at least the wiring and plumbing would indicate that. The rest was probably a warehouse of some kind."

"Laboratories? Like in virus?"

"It's possible, but we can't be sure. We found no trace of any viruses or bacteria. And the labs weren't top-security at all, just regular labs. If these people were playing around with something deadly, they were pretty casual about it."

"So you don't know any more than you did before?"

"I didn't say that, sir. We did find traces of other chemicals."

"What chemicals?"

"Arsenic, mostly. Found on the concrete floor of the warehouse. Also, we took your advice about looking for a religious connection. We checked out this Genflex; it's a California corporation, legally organized. The incorporators were all California residents, but none of them lived any longer at the addresses they listed. However, the neighbors remembered one of them, an Irving Ewell."

"Yeah?"

"He's a member of the Church of True Atonement."

●●●

Tuesday, January 23, 7:10 P.M.

In the Sweetwater, Montana, public library, James Walker sat at a reading table, leafing through a newspaper. As he turned the pages of a week-old *Rustler,* Sweetwater's weekly paper, he was irritated with himself. He'd been searching for Michael for four days without success. Finally, it had occurred to James to backtrack and see if he could find word of Lopak, the closer. If something had happened to him, an accident or an arrest, it might have made the local papers. And that could give James a line on Michael. But there was nothing in this edition. He threw the paper aside and picked up the previous week's.

And stopped. There. Front page. "ATTEMPTED ASSASSINA-TION AT RINGER RANCH." He stared at a photo taken by a

Bozeman TV crew of two men struggling. Lopak was one of them; James could see the face. And who was that with his face nearly turned away?

He sat back in astonishment. Michael? In the Church of True Atonement? He couldn't believe it. What was he doing there? Lopak must have located him and followed him into the ranch. And somehow Michael had recognized him.

James read the story beneath the headline, his amazement growing. Lopak had been attempting to assassinate Mother Mary but was prevented by the quick action of a loyal follower, whose name was not given. Lopak? Trying to kill Mother Mary? He shook his head. Unbelievable. And Michael a loyal follower? What the hell?

Unfortunately, the story went on to say, the assassin had escaped and his whereabouts were unknown. James smiled grimly. He doubted it. If Lopak had escaped, he would have heard from him. The Ringers must still have him.

He put down the paper. So Michael was on the Ringer ranch. *If you went in there to hide, Michael,* he thought, *it didn't work. I still found you.* He gnawed his lip, thinking. He could phone the Ringers and tell them Michael was an impostor. But that was too uncertain—James didn't know what their reaction would be. Michael had to die without drawing attention to him, and the only way James could be sure that would happen was to kill him himself. To do that, he would have to go inside the ranch. He shook his head. That would take some explaining.

He checked his watch. Too late to do anything today, but first thing in the morning he'd drive out to New Jerusalem and see what he could do.

31

Nestor Pruitt sat in the cabinet room of the White House and tried not to fidget. He was sticking his neck out here, he knew. It was his career on the line. Heck, what was he thinking? As soon as they found someone to replace him, his career was probably over anyway.

He was sitting at the end of the table, the least important position. Director of the Task Force for Disaster Control. TFDC. The initials had become a joke. They were calling him The Fucked-up Disaster Coordinator, good gracious. Well, maybe he hadn't done a great job, but he'd done the best he could. He'd never asked for the job anyway.

The weather outside was warm and muggy, typical for Washington in summer but not for Washington in January. And it didn't seem much cooler in here, although the air-conditioning was running. A trickle of sweat ran down the inside of his arm.

He glanced at Annie Soares sitting next to him, who seemed a little awed by the White House. She was the one who should have been director of the task force, he thought. But she never would be—no political advantage to the president. That was the way Washington worked.

At the other end of the table sat the president's chief of staff, a man named Sloane. With that patch over the left eye he looked like a darn pirate instead of a political adviser. Wore it for effect, Nestor suspected, like that guy in the ads in the fifties—who was he?—the Hathaway shirt guy? But a man needed both eyes to see the road ahead. Couldn't see out of his left eye; maybe that was why he kept nudging the president to the right.

Sloane was ignoring Nestor, talking baseball with the attorney general. Next to the AG sat Billy Massey, director of the FBI, not talking. He was a civilian now, but he was still a general underneath; anyone could tell. The guy even sat at attention. Ugliest man in Washington, Nestor thought. Looked like a darned frog with a chest. Nestor had talked to him, tried to sound him out on this, but Massey had refused to commit himself. Right now he was scraping skin from his bald head with the blade of a pocketknife, looking at it, and wiping it on his pants.

The door opened and President Bishop strode in. "Morning, gentlemen." Distinguished gray hair. The president from central casting. He pulled out his chair and sat, giving Nestor a grudging nod. "I believe I know everyone here but this attractive lady."

"Mr. President," Nestor said, "this is Dr. Annie Soares. She's been working with me on the task force."

The president favored her with his warmest baby-kissing smile. "Welcome. Well, let's get right to it, shall we? Nestor, what do you have for us?"

Nestor outlined the plot as he understood it, then turned it over to Annie to explain the details—she sounded a lot more convincing. He watched the president's expression change from disbelief, to astonishment, to worry, and finally to anger.

Annie said, "And we believe, Mr. President, that the New Mexico deaths were a test of the virus. In the cult's vision, the seventh vial. They're getting ready for the death of the Great Babylon."

"Babylon? What's that?" he said.

"Babylon is a city that was regarded in the Bible as particularly evil. We think the Ringers are getting ready to use the virus on an

American city, one that they regard as evil. And we think they're going to do it soon. Unfortunately, we don't know which city that is."

President Bishop turned to his science adviser, a tweedy older man with an Old Testament beard who was a Harvard professor. "Is this possible, Dr. Dunleavy? Can people really make viruses?"

The adviser nodded. He kept licking his lips, Nestor noted, his tongue pink like something skinned. "With genetic engineering, it's a simple-enough matter to insert genes in order to encode just about anything into the DNA or RNA of a virus. Nowadays, any crackpot with a few thousand dollars' worth of equipment and a biology degree could insert, say, Ebola Zaire genes into a virus adapted for respiratory transmission. Influenza, say. Or, in this case, apparently hantavirus." He licked his lips. "This is not science fiction anymore, Mr. President."

The president's scowl deepened. "Billy, what do you know about this cult?"

The FBI director had put his pocketknife away. "Organized in California in 1989 by one Paula Sue Tully," he said. "We don't know much about her early life, except that she's from Arkansas. She's charismatic, has a real knack for separating people from their money, and it's our belief she's a paranoid schizophrenic."

"Schizo? Is she crazy enough to kill millions of people?"

"She's unpredictable. She preaches a violent form of judgment. Apparently she has apocalyptic visions. It's possible, given the technology, that she could translate her visions into mass murder and justify it theologically."

"What about her followers? How big is this cult?"

"Fifteen to twenty thousand that we know of scattered across the country. Maybe four thousand are living at her headquarters in Montana."

"Are they armed?"

Massey looked uncomfortable. "I'm afraid so, Mr. President.

ATF was already investigating them, and since we traced the virus to their lab we've had them under surveillance. Our intelligence indicates they're heavily armed. AK-forty-sevens, Uzis, TEC-nines, at least one Vulcan. That's a high-tech Gatling gun, state-of-the-art. Six twenty-millimeter barrels, fires three thousand rounds a minute."

"Jesus. What about this virus? If they have it, where is it?"

"The evidence is circumstantial. Manufacture of the virus was traced to a lab in Livermore, California, which was owned by the cult. When we searched it, the lab was empty, stripped clean. But if they have manufactured this agent in quantity, they could hide it anywhere. Enough virus to wipe out the whole country could be stored in a medium-sized room."

"So we don't even know where we're supposed to look?"

Massey hesitated. "We have a good idea." He signaled an aide, who spread out a map and a series of photos on the table. "These are satellite and high-altitude overflight photos of Heaven's Door—that's the name Mother Mary uses for her retreat in the center of the ranch." He took out a pen and pointed to one of the photos. "The compound is built on an abandoned mining camp. This is her mansion here, butting up against the mountain. This structure, here, is a mine she turned into a fallout shelter, probably with biological hazard protection. If I were her, I'd store the virus there. It would be the safest place.

"Where's that other photo, Lon? Oh, there it is. See the panel truck being unloaded in this one, Mr. President? That plastic case those two men are carrying into the shelter? According to our experts, that's the type of protective container laboratories often use to transport hazardous material. Liquids, I'm talking about."

"Can you tell what's in it?"

"No, sir. We can only surmise."

"Surmise. And what do you surmise?"

"That this is the virus, sir."

The president studied him. "How confident are you in that conclusion?"

"Well, under normal circumstances we'd wait until we had direct evidence to substantiate it."

"I'm asking you, Billy. Given the other information we have, do you think your conclusions from these photos are reliable enough to act on?"

Massey squirmed, glancing at Nestor. *Crunch time, Billy,* Nestor thought. "As I said, sir, we normally wouldn't act on the basis of this alone. But, given the seriousness of the situation, this may be the only corroborating evidence we'll get, and . . ."

President Bishop's scowl deepened.

The FBI director exhaled. "Yes, Mr. President, I think we have to trust the information. And I think the situation warrants rapid action."

"What kind of action would you suggest?"

The director seemed more comfortable discussing tactics. "Assuming the agent is stored inside the compound, we have to make sure it stays there at all costs until it can be destroyed. Since we don't know which city is the target, once the virus leaves the ranch we probably won't be able to stop it in time." He tapped the map with his pen. "Heaven's Door is located in an isolated area of the mountains. If we can quarantine the virus there, we have a good chance of preventing its spread."

He looked up. "We can go one of two ways, Mr. President. We can surround Heaven's Door, creating a blockade which would prevent the agent from leaving, while we negotiate with them. Or we can use the element of surprise, insert a strike force directly into the compound to take out her paramilitary guards, then search for and destroy the agent."

Sloane raised his eyebrow above his eye patch. "He's talking about another Waco here, Mr. President. We're still getting flak about that fiasco—a small bunch of religious kooks assaulted by the might of the federal government. We need to avoid another disaster like that."

"This is a hell of a lot more serious than Waco," Massey retorted. "These people are responsible for casualties in the thousands already. So far we've had anthrax in twenty-three cities. The water supplies of seven cities were contaminated. And thousands of people had to be relocated away from the Gulf Coast, not to mention the ones forced out of their homes because of the arson-caused forest fires."

"I agree." The president looked at Sloane. "Losing a couple million people in New York or Washington would be a hell of a political liability if I *don't* act. So which option would you suggest, Billy?"

"As I said, this woman is dangerously insane. If we attempt to negotiate, she could release the virus, causing high casualties among our agents. I believe our best chance is a surgical strike on the compound."

The president pursed his lips. "What about the possibility of a hostage situation?"

"Our information is that there are no outsiders within the Heaven's Door compound," Massey said.

"Any children?"

"No, sir. All children are kept on the lower ranch. Mr. President, there's another reason for a quick strike. This woman has more firepower than many third world countries. If she has a chance to get entrenched, our casualties could be very high."

President Bishop rubbed his jaw. "How soon could your men be ready?"

"We can have a strike force in there within twenty-four hours."

The president sat silently a moment, then slapped the table with his hand and stood. "Gentlemen, I'm not going to sit by and watch some nutball cause the end of the world, not on my watch. Billy, I want a strike force in that compound in twenty-four hours."

•••

Thursday, January 25, 7:30 A.M.

Darby Mackenzie's van bounced up the Boulder River road. On this stretch the gravel road was only wide enough for a single car, and she knew if she met someone now at this speed, one of them would go into the river. Probably her, since the water was on the right side.

Damn it, why did that cake oven always pick the worst time to act up? The thermostat read too low and Mother Mary's huckleberry chocolate cake had burned. Darby had to bake another one, and it had made her late for her delivery. If she was more than an hour behind her scheduled time the guards wouldn't let her on the ranch.

Concentrate, Mackenzie. This road is bad enough when you're paying attention. She turned her thoughts back to her driving just in time to avoid ramming a spruce tree. The van swerved, but she got it under control and kept going. Dodging rocks, she stepped on the gas, and the van rattled along faster.

Damn! She nailed that one and it was sharp. She hoped . . .

The van began to slew, and the steering wheel pulled to the left. Darby's heart sank. *Not a flat, God. Not here. Whose side are you on anyway?*

She took her foot off the gas and braked, got out, and looked. The left front tire had gone completely flat. She glanced up the road, calculating her chances of making it the remaining five miles. Slim. She'd have to change it.

She flung open the rear doors and unscrewed the bolt holding the spare tire to the side of the van, hoping it had air in it; she hadn't checked it in at least a year. As she pulled the tire out of the back, a car came around the corner behind her. She glanced around and realized she was blocking the road. The car, a Toyota, pulled up behind the van and stopped, dust swirling around it. A man got out.

"Problems, miss?" He looked irritated.

Darby glanced at him, then did a double take. He was tall and looked a little like Matt, except he was blond. Could they be related? She looked closer, then decided probably not. There was a hardness in this man's face that Cooper didn't have. He resembled Matt like an arrow resembled the bird it killed.

She smiled at him. "I hit a rock. Wiped out my tire. I'm sorry I'm blocking the road."

"Well," he said, "I'd help you, but I'm late. I'll see if I can get around you."

She'd pulled off the road as far as she dared. On her right was the river fifty feet below, on the left a rock face. The man got into his car, eased it around the rear of the van, backed up, jockeyed, and drove forward again. She could see he wasn't going to make it.

Finally, his face red with anger, he backed the Toyota up and rammed the bumper of the van. It jumped forward. She gasped. The front of the van tilted a little.

He eased the Toyota around the van and sped off.

"You bastard!" Darby flipped him the bird, then went around to look. A trickle of gravel slid from beneath the right front tire into the river below. She didn't dare change the tire with the van leaning like this. Maybe she could back it up.

She climbed in, holding her breath as the van rocked a bit. Murmuring a prayer, she started it and slid the gearshift into reverse. Slowly she stepped on the gas. The rear wheel spun and the van tilted more. Frantic, she gunned the engine. Gravel sprayed and the van began to slide over the edge. *Shit! Please don't! Please!* Then the right wheels caught on solid rock and the van shot backward onto the road.

She stomped on the brake and sat slumped over the steering wheel, trembling and crying.

When she was recovered enough, she wiped her eyes and got out. That jerk! She put the wrench over the lug nuts and stood on the handle to loosen them. Wait until she saw him again! One by one she unscrewed the nuts, then jacked up the front of the van and pulled off the flat. She should report him to the cops. She wrestled the spare into position and tightened the lug nuts.

Still fuming, she lowered the jack, threw everything into the back of the van, and drove on toward the ranch.

32

In a large clearing in the Gallatin National Forest twenty miles south of the Ringer ranch, Special Agent in Charge Willard Perkins watched as the second of two C-141 transport planes touched down on the makeshift runway. He'd gotten his transfer, he thought wryly, and with a vengeance—appointed SAC of the assault on Heaven's Door, code-named Operation Dry-clean. According to Director Massey, it was because of his special ops training and the fact that he'd been in on the case from the early stages. That he had three other SACs to back him up, plus the commander of the Hostage Rescue Team, was some comfort, but not much. If he screwed this up, he'd be shuffling papers the rest of his career.

The plane taxied toward the trees, its engines roaring as it reversed thrust to slow. Inside would be the rest of the Hostage Rescue Team from Quantico. As good as any counterterrorist unit in the world, Willard thought, but with only a hundred men, there just weren't enough of them to handle this situation. So he'd asked for, and received, four regional FBI SWAT teams in addition to the HRT. Add to that a Critical Incident Negotiation Team and four agents from the Behavioral Science Unit and they were as ready as they were ever going to be. If the weather would cooperate.

He raised his radio. "What's the wind doing now?"

"Picking up, sir. Gusts up to twenty-five knots."

Not a problem yet for the helicopters, but it would hamper the efficiency of the tear gas. As they inserted a strike force into Heaven's Door, he intended to employ massive quantities of CS gas and flash-bangs to disorient the cult guards. He didn't anticipate interference from the cult members living on the lower ranch, but the Bradley Fighting Vehicles and Abrams tanks that would enter the ranch through the main gate would ensure that. Only if his agents were fired upon would they return fire. But if they had to, they would play for keeps.

He hoped to hell the intelligence reports were accurate. If the compound turned out to be empty of anything dangerous, this assault was going to be hard to explain to the American people. And guess who would be the scapegoat.

The plane had stopped and began disgorging men. Willard strode forward to greet Donald Post, commander of the HRT, a skinny man with big ears and a leathery face who was wearing fatigues.

Post turned his head and spit a stream of chewing tobacco into the dirt. "I want my men protected from this damn virus," he said, shaking hands with an iron grip.

"They'll all be in biological hazard suits, Commander," Willard said, knowing Post had already been briefed. He didn't blame him for double-checking. "If things go right, we won't need them."

"When have you ever known things to go right?" Post growled. "Where's our forward command post?"

"At the gate of the compound. Heaven's Door."

"Heaven's Door." The commander snorted. "More likely the gates of hell. You got enough choppers?"

"We've got enough."

As the HRT and SWAT teams scrambled to put on protective suits in the tents erected in the staging area, Willard and Post finalized tactics and timetables. When the commander finally ran out of questions and suggestions, he said, "If we're gonna do it, by God, let's do it."

For the tenth time that morning, Willard spoke into his radio. "What's the wind doing?"

"Between gusts at the moment, sir."

Willard looked at the commander and nodded. "Load your men."

Darby pulled up to the gate at Heaven's Door. What was this? Two guards? There'd never been two guards at the gate before.

Both of them came out of the gatehouse and strode toward her, looking even grimmer than usual. She took a deep breath and brushed her hair out of her eyes, smiling at them.

"You're late," one of them said. He was big enough to be a pro football player, and he'd been at the gate before. He looked her over, not returning her smile. "What happened to you?"

She looked down at her sweatshirt, streaked with dirt. Her face was dirty, too, she supposed. "I had a flat tire. I'm not very good at changing them." That ought to appeal to his woman-hating ego.

"Step out of the van."

"What?"

"We're going to search your van."

"Why? It was just searched at the lower ranch. You've never done it here before."

"Why is not your concern. Step out of the van."

She opened the door and got out, watching as the guards went around to the back. One of them opened the doors, and the other climbed in. She could hear him opening and slamming the doors of the cabinets she'd installed.

Through the gates she could see groups of men running in the distance, some kind of training exercise. She wondered where Matt was. She'd heard nothing from him, and when she drove through the lower ranch she'd looked for him, but there'd been no sign of him. Her worry had turned into fear for his safety. Had he been found out? Maybe he was up here. She chewed a rough spot on her fingernail as she waited for the guards to finish their search.

Behind her the gatehouse stood empty. As she glanced at it a thought came to her. Every time she'd made a delivery, the guards had logged her in. If Matt was in Heaven's Door, there might be a record of it in the gatehouse. She looked at the guards. Neither of them was paying any attention to her.

She eased away from the van, then hurried over to the gatehouse. The door was closed. She tried it. It wasn't locked. With a glance over her shoulder she opened it and stepped in.

It wasn't much bigger than a telephone booth and smelled like a locker room. On a shelf sat a black phone and a walkie-talkie. And the logbook. She glanced at the guards. One was still in the van; the other was standing behind it, saying something to him. Part of her mind screamed at her, *What are you doing!? Get out!* She didn't know what they would do to her if they caught her, but she knew it wouldn't be pleasant.

Heart pounding, she lifted the cover of the book. The pages were marked by date, and each page was divided into IN and OUT sides. She turned to today's date and scanned the page. There were three names but no Matthew Cooper. The OUT side was blank.

She turned to yesterday's page. Eight names in and six out. No Matthew Cooper. Was he using an alias? With sweating hands she flipped the pages, going backward in time, scanning them for Matt's name.

A bead of sweat trickled down her chest into her bra. *Hurry, Darby.* She was turning the pages so rapidly she had gone past Matt's name before she recognized it. She backed up. There it was. January 18. Matthew Cooper, IN. She skimmed the OUT entries again since that date. No Matt. He was still in there.

"Having fun, lady?" The big guard stood at the door staring at her.

She gasped and slammed the book shut, her heart jitterbugging. "Oh, I, uh, was just curious. I'm sorry. I know it's none of my business—"

"You're right. It's none of your business. What were you looking for?"

"No one. In particular. I, uh, just wanted to see if I knew anyone here. Just killing time. Are you through searching?" She was babbling, she knew. "I'll just leave the stuff here and be on my way." She started past him.

"No, you won't." The guard held up a robed arm and blocked her exit. "You'll tell us what you were looking for."

"I told you. No one."

The other guard strode up, scowling. "What do we have, a spy?"

"Looks like it, Brother. I caught her snooping in the logbook."

"Guys, look; you know me. I'm just the bakery girl. I've been delivering stuff to Mother Mary for months."

"For all we know, you've been spying for months. We're going to have to take you inside for questioning."

"Are you serious?" She fought down panic. "All right, I was snooping; I admit it. It's one of my bad habits. But I'm not a spy, for Christ's sake. Why would I spy on you?"

Without answering they seized her arms and hustled her toward her van.

This was America, she thought. This couldn't be happening. Fear turned to outrage. "You people are seriously paranoid; you know that? Ouch, let go."

They pushed her into the passenger seat of the van. One of the guards went around to the driver's side and climbed in.

"You're gonna hear from my lawyer about this!" she shouted.

"You're a trespasser," the guard said, turning the key. "You don't have any rights here." He gunned the engine and they roared toward the mansion.

•••

Thursday, January 25, 8:21 A.M.

Salway plumped up the pillow on his desk chair and sat down, picking up his cup of Ovaltine to sip it while he planned the day's schedule. If it weren't for his oversight of the operation of the ranch, it would, he knew, fall apart. Mother had no head for business, although there was no doubt she was a brilliant strategist. The apocalypse plan, for example. He wished he'd thought of it. But he was brilliant, too, in his own way, and someday she would see that. Then maybe she would love him the way he loved her.

He sighed. As usual, there were a dozen administrative details, but today they could wait. This morning he would supervise the loading of the Agent of Judgment. By noon it would be on its way to New York, the Great Babylon. Once it was out of Heaven's Door, there was no way it could be stopped. By tomorrow the entire city would be infected, dying. Then the world would listen. The world would come to their door. *The best part,* he thought as he set his cup down on the plastic coaster, *is that enough of the agent to wipe out an entire city will fit into the trunk of my Buick.*

The phone rang and he picked it up in irritation. "Yes?"

"Salway? Brother Ezekiel. I'm in Duluth, Minnesota."

"Yes?" For a moment Salway couldn't remember why he'd sent him there.

"He's a fake."

"Who is?"

"Matthew Cooper. We located the real Cooper. He's in jail for delinquent alimony. Your Cooper's a spy."

"Ah. I suspected it. What's his real name?"

"I don't know that yet. Do you want me to find out?"

Salway thought a moment. "No. That won't be necessary. We can get the information from him more quickly ourselves. Come back here. I have more important things for you to do." He hung up. Another administrative detail. He would tell Saul to interrogate the spy.

The intercom on his desk buzzed. "Brother Raguel is here to see you, sir."

"Raguel? Here?"

"Yes, sir. He says it's urgent."

He hesitated. If Raguel was here in person, it meant trouble. Better get Mother in on this. "Send him into Mother Mary's office."

•••

Thursday, January 25, 8:25 A.M.

In her wheelchair, Jocelyn Yates opened the door to her cabin and looked out. A few hundred feet away a group of men were doing wind sprints on the parade ground. She looked in the other direction, where a crimson-robed guard strode up the steps of the mansion. As she watched, he disappeared inside. Except for that activity, the grounds seemed deserted. It was now or never.

After Ursula Walker's brother had left her two nights ago, her shame had risen, like the covers, to her chin. And it kept rising. She was suffocating in shame, and she knew she could take no more of it.

She wheeled her chair back from the door so she could open it. Then, trying not to show the fear that nearly incapacitated her, she guided the chair down the ramp. The air was cold and she hesitated, wondering if she should go back and get her coat. Then she realized it didn't matter; she probably wouldn't be alive long enough to need it. She turned her chair and rolled toward the mansion.

33

Michael held his blanket over the window of his cell and swung his sandal at it. Glass cracked. He swung again, not too hard. He wanted enough big pieces left to make a weapon. Tossing the blanket away, he checked his work. There, that one would do, a shard shaped like a long triangular blade.

Carefully he pressed inward on the fragments of glass surrounding the one he had chosen, then worked his new knife free. A strip of sheet from his bunk would make a handle. He wrapped it around the wide end of the shard, then inspected his weapon. It'd have to do. Tonight, he suspected, was the night they'd make him dance with the wolf. He didn't plan to do that. The glass knife wouldn't help him escape, but he might take a few guards with him before they killed him.

Outside, he heard the sound of a vehicle rattling toward the jail. His knife in one hand, he went to the window and peered out, but he couldn't see the vehicle. Somewhere behind the building it stopped. He heard voices.

No, just one voice. A woman's. Furious.

Darby?

He felt like he'd been kicked in the stomach.

"This is America!" she was shouting. "You can't just kidnap an

American citizen. I'll sue your miserable butts for every penny you've got!"

Darby, no question. Somehow they must have linked her to him. Taken her when she made a delivery.

The inside of him fractured and collapsed. He'd prepared himself for his own death, but Darby in the hands of the Ringers was something else. He sank to the bed. She was going to die, too, and it was his fault.

"Get your hands off me, you smelly bastard!" she shouted. "You can't do this! I want a lawyer."

The door of the empty cell next to his creaked open.

"Ouch!" a man's voice yelled. "You little slut. Get in there; maybe we'll teach you some manners before we're done with you."

The door slammed shut and Michael heard a key turn in the lock. "Whore of Satan," the guard's voice muttered. The sound of footsteps receded.

"That's the last cake you'll ever get from me, buster!" she shouted, her voice muffled through the wall. Then a softer, "Shit."

He waited until he thought the guard was out of hearing, then stood and walked over to the wall. "Darby?" he said.

"Matt? Is that you? Oh, thank God."

"Don't thank him yet. I'm not exactly in a position to help you. What happened?"

"I was trying to save your worthless hide. I didn't know what happened to you. You could have at least let me know where you were."

"I haven't been able to get to a telephone."

"How did they find out about you?"

"It's a long story," he said. "What are you doing here?"

"I was worried to death about you, so I snooped in their logbook a little; that's all."

"That was dumb."

"Yeah? Well, it doesn't look like you were any smarter. You're a prisoner, too."

"I'm working on it. I almost had a plan figured out."

"Oh, right. Let them hold you until they get bored to death. Good plan."

"Listen," he said. "I may not be here much longer—"

"Where are you going?"

He ignored the question. "These people are psychos," he said. "Don't do anything to aggravate them. When they question you, be nice to them and tell them you're very sorry. Maybe they'll lecture you and let you go."

"Where are you going?" she said again.

He didn't answer.

"Matt?"

"They, uh, may be moving me to another cell, is all. Just remember what I said. Be humble. Grovel, if you have to. I know I'm asking the impossible, but being sweet wouldn't hurt, either."

"Sweet to these bozos? I don't think so."

"Darby, promise me."

She hesitated. "All right, all right. Why are they moving you to another cell?"

A key scraped in the lock of his door.

He bolted for his knife, grabbed it, and waited behind the door. Another scrape, as if the person on the other side was fumbling for the right key.

He heard the tumblers clink, and the door opened inward.

He reached around the door, grasped a wrist, and jerked, hard. A body flew into the room with a shocked gasp. Michael pinned it to the floor with his knees and put his knife to the throat.

"Please! Don't hurt me."

"Dr. Yates! What . . . ?"

Darby's voice came through the wall. "Matt, what's going on?"

"I'm sorry," he said, helping Yates to sit. "I thought you were someone else. Did I hurt you?"

"I . . . don't think so. My arm . . ." She rubbed her wrist. "Please, I need my chair."

Michael looked at the wheelchair in the open door. A ring of keys hung from the lock. He pulled the chair into the cell, jerked the keys from the lock, then scooped Yates up and set her in her seat. "Thanks," he said. He headed for the door.

"Wait!" she said. "There's something you need to know first."

"What?" He paused at the door and scanned the grounds. The guard at the door of the mansion had his back turned. Most of the other Ringers would be at breakfast.

"It'll take a few minutes to explain."

"I don't have a few minutes. Someone may have seen you come in here."

"I don't think so. No one pays attention to me; they're used to seeing me around the compound. And today they're distracted. Salway's in with Mother Mary. That's how I got his keys from his office."

"Whatever it is, it'll have to wait a minute." He ducked out the door and ran to Darby's cell. Which key? He tried the one that had worked on his own door. No. Glancing around, he tried another, then another, He swore. There. That one. The tumblers of the lock turned, and he pushed the door open.

Darby was standing against the wall, trying not to look frightened. Her long brown hair was disheveled and her face and sweatshirt smudged with dirt. "Matt?"

She flung herself at him, wrapping him in a fierce hug.

He hugged her back for a moment, then took her by the arm. "Come on, let's get out of here."

"What's going on?"

"I don't know. I'm going to find out." With her in tow he ran back to his cell.

Yates was hunched in her wheelchair, rubbing her wrist. "Could you please find my glasses?"

He picked up the wire-rimmed glasses from the floor and handed them to her, then closed the door. Kneeling, he took the woman's arm and flexed her wrist carefully. Nothing seemed broken. "I'm sorry I hurt you. Thanks for letting us loose. Why'd you change your mind about helping me?"

He saw she was weeping. "Shame, Mr. Walker. It's too late for my soul, but there's a limit to how much shame any person can stand."

"Who's this?" Darby said.

"Jocelyn Yates. She handled my sister's artificial insemination."

"The one who gave you the note?"

"Yeah."

"Why did she call you Mr. Walker?"

"It's a long story. I'll tell you later."

"It wasn't artificial insemination," Yates said. "It was much more complicated than that."

"Tell us what's going on," he said. "Quick."

She wiped the tears from her cheeks. "I'm a geneticist and I'm brilliant. Do you believe me?"

"Whatever. Sure."

"I'm not boasting," she said, "only explaining. I have an IQ of one-ninety-three. I graduated from MIT first in my class. Two doctoral degrees. My work in genetics is recognized worldwide. I would have received the Nobel Prize, in time; I'm convinced of that. But instead—"

"Get to the point, please." He glanced through the window. A white Buick was driving toward the mansion. The driver wore a scarlet robe.

"A few years ago I was contacted by a laboratory in California," Yates said. "The director was a classmate at MIT. He wanted to hire me to supervise a new line of research into genetic cloning."

"Genflex?" Michael said.

"Yes. They offered me more money than I'd ever made before. But it wasn't the money. It was the challenge, to do something that had never been done before. Can you blame me for accepting?"

"What did they want you to do?" The Buick had driven behind the mansion and was stopping beside the JetRanger helicopter.

"To clone a human being."

Michael turned back to her.

"Oh, not just duplicate a human embryo; that's nothing new. But clone an adult cell. That, now, is much more difficult!" Yates leaned forward, a spark of life in her eyes for the first time. "You see, all cells contain within their DNA the information required to reproduce the entire organism. But in adult cells, access to parts of that information has been hidden. No geneticist has learned how to access it. Until now. I unlocked that door, Mr. Walker. I succeeded."

"You cloned—"

"I found the master molecule that would dedifferentiate a blood cell, cause it to lose its specialty. Don't you see? Once it was dedifferentiated, it would behave exactly like a fertilized egg cell. It could develop into a whole new human being, genetically identical to the person from whose blood it came."

She sat back in her chair. "Of course, I wasn't told who I was cloning. I was just given a strip of bloodstained fabric. From the blood I extracted DNA."

"Whose blood was it?"

Yates hesitated. "Have you ever heard of the Shroud of Turin?"

"Shroud of Turin?" Michael thought a moment. "That thing that's supposed to be the burial cloth of Christ? Yeah, sure." He stared at her, realization dawning. "You're kidding."

"It was the very cloth they wrapped Jesus in after they removed him from the cross," Yates said, "or so many people claim. There was an image etched into the shroud, one which looked very much like Jesus himself might have looked. And there were bloodstains that matched the wounds inflicted on him according to the Bible."

Michael remembered the *National Enquirer* headline in his trailer. "It was stolen about a year ago," he said. "By aliens, supposedly. Anyway, it's a fake, isn't it?"

"Fake? In a sense, I suppose. The shroud has been the subject of controversy for hundreds of years. In 1988 the Church permitted C-fourteen testing on it. Radiocarbon dating. Bits of the shroud were tested by three different universities. All of the pieces carbon-dated to a time around A.D. 1350."

"So it couldn't have been the burial cloth of Christ."

"No. Not according to those tests, although some scientists disputed their accuracy. The point is, many people still believe in the cloth. Faith is never destroyed by science." She bit her lip. "One thing, at least, on the shroud was not faked. The bloodstains were real."

Michael sat down abruptly, knowing what was coming.

"When I learned what the cloth was, it didn't require a genius to guess the subject. And then, you may be assured, I thought about what I was doing, long and hard. But I concluded it could do no harm. Scientific evidence had shown that the man who bled on this cloth was just an ordinary man. What harm could it do to clone him?"

He stared at her. What harm? What world did this woman live in?

"Then I discovered who the laboratory belonged to."

"The Church of True Atonement."

"Yes."

"But how did Ursula get involved with them?"

"She didn't know about them. The in vitro fertilization clinic was legitimate, although it was a front. Her involvement is my fault."

"You?"

"The recipient of the embryo I produced from the shroud was supposed to be Mother Mary. The first time I ever met her was when we discussed the procedure." Yates shook her head. "I had no idea how psychotic she is. She plans to use the child to gain unlimited power."

She looked at Michael, pleading for understanding. "I'm not without conscience, Mr. Walker. When I learned her intention and found out how disturbed she is, I was horrified at what I had done. So I switched embryos. The embryo I implanted in Mother Mary was defective. I knew it would die. I implanted the shroud embryo in your sister. She was the only suitable patient available. Perhaps I should have destroyed it, but I couldn't bring myself to do it. I'm sorry. I didn't intend to endanger Ursula's life."

"Well, you did."

"I'm sorry," she said again. "The switch would never have been discovered, but the embryo received by Mother Mary lived longer than I anticipated. It died, but only after it had developed enough to be obvious that it was a girl. After the initial confusion, the Ringers searched the lab records and discovered what I'd done."

"The Shroud of Turin. Jesus."

"I doubt it, Mr. Walker."

He tried to comprehend. "But why? What does Mother Mary get from this?"

"Power, of course. If she can prove the procedure was actually performed, millions of people will believe she's the mother of Jesus Christ. That's why they need me, to verify the child's identity when she makes her announcement. After that, I suspect they'll . . . kill me."

"What announcement?"

"Her announcement that God has selected her to bear his son. The Second Coming, don't you see? To prepare the world for it, she's planning to create Judgment Day as proof."

"Judgment Day?"

"By fulfilling the prophecies of the Book of Revelation. She thinks she was appointed by God to bring them about."

Michael was trying to absorb what he was hearing. "How can she do that?"

"She's already done it, she thinks, many of the prophecies, at least. She and her Avenging Angels. And she has plans to make the rest of the prophecies come true, partly through the biological research they were conducting in the lab. Her coup de grace is coming very soon."

"There's worse to come?"

Yates nodded. "Do you know about the virus outbreak in New Mexico?"

"I read about it," Darby said. "It killed everyone in town. It sounded horrible."

"It was developed in the church's laboratory. It's deadly and they're going to unleash it on a city in the United States. I don't know which one."

Darby was staring at her, incredulous. "And you sat back and let them do all this?"

"You weren't there," Yates said bitterly. "It's easy to be brave when your life isn't in the hands of psychopaths. Besides, I didn't know about the virus until very recently."

"So what do we do now?" Darby said.

Run! Michael wanted to say. *Escape any way we can.* But there was something he had to do first. "Where's your van?"

"Behind the jail. They brought me here in it."

"Are the keys in it?"

"No, they took them," Darby said. "But I can hot-wire it."

He blinked. "Someday we'll have to talk about that. Wait here. I'm going to try to get the baby. If I'm not back in twenty minutes or if someone comes to get you before that, take Dr. Yates to the van and get out of here. Just point it toward the gate and keep going, you understand? Don't stop for anything."

"Matt, it's broad daylight. You can't just walk in there—"

"You have any better ideas?"

Her eyes were fixed on him, pleading, and her face betrayed the fear she felt. *Don't beg me not to go,* he thought. *I may not have the strength to refuse.*

She looked away. "I guess not."

"Which one of these is for the west wing door?" he asked Yates, holding up the ring of keys.

"I'm sorry, I don't know."

He stuffed the keys in the hand-warmer pockets of his sweatshirt. "You didn't happen to steal a gun, too, did you?"

"No. I didn't think of it."

His mind raced. *A plan, Michael, come up with a plan.* The only thing he could think of was . . . "Is there a broom closet near the nursery?" He pulled his brown robe over his head and fumbled with the buttons.

"Broom closet?" Yates looked puzzled. "I . . . let's see. I think so, yes. First door on the left as you go in the west wing."

He handed Darby the makeshift knife. "Take this; it's better than nothing." He opened the door a crack and peered out. The Buick was parked beside the helicopter, but the driver had disappeared. At the base of the mountain a few hundred feet beyond the helicopter, the steel door of the judgment shelter stood open. He glanced at the mansion. From this angle, the front door guard wouldn't be able to see him, he didn't think. And no one else was in sight, except . . .

Brother Saul. Michael swore. The bald guard was coming down the front steps of the mansion with the door guard. Where had he come from? He must have been inside. They stood on the bottom step of the mansion in earnest conversation. *Come on, you cone-*

head, he thought. *Get out of here.* But they kept talking.

Sweat broke out on his forehead. Two minutes, three. Breakfast would be over any time now. The place would be crawling with guards. The door guard was talking now while Saul listened, shaking his head occasionally.

Finally, the door guard said something, angry, and went back up the steps of the mansion. Saul stared at his back for a moment, then stalked after him, his white robe whipping around his ankles.

When they disappeared inside, Michael opened the door and sprinted toward the west wing of the mansion.

Whoa, slow down. He pulled up his hood and forced himself to walk, trying to look like he was on business. Behind the mansion, a scarlet-robed Angel appeared at the door of the judgment shelter carrying a small aluminum case with a handle. Michael kept his head down, the hood pulled low over his face. From the corner of his eye he saw the Angel deposit the case in the trunk of the Buick and walk back to the shelter.

Fumbling at the buttons of his robe, Michael stopped at the west wing door. *Great idea,* he thought. *Put the keys inside your robe.* There, he had them. He chose one that looked the right size and inserted it in the dead bolt.

It wouldn't turn.

Fighting the urge to run, he chose another, but this one wouldn't even go into the lock.

He took a deep breath to steady himself and tried a third, with the same result. Then a fourth. Panic seized him, making his fingers clumsy. Maybe the mansion keys weren't even on the ring. He tried another, unsuccessfully. Then the last key. It wouldn't turn in the lock.

No, come on; it has to work. Please! A hundred feet to his right, the Angel appeared at the door of the shelter, another aluminum case in his hand. He glanced at Michael.

He jiggled the key in the lock, tried it again. His back tingled as he imagined bullets ripping into it. The key turned and the lock snicked back. He opened the door and stepped inside.

Leaning against the door, he blew out a sigh of relief. Ahead of him was a long log-walled corridor, a half-dozen closed doors on each side. About halfway down the corridor, a guard was standing in front of one of the closed doors, an assault rifle in his hands. It had to be the nursery. The guard was looking his way, frowning.

As he watched, a green-robed woman stepped out of another room and hurried away from him, toward the reception hall, diverting the guard's attention for a moment.

Michael opened the first door on his left. Inside was a large utility sink, a bucket and mop, and a cart full of cleaning supplies. With the mop in one hand and the bucket in the other, he backed out of the closet.

Head down, he walked as calmly as he could toward the guard.

34

Salway's conference with Mother Mary and Brother Raguel was interrupted by an insistent knocking on her door. Salway looked at her apologetically and, when she gestured permission, got up and answered it. His secretary stood outside, looking worried.

"Sir, there's a call from the perimeter guard. He says it's very, very urgent."

He hesitated for an instant, torn between crises, then ran back to his own office. He picked up the phone and snapped, "What is it?"

"Sir, helicopters." The man was excited. "Dozens of them. They're heading for Heaven's Door. I think we're under attack."

Michael walked toward the guard, his posture one of humility.

The guard was watching him again, alert.

Thirty feet to go. Twenty-five.

"You!" the guard said.

He kept walking. Twenty feet. Fifteen.

"I'm talking to you, Novitiate," the guard said. "What's your name?"

Ten feet. He didn't answer. Five.

The assault rifle came up. "Stop right there."

He stopped in front of the guard, pretending surprise. "Me, Brother?"

"What are you doing here?"

"I was told to clean the nursery."

"No you weren't. Novitiates aren't allowed in here."

With all his strength he brought the mop handle up into the guard's solar plexus, just under the rib cage. The man gave a strangled gasp and doubled over. Michael wrenched the rifle from his hands and brought the butt down on the back of the guard's neck. He collapsed face-first onto the tile floor, unmoving.

Michael opened the door of the nursery and went in.

Brother Saul stood inside the front door of the mansion, waiting for Salway, thinking he knew what he'd summoned him about, thinking how fun it was gonna be to have him turn that maggot punk over to him. *What I'm gonna do first*, he thought, *is the rabbit; that'll be fun. No, wait; maybe work him over a little first, make him good and scared.* Wishing Salway would hurry up, he wanted to go into Holy Mother's office and interrupt, say, "Is it about Matthew Cooper? I knew it." He wished he could interrupt, but he knew Holy Mother would get mad, and he didn't want to face her when she got mad.

The lights flickered, then went out.

What's going on?

The lights came back on, but a little dimmer, yellower than before. Generators must have kicked in.

Mother Mary came striding from the east wing, coming toward him with that terrible look in her eyes. He lowered his eyes.

"Brother Saul," she commanded, "assemble the Holy Guards. Defensive positions."

A drill? Wasn't one scheduled today. He looked at her, confused.

"Do it," she said. "Now! We're under attack." She turned and strode back toward her office.

He hurried to obey.

Michael stepped into the nursery, closing the thick wooden door behind him.

A woman was on her hands and knees in the middle of the floor, playing peek-a-boo with a baby in diapers, who was lying on his back on a powder blue blanket, grinning up at her.

Michael stared at the baby. It was Ursula's; he'd recognize it anywhere.

The nurse looked up. She was thin and plain, her hair bound tightly behind her head. Unlike most faces he'd seen here, hers had intelligence in it. "What do you want, Novitiate?"

He started toward her. "I need help, Sister. I just came from an audience with Holy Mother and I got lost." *Lame, Michael. Lame.*

She looked suspicious. "Where's Brother Daniel? Why are you armed? Novitiates can't carry weapons." Frowning, she got to her feet.

He moved closer to her.

"Leave!" she ordered "This minute."

The baby studied him seriously, two chubby fingers in his mouth.

Michael aimed the rifle at the nurse. "I don't want to kill you, lady, but if you yell, I will." He gestured toward an open bathroom door. "In there."

The nurse screamed.

He clubbed her with the butt of the rifle and she fell senseless.

Hoping he hadn't killed her, he ran to the door and looked out. No one coming yet, but that shriek would bring them. He dragged the guard into the nursery and stripped off his white robe, then his own.

The baby began to cry. Michael stooped and gathered him up.

"Shh, shh, you remember me, little guy? Come on, we have to get out of here."

A chest carrier hung from a coatrack in the corner. He worked the baby's feet into it, then held him against his chest while he secured the Velcro strips behind his back. "Don't have time to dress you, pardner." He grabbed the first baby clothes he saw, a blue sleep suit, and stuffed it into his sweatshirt.

"Let's play pat-a-cake," he whispered, shrugging into the guard's white robe. He buttoned it, covering the baby, then unfastened two buttons, took the baby's hands, and patted them together. The baby had begun crying again, but now he stopped. He looked up at Michael solemnly.

"Pat-a-cake," Michael said, and patted the hands together again. This time the baby gave him a small smile. He covered him once more. "You stay under there and I'll try to find you, OK?"

He started out of the nursery, then spotted Brother Daniel's assault rifle. May as well take that, too. He picked it up and stepped into the corridor. Two white-robed women were hurrying toward him from the reception hall. He turned and strode toward the door at the other end of the corridor.

"You there, Guard," one of the women said. "What are you doing?"

He reached the door.

"Stop!" the woman yelled.

He slammed the kick bar with his foot and the door swung open. He was outside.

A siren on the roof of the mansion went off, a metallic growl that climbed in pitch to an ear-piercing wail. Over the top of the mountain came a flock of crows. They quickly grew to be helicopters, dozens of them. Their droning filled the air. He watched in astonishment as they swept toward the compound, the thump of their rotors growing louder.

Guards in white robes erupted from the mess hall and barracks, sprinting to defensive positions in bunkers and fallout shelters.

Saul, leading one squad of guards, saw Michael. He unslung his assault rifle.

Michael ran. *He doesn't know I've got the kid,* he thought frantically, *He's going to shoot.*

Saul's weapon chattered. Bullets pocked the ground in front of Michael, cut a swath inches from his legs. He turned, kept running, *please, God,* zigzagging toward the bunkhouse as bullets hissed past him.

The helicopters were landing, kicking up swirls of dust as they settled to the ground. Men erupted from them, spreading out and running at a crouch, all of them wearing orange suits and some kind of helmets and carrying rifles.

As he neared the jail, a guard stepped from the building next to it and raised a machine pistol. Michael ducked, but the guard fired past him at the invaders, bright brass shell casings flying from the magazine.

More rifles popped. The guard grunted and staggered backward, then sat down. He looked at Michael, surprised, blood pumping from his robe, then he slumped over on his side.

Michael reached his cell and burst inside, nearly knocking over Darby, who'd been trying to see through the window of the door. Yates sat with her head buried in her hands. He slammed the door shut.

"What's happening?" Darby said.

"I don't know. I thought the siren was for me, but they've got worse problems now. Feds, maybe."

He unbuttoned the white robe. The baby was clinging with tiny fists to the straps of the chest carrier and crying, his face screwed up.

"Matt, you found him!"

"Yeah, but he might have been better off if I hadn't." He lifted the baby from the chest carrier and handed him to Darby. "Here.

I think he'll be safer with you." He pulled the sleep suit from beneath his sweatshirt and gave it to her. "I didn't have time to dress him."

"Poor little guy." She took him. "What a cutie. Are you cold, sweetie? Let's get you dressed, huh?" She hurried with him over to the bed and began working the sleep suit over his legs. "Even built-in feet and hands to keep you warm." Over her shoulder, she said, "What do we do now?"

Michael unstrapped the baby carrier as he looked out the window. Most of the Holy Guards had reached defensive positions, and gunfire spewed from bunkers and the mansion. Clouds of white gas drifted across the drill field. Tear gas. It had to be the feds. "We could wait here, hope the good guys win, then surrender," he said. "It's probably the safest thing to do."

Then he saw Saul. He was crouching near one of the bunkers with another guard, struggling to load a rocket launcher. An LAW. *Oh, shit. Hell on choppers and light aircraft.* Except Saul wasn't looking at the helicopters, he was looking in Michael's direction.

"We have to get out of here. Is the kid dressed?"

"Almost. Why? I thought you said we'd be safer—"

"The wolf is about to blow our house down. Come on, let's go."

She stuffed the last arm in the suit and zipped it up.

Michael stripped off the white robe. "Here, wrap him in this. Do you want to go with us, Dr. Yates? Once they see us leave, you might be safer here."

"Please, take me with you."

"You take the baby," he told Darby. "I'll carry the doctor."

He looked out the window again. Saul was having a problem with the LAW. For the moment his full attention was on the launcher. "Let's go. Now! Head for the van and don't stop." He picked up the woman. "Ride's gonna be a little rough, I'm afraid."

She nodded.

Darby opened the door with one hand, the baby a white bundle in the other. She sprinted around the corner of the bunkhouse, and he followed with Yates in his arms, the rifle slung from his shoulder.

Darby's van sat behind the building. She opened the rear doors and laid the baby on the carpeted floor, then ran around to the driver's side and yanked open the door. While Michael deposited Yates in the front passenger seat and fastened her in, Darby dived under the steering wheel and jerked down two wires. A moment later the van lurched and the engine started.

"Where's the safest place in here?" he said.

"Uh, in the back, by the warming oven, I guess."

"Get back there with the baby and hang on."

She scrambled into the back of the van, picked up the baby, and crouched on the floor, shielding him with her body. He climbed into the driver's seat and gunned the engine. Gravel flew.

"Where are we going?" Darby shouted.

"The gate's our best chance!"

The compound was a war zone. The van rounded the corner of the jail and accelerated. He aimed it for the entrance a half-mile away, where a column of Jeeps and armored cars was streaming through the gate.

A concussion slammed him into the door and the van skidded. He fought the steering wheel and for a moment gained control. In the rearview mirror he saw the bunkhouse erupt in flames.

A rear window shattered. Darby screamed. Something hit the side of the van, a series of metal *thunks* that worked their way forward. More glass burst. The van swerved again, then slowed. He pumped the accelerator, but black smoke billowed from the engine. They coasted to a stop. He ground the ignition. Dead. In the van, glass lay everywhere.

"Are you hit?" he shouted to Darby.

"I don't think so." Her voice shook. "But she was."

Beside him Dr. Yates's head lolled to the side, her eyes staring sightlessly. Bloodstains were spreading on her jacket. He checked her neck for a pulse and found none.

"She's dead. We're sitting ducks here. We've got to get out!" He grabbed the rifle, jumped from the van, ran around to the back, and wrenched open the doors.

Darby handed him the baby.

"Is he OK?" he said.

"I think so. The robe caught most of the broken glass."

As she slid out, something landed near them and exploded. White gas enveloped them.

"God! I can't see!" Darby shouted. "My eyes!"

Michael got a whiff of something pungent and peppery; then his lungs were on fire. He sneezed. His eyes slammed shut and he couldn't open them. "CS gas." He coughed. "Don't rub your eyes."

Forcing his eyes open a slit, he saw a watery outline of Darby bent over the baby. "Let's get out of the open." He grabbed her arm and pulled her away from the van.

"I can't see."

"It'll wear off." The nearest building was a brown blur in the background. He led her toward it, Darby coughing and retching, the baby wailing.

When they reached it, he pushed her down beside the log wall and crouched in front of her. His eyes burned and his hands and face itched from the gas.

"God, this is awful," she gasped. "How long does it last?"

"Five or ten minutes." He coughed and blinked the water out of his eyes long enough to see that they were still exposed. "Come on, we're out of the line of fire, but we've got to find a place to hide." Still crouching, he led her to the back of the building and around the corner. "Stay here. I'll see what's inside."

He ran to the door and threw it open, then dived in and rolled, ready to fire as he hit the floor. It was a classroom with folding chairs facing a chalkboard to his right and a pair of windows on the opposite wall. He backed out and ran back to her. His sight was beginning to come back. Squinting at her through watery eyes, he said, "Come on, we'll be safer in there." He led her into the room and closed the door.

She uncovered the baby's head. "Poor thing. What an awful thing to do to a child."

"It's supposed to be harmless to infants," Michael said.

"It better be." She coughed. "There, there, it's all right. Shh, shh."

He ran to the windows in a crouch. The drill field was chaos, littered with bodies and the wreckage of UH-1 helicopters. The LAW, probably. The battle still raged, but many of the guards had retreated to the mansion, where they formed a protective phalanx around it. Gunfire poured from the windows.

Behind the mansion, a flurry of activity surrounded Mother Mary's helicopter. He blinked to clear his eyes. Scarlet-robed Angels were moving aluminum cases from the Buick to the JetRanger. As he watched, they put the last case inside and shut the hatch, then backed away.

The rotor blades began to turn, slowly at first, then faster. A few seconds later, the chopper lifted from its pad and rose into the air.

At his forward command post outside the compound gate, Special Agent in Charge Willard Perkins listened with dismay to the crackling message coming over his radio. "Say again, Eagle!" he shouted.

"... said we counted six cases, Sierra One. We think it's the virus."

"Who's flying it?"

"Some dude in a red..." The voice broke up. "... not with them."

"Say again."

"I said Mother Mary's not with them, sir. She's still in the mansion. Shall we bring it down?"

Willard stared at the helicopter lifting above the roof of the mansion. They should have taken it out with the first wave; he'd given clear orders to do it. But what was clear in the planning somehow hadn't gotten accomplished in the assault. The Ringers had been much better trained than they'd thought, and intelligence had missed the LAW rocket launcher. Game slippage. Things never went exactly as planned. This time, the consequences could be devastating.

"Sierra One? I said, shall we bring it down?"

"Copy. Stand by on that." He thought quickly. If he didn't bring it down and the helicopter escaped, millions could die. If he brought the chopper down, he was putting his own agents and himself, as well as hundreds of other people, at risk from the virus.

There was no right choice.

Still, the area was isolated; the damage here could be contained. He made the only decision he could. "Eagle, this is Sierra One. Bring it down."

"Roger. Out."

Just about the only thing the virus seemed to be susceptible to was fire. Maybe, just maybe, if they were very lucky, the chopper would explode and burn when it was hit. Or when it crashed.

But today, Willard didn't feel lucky.

From the classroom Michael watched the helicopter gain altitude. A withering barrage of fire came from the mansion as the guards laid down a protective screen. When the chopper was above the roof of the mansion, it turned and flew out over the meadow, gaining speed and altitude. Michael wondered if Mother Mary was in it. As he watched, a small cigar-shaped missile streaked skyward from somewhere near the gate. A second later the rotors of the helicopter exploded, fragments spinning away from it. The body of the JetRanger seemed to hang in the air a second longer; then it began falling in an arc, carried forward by its momentum. He thought he heard a scream.

The helicopter struck the ground near the flagpole and crumpled. The cockpit window shattered and glass flew skyward, then rained onto the field.

For a moment the fusillade continued from the mansion. Then a faint pink fog rose from the wreckage of the helicopter. The shooting dwindled and finally stopped. The mist spread slowly in the still air and began drifting toward the entrance gate.

Downwind of the fog, three Holy Guards burst from a bunker and ran toward the mansion.

Darby crouched beside Michael. "What's going on?"

"The feds just brought down Ma's chopper."

"What's that stuff?"

"I don't . . . Oh, my God."

They looked at each other, realization growing. "The virus. Oh, shit. Oh, Matt."

A gust of wind blew through the fog, and it eddied and swirled outward at ground level. A moment later the back door of the mansion opened and a dozen Holy Guards burst out, led by three scarlet-robed Angels. Behind them hurried a tall woman in a purple robe, followed by a tiny man in a business suit. The guards formed a protective wall around them, and they moved quickly toward the judgment shelter. One of the Angels opened the steel door, and Mother Mary and Salway disappeared inside. The Angels followed them, then the guards. The steel door slammed shut.

"We have to get out of here," Michael said.

Darby ran to the baby and gathered him up. "Where?"

"I don't know. Upwind. Maybe we can get above it. Let's climb up the slope." He led the way to the back door, opened it, and glanced out. "Everyone's scrambling for cover. Come on."

They raced toward the mountain, dodging from wall to wall until they ran out of buildings. A strange silence had descended on the compound. Even the baby had stopped crying. Except for the bodies, the place looked deserted.

Ahead, the ground sloped upward, the foot of the mountain strewn with boulders and talus, loose rock fragments that would make footing treacherous. Two hundred feet above the talus, the forest began.

Michael pointed. "Head for those trees. At least we'll have cover."

She began climbing and he dropped behind her to cover their retreat, scanning the compound. There, on the roof of the mansion. Three guards. They were crouched on the back side of the roof, their backs to him, peering over the ridge at the approaching mist. He edged up the slope behind Darby, keeping the guards in sight.

The slope grew steeper and she shifted the baby to one arm while she steadied herself with the other. Then a rock slid out from under her foot and she fell with a gasp, twisting onto her hip to protect the baby. She rode a small rock slide four feet down the slope before it stopped.

One of the guards heard the noise and turned. His rifle came up.

Michael fired a short burst from his assault rifle. The guard screamed and tumbled down the roof, dropping off the edge. The others scrambled over the ridge and turned, firing back at Michael. Bullets hissed and rock chips flew near his head.

Darby got to her feet and scrambled up the slope. He fired another burst, keeping the guards pinned down.

"We need cover!" he shouted. "Right now!" He looked around. The trees were still too far. Thirty feet away across the slope the timbers of an abandoned mine shaft protruded from the rocks, its entrance covered with old boards.

"There." He pointed. "Head for that."

She made her way across the scree, slipping but managing to stay on her feet. Rocks cascaded down the slope. He followed, firing a round every time the guards on the roof lifted their heads. The rifle had a twenty-shot magazine. He estimated he had about five rounds left.

They reached the entrance to the mine shaft. Rotted boards covered it. He kicked one and it split, opening a hole. He ripped it off, then kicked open a gap big enough for them to squeeze through.

She eased through the hole with the baby. The guards fired again. Bullets splintered the wood of the entrance and pain seared Michael's leg. He turned and emptied the rifle as he ducked into the mine shaft. One of the guards toppled backward.

Enough dusty light filtered through the opening to see. Down the center of the tunnel ran a rusty ore-car track that disappeared into the gloom.

Darby stood waiting inside the entrance. "What now?"

"Keep going," he said. "We have to get solid rock around us."

Limping, he followed her deeper inside. The air smelled musty, and cobwebs draped across his face.

Behind them, more shots thunked into the wood.

"Goddamn it! Why are they shooting at us?" she shouted. "They might hit the baby."

"They were aiming at me."

She glanced at him and noticed his limp. "They hit you, too. Oh, Matt. There's blood on your sweatpants. Sit down, let me look."

He eased down against the rock wall of the mine shaft. His calf was on fire. She handed him the baby, then pulled up his pant leg.

"Ow."

"Sorry." She inspected his leg in the dim light. "Looks like the bullet went through the muscle." She looked up at him, relief on her face. "There's a lot of blood, but I don't think it did much damage."

"Are you kidding? I could be bleeding to death."

"Oh, don't be such a baby."

"Well, it hurts, damn it."

"Do you have a handkerchief?"

"No."

She took the end of the robe that was wrapped around the baby and, grunting, ripped off a strip. She wound it around his calf and tied it. "That'll stop the bleeding, Arnold."

"Even Schwarzenegger hurts when he gets wounded," he grumped.

The baby began to fuss. "I'll take him back now."

He handed the child to her.

"You spit up, didn't you, sweetie?" she said. Orange baby food was smeared around the baby's face. She wet a corner of her sweatshirt with spit and wiped it off. "There, I guess we'll live." She jiggled him in her arms. "So what do we do now?" she said, looking around.

"Hope the virus doesn't drift up this far."

He got to his feet, limped back to the entrance, and peered through the hole. The pink mist had dissipated; it was impossible to tell where the virus had spread. Or was still spreading.

The battle seemed to be a stalemate, the mansion and Mother Mary's shelter still under control of the Ringers, the rest of the compound in the hands of the feds. At the moment, both sides were probably more worried about the invisible threat of the virus than they were about each other.

He walked back to Darby. "I think we'd better move farther in. The more distance we put between us and that virus, the better off we'll be. And the Ringers aren't beaten yet. They know we have the baby. Sooner or later they may come looking for us." He eyed the roof of the tunnel, gray rock shored up in places with rotting timbers. The thought of them dying a horrible death in the darkness of a dead-end tunnel made his knees weak. Keeping his voice, he hoped, calm, he said, "Not much clearance. Keep low and stay close behind me." He started down the tunnel, following the ore-car rails.

For a few moments the only sounds he heard were creaking timbers and the scrape of their shoes on rock. The tunnel grew darker, only a few rays of dim light penetrating from the entrance. "How deep is this thing?" Darby asked quietly.

"I don't know."

"I hate caves," she said. "I always used to have nightmares about being lost in caves."

"Freud would have something to say about that."

"Freud hated women; what did he know? Yuck, cobwebs." She followed him. After a moment she said, "Matt?"

"Mm?"

"Do you believe her? Dr. Yates, I mean."

"What, that she cloned a human being? I guess I have to. The kid's real."

"I mean, do you think he's really . . . ?"

"No. You heard her. Radiocarbon dating doesn't lie. He's just a baby we had no business bringing into the world."

"Whoever he is," she said, "he's a sweet child."

A broken roof timber caught Michael in the forehead. "Ow!" He bent over. "Damn."

"Will you quit hurting yourself?"

"I'm trying to, damn it." Rubbing his forehead, he crouched lower and went under the timber. "Watch that thing."

Ahead, the roof had collapsed and a pile of rocks partially blocked the tunnel. "We'll have to climb over," he said. "You can hand me the baby when I'm over the top."

"How much farther do we have to go?"

"Maybe we can wait on the other side of this."

Cautiously he climbed up the pile, then worked his way down the other side, where the darkness was almost complete. Sharp tentacles of pain wrapped around his leg. When he was back on the floor of the tunnel he looked up and waited for the shadow of Darby's head to appear, then held up his hands for the baby.

She passed him over carefully. "He's exhausted, poor little guy." He had fallen asleep, his face scrunched up as if he were smelling something bad. She crawled over the top of the pile and backed her way down the other side on all fours.

A noise came from behind them, near the entrance. "Shh, shh." Michael held his breath to listen.

"What?" She stopped.

They waited in silence, but the sound wasn't repeated. "Nothing, I guess. Creaking timber."

"I'll take him again," she said.

He handed the baby to her and eased himself to the ground, leaning his back against the rough rock wall. He could feel Darby looking at him.

After a moment, she said, "Who are you?"

"What?"

"You heard me. Dr. Yates called you Walker. Is that your real name?"

He hesitated. "Yes."

"What's your first name?"

"Michael."

"You lived with me under a fake name?" Her voice trembled with anger. "I should hate you."

"When this is over, I give you permission."

"Why did you lie to me?"

He sighed. "It's a long story, Darb."

"I seem to have some time here."

He was tempted to invent a lie. If she didn't hate him now, she soon would. But he was tired of lying, tired of running. And they were probably going to die anyway. He said, "There's an organization after me. They want to kill me."

"Organization? You mean other than the Ringers? What kind of organization?"

"A bad one."

"What did you do? Something illegal?"

"Yeah." Might as well start at the beginning. "When I was in the army I was trained to be a sniper, to kill people. Then, when I was in prison—"

"You were in prison?"

"Yeah. But I was set up, Darby. Customs found cocaine in my duffel. I think my brother did it."

"You have a brother?"

"James. You want me to hold the kid awhile?"

"Don't change the subject. How long did you spend in prison?"

He scuffed his sneaker in the dirt. "A few months. I was lucky." He heard the bitterness in his voice come through. "My brother got me out."

"He did? How?"

"He works for the organization. It's called the Arm, some supersecret government agency. James, or someone above him, pulled some strings with the sentence review board, got me out. But there was a condition."

"What?"

"That I serve the rest of my sentence working for my brother."

"That doesn't sound so bad. What were you supposed to do?"

He didn't answer, thinking, *Don't tell it all; there may still be a chance for us.* But he found himself saying, "Kill people, Darby. That's what they did. Still do, this little group. Assassinations."

There was silence. Then, "Did you kill anyone?"

"Yes."

She hesitated. "How many people?"

"One, for them. I've been running since then, hiding. That's why the Arm's looking for me; they think I know too much."

"Why didn't you tell me?" The anger had left her voice, but she had left with it. Her casual question was in the tone she would use with a stranger. "I mean, I guess I can understand why you didn't at first, but after we'd lived together for two years, why didn't you then?"

"I was afraid you'd leave me."

"I did leave you."

"See? I had good reason."

"It's not funny, Matt. Michael. Whoever you are."

"No, it's not." He waited, then said, "Darby, the man I killed?"

"Yes?"

"He was a good man. He didn't deserve to die."

She didn't say anything. He shifted next to her and felt her pull herself in tighter. Finally she said carefully, taking her time, "What else do I need to know about you?"

He thought. "Nothing." He was about to say something else, to try to explain, when a dull boom sounded somewhere outside, an explosion muffled by hundreds of tons of rock. The ground shook and dust rained down on them.

She jumped up. "My God. What's that?"

"I don't know." He got to his feet.

Another boom, louder, deafened him. Rocks cascaded down around them.

She shrieked and huddled over the baby, who started to cry again.

Michael covered his head with his hands until the slide of rocks stopped. Then he cautiously lifted his face and stared at the pile of rocks between them and the entrance, straining to see. The pile had grown. The rocks now reached almost to the roof. Fighting growing dread, he climbed up on all fours, testing each rock. The smell of dust hung thick in the air. Below him, Darby made soothing noises to the baby.

When Michael got to the top he groped in front of him. A small opening remained between the pile and the roof. He peered toward the tunnel entrance, blinking.

"Can we get back over it again?" she said.

"Maybe. But I don't think it would do us any good if we did."

"What do you mean?"

"Someone must have blown up the entrance. There's no daylight." He stared with stunned eyes, willing his eyes to see light, thinking maybe the dust was too thick to let it through. But he knew better. Finally, with the sick certainty they were going to die here, he gave up and worked his way back down. "It's gone. There's no entrance left."

"Oh, my God." Her voice was hoarse. "Why?"

"Who knows? I don't even know which side did it. It might have been an accidental hit. But we're not going out that way."

"We're trapped?"

He nodded, knowing she couldn't see it. The darkness was total. But he said, instead, "Maybe not. We can go in deeper. Maybe there's another entrance." *Fat chance of that.* Fear crackled in his head like heat lightning, and he forced himself to take slow, steadying breaths.

"I can't see anything," she whispered.

"Doesn't matter. We can't get lost." Just step into a pit, he thought, or die in a cave-in. "Here, hold onto my sweatshirt. We'll follow the rails."

Her hand touched his back tentatively, a brushing stroke, then gripped a fistful of sweatshirt. Arms out, eyes wide, he stepped slowly along the track, straining and failing to see something, anything, in the darkness.

They groped their way deeper into the mine, their footsteps

making soft, quick echoes, their breathing raspy in the thick air.

The baby coughed.

"It's getting hard to breathe," Darby said.

He said nothing. He knew the deeper they went, the worse the air would be. It might even become lethal. He wanted to make some reassuring comment, but he couldn't think of any.

For what seemed hours they plodded on. His mind assaulted him with recriminations. He'd been stupid to try the rescue; all he'd managed to do was get Darby and the kid killed, along with himself. He should have stayed in San Francisco.

Ahead, he heard a trickle of water. Gripped by sudden thirst, he shuffled faster toward the sound, his arm outstretched. His hand touched cold, wet rock. Water ran over his fingers from some small seep in the side of the tunnel. He put his mouth to the water and drank, and it tasted cold and wonderful. Then he guided Darby to it. She drank, filled her cupped hands, and managed to get the baby to swallow a little.

They moved on, not talking. What was there to say? The baby had stopped crying but was fitful and fussy. Once, Michael thought he heard another scraping noise far behind them, but when he stopped and listened he heard nothing. He didn't mention it.

A few steps later the rail seemed to curve to the left.

"Uh-oh." He stopped.

"What is it?"

"Stay here." He stepped across the rails and walked forward in what he hoped was a straight line. A few steps later his outstretched palms scraped solid rock. He moved them to the left. Empty space. He moved them to the right. More empty space. "A fork in the tunnel," he said. He turned and made his way back to her.

"Which way?" she said.

"Your guess is as good as mine."

He heard her groping along the rails with her feet. "I say left."

"Why?"

"The track goes that way. It's the main tunnel."

"If it's the main tunnel, it probably just goes deeper into the mountain."

"Left," she said. "I've got a feeling about this."

He shrugged. "Why not?" They trudged into the left branch.

A thousand steps, two thousand. The air grew staler, harder to breathe, and their breaths came in ragged gasps.

His mind began to wander. He found himself thinking about the touch of Darby's hand on his back, remembering times when her hand had caressed him with love, wishing . . . He forced himself to think about something else, then discovered that everything else was worse.

Abruptly he stumbled into solid rock. "Ouch!" He rubbed his bruised knee.

Behind him Darby stopped, still gripping his sweatshirt. "What's wrong?" She sounded tired, defeated.

He groped along the rock wall. "That's it. Dead end. Far as we can go."

"Oh, no. Oh, Matt, I'm sorry." She let go of him and slid down against the wall.

He didn't remind her of his real name. It didn't matter. In despair, he slumped down against the rock beside her. Except for the eerie creaking of timbers, the silence was that of a tomb. Only their own ragged breathing and the occasional whimper of the baby intruded.

"I'm sorry I got you into this," he said.

"You didn't. It was my decision to snoop."

After a moment she said, "Matt, when you refused to marry me? All that talk about not wanting to be tied down was a lot of crap, wasn't it?"

"Yeah. I didn't want to get you involved. That's a hoot, isn't it?"

As if agreeing, the baby grunted.

"It's too bad you're not really who they claim you are, kid," Michael said. "We could use a miracle here. Just a small one. Fresh air, maybe. A flashlight at least."

Instead of fresh air, he got a whiff of dirty diapers.

35

Michael caught himself nodding off. Sleep seemed such a pleasant idea, just a little nap. What was the point of prolonging the torture? But part of his mind wouldn't let him quit. He opened his eyes and forced himself to his feet. "Come on, no sense waiting here to die. Let's see if we can get back to that other tunnel."

"Mmm?"

"Darby, wake up. Let's go."

"I don't want to. Leave me alone."

He stooped and took the baby from her, listening for his breathing. It was there, but shallow and rapid. With one hand Michael grasped her arm and pulled her up. "Come on, tiger. Don't give up on me."

She coughed and jerked her hand away, but she remained standing.

"You all right?"

After a moment she said, "I'm awake. Give me the baby."

He handed him back to her and she wrapped her fist in Michael's sweatshirt. They trudged back the way they had come.

It seemed to take forever. He tried to remember how many steps it had been from the fork, two thousand and . . . something. In the dark they could easily walk right past it. "Did you count the steps?" he said.

"No."

He angled over to pick up the left wall and ran his hand along it to guide him. Forced himself to concentrate. At 2,329 steps the left wall disappeared.

"We're here," he said. "Now all we have to do is walk down the other shaft. . . ." And hope it doesn't dead-end, too.

They turned into the tunnel. Michael groped his way along the wall. Instead of growing fresher, the air grew heavier somehow, even staler than in the other fork. No, not stale; dark, some kind of faint odor. He sniffed. Mold or mildew, probably.

But the stain in the air got darker, stronger. Now it smelled like something dead, something he'd smelled before, but he couldn't place it.

"What stinks, anyway?" Darby said.

"I don't know." He stepped to the center of the tunnel, turned his head left, then right. The air on the left side was . . . not exactly fresh, but at least it wasn't as bad. The smell came from the right side of the tunnel. "Wait here."

He moved straight ahead, hands out, and came to a point of solid rock that sloped sharply back on both sides. Wearily he moved back to Darby, guided by her breathing, and touched her shoulder with his outstretched hand.

"Another fork."

"Oh, no." Her voice was small. "Which way?"

He hesitated, trying to remember the odor. Something he needed to know.

"What *is* that smell?" she said.

Then it came to him. Where he'd run into it before, hiking in the mountains. "It's a rattlesnake den! Smells like they're in the right tunnel."

He felt her shudder. "Oh, God." She moved toward the left.

"Stop," he said. "We have to go to the right."

"Are you crazy?" Her shout echoed from both tunnels, a weird, hollow sound followed by the rasp of gravel falling from the roof. "No! I won't do it!"

"That's our way out," he said. "Rattlesnakes don't stay underground. They go to the surface to hunt. We have to go through them. There must be an exit on the other side of the den." That it probably wasn't an exit big enough for them to get through he didn't want to think about. It was their only chance.

"No!" She was sobbing now. "I want to go home."

He moved close to her and wrapped his arms around her. The baby was between them, crying again, too. She buried her head in Michael's chest. "I just want to go home!"

"It'll be all right." Telling himself it wasn't a lie, it really could be all right. In another life. "Just move slowly. They won't strike unless they're alarmed, and at this temperature they'll be sluggish."

"Do we have to?"

"Yes. Just try not to step on one."

"How?" she quavered. "I can't even see them."

"We'll go slow. Ready?"

"No." But she held onto his sweatshirt and followed when he walked slowly into the right tunnel, the baby still crying.

"It's all right," she whispered to the baby. She sniffed. "Shh, it's all right."

The evil smell grew worse, became a stench, a dead thing that overpowered him, gagging him.

"How many of them are there, for God's sake?" she said.

"I don't know. Lots, it smells like."

He heard, or thought he heard, slithering sounds now, the rasping of snakes sliding over dry rock. His imagination. He slowed even more, one foot reaching carefully out, trying to sense what lay on the tunnel floor ahead, trying to see in the darkness, putting it down gently, then the other.

"Most of them will be asleep," he said. He hoped. Even though it was winter, the weather outside was warm enough for some snakes to be awake.

"Can't they hear us talk?"

"I don't think so. They just pick up vibrations from the ground."

"I hate this."

He sensed snakes all around them. His body whittled down to bare nerves, he moved along the wall, using his hand to steady him while he groped with his feet. His right foot came down slowly and something moved beneath his shoe. A knot of snakes. Writhing. Shit.

He lifted his foot and froze with it in the air as the snakes hissed and began to rattle.

"Don't move," he whispered, but behind him Darby was already motionless.

They waited, his left hand on the rock wall, his right foot in the air. Somewhere in front of him another snake began to rattle, then another in the center of the tunnel, the rattling spreading from snake to snake until the tunnel seemed full of it, alive with buzzing.

Seconds dragged. He was acutely conscious of the pain in his calf. Worse, his leg was cramping, his thigh muscles demanding release. Sweat trickled down his face.

The baby had quit crying and lay still in Darby's arms, silent now except for the sucking sounds of two fingers in his mouth.

Gradually the buzzing grew less. A snake slithered across Michael's foot. He heard other snakes slide slowly away as the knot dissolved. Several of them were still rattling.

With his muscles screaming he waited another minute, then slowly lowered his foot onto . . . rock. He could have wept.

"Come on," he whispered.

They moved on, inching their way along the wall. Darby gripped his sweatshirt, pressing against him, making tiny whimpering noises. The stench seemed to decrease, or else his sense of smell had burned out. But there were still snakes around them; he was sure of it. He tried not to hurry.

Then he sensed something else. A wisp, a lightening of the air here. Now it was gone, but two steps later he smelled it again. Fresh air. Real, outside air.

"Oh, God," she said.

"Hang on. Don't hurry."

"I can see you," she whispered. "Just barely. I can see the baby."

The tunnel turned to the right. He inched around it. And stopped.

A hundred feet ahead, splinters of daylight filtered through wide boards. He blinked at the brightness. His legs went weak with relief.

Darby let go of his sweatshirt and gave a little sob of relief.

"We're not clear yet." He pointed to a pair of rattlesnakes ahead of them, wound into their resting coils along the side of the tunnel. "They're probably asleep, but don't rush."

He could see well enough now to leave the wall, and he moved out into the center of the tunnel, his own steps quickening in spite of his warning to Darby.

When the snakes were behind them, he ran.

The last ten feet of the tunnel consisted of rotting wooden timbers and boards holding up loose dirt. Across the opening, rough two-by-six boards had been nailed. Michael kicked one and dust flew. Dirt trickled from the ceiling. He kicked again, knowing someone might hear him or the whole roof could collapse but not caring. Needing to be out of here, into daylight. Now! He kicked again. Nails screeched. One more kick and the board dropped away with a clatter.

He kicked off two more boards, enough of an opening for them to squeeze through. Then he stood back and took the baby from Darby and she squeezed through the hole, laughing, tears running down her cheeks. He handed the baby through to her and followed.

And stepped squinting into sunshine, warm, blinding, wonderful sunshine. He sneezed and looked around, blinking.

They were standing on a pile of mine tailings on the side of a timbered slope, at least two hundred yards above the floor of the valley. To their right, a mile or more away, smoke drifted up from the fir trees. The compound. He heard the distant pop of small-arms fire.

"We're outside the perimeter of Heaven's Door," he said. "But it looks like we're still inside the ranch. If we cross that creek down there and climb up the other side, then go down into the next drainage, we should be off Ringer property."

Darby looked at him, grinning. "Here's your miracle."

He smiled and looked down at the baby, who was squirming and stretching out his arms, wanting down. "Thanks, kid." As she put the baby on the ground, he eased down on a rock, reaching back with his left hand to steady himself.

Something stung his hand. He jerked it away and glanced down. The rattlesnake had struck and was retreating, still in his striking coil, head weaving above his body, tongue flicking up and down.

"Goddamn!" He grabbed a rock and threw it at the snake, who struck at it, then disappeared into a crevice between rocks.

He checked for other snakes, then looked at his hand. Two drops of blood glistened from twin puncture marks just behind the knuckles. "Some miracle," he said.

"Let me see." She examined the bite, put her mouth to it and sucked, then spit. She sucked out the venom twice more, then ripped off another strip of the baby's robe and tied it around Michael's arm below his elbow. "Maybe that'll hold until we get you to a doctor."

"Let's get out of here."

They made their way down the slope, stepping carefully through the tailings and granite talus, trying not to cause a slide. Twenty minutes later they entered the forest, where they crossed a game trail and followed it down to the creek on the valley floor.

It was a small stream, drought-shrunken to a thin trickle over moss and rock. But the thread of water that flowed in the center was clear and cold, and they stopped and drank. Then they splashed across and moved on, up the other side.

The adrenaline from the snake attack was wearing off. Michael was exhausted, and he knew Darby was just as tired, or more so, from carrying the baby. His wrist was aching and starting to swell.

The baby began crying again. "He's hungry," she murmured. She plodded behind Michael, seeming half-asleep.

"You want me to take him?"

"No."

They climbed, zigzagging up the steep slope, pausing every hundred steps or so to catch their breath. The sparks of pain in his wrist were shooting now to his elbow. He moved more and more slowly to let Darby keep up, but the slower he climbed, the farther she lagged behind.

At the top of the ridge he stopped and waited for her. She stumbled and almost fell. He scrambled back down to her and took the baby from her arms, and this time she didn't resist.

From then on he let her set the pace, knowing they needed to hurry but relieved at the slowness because he felt dizzy. At the top they both sagged onto a log.

"Hard part's over," he gasped. "All downhill from here."

"Where . . . ?" she began, then coughed and kept coughing, unable to catch her breath. She put her hands to her mouth and coughed up something red. It oozed through her fingers.

He stared at her, not understanding, then not believing.

She looked at her hands, blood dripping from her fingers, then at him, panic in her eyes. Quickly she turned her face away and wiped her mouth with her sleeve.

"Can you walk?" he said.

She nodded, her face scrunched up, fighting to keep the tears inside.

"We'll make it." Not knowing what else to say.

The baby in his right arm, he helped her up with his left. An electric spear of pain forced a groan. "We'll get help," he said. "There's a road at the bottom of the hill. We can catch a ride."

She managed to stand, weaving, but the effort made her cough again. She gagged and spit red. When she could breathe, they started down with her leaning against him. Michael kept an eye on the baby. He was cranky and fussing and his diapers stank, but so far he hadn't coughed.

She slipped and slid to her knees. Michael helped her up and they stumbled on. A few minutes later she fell again. He put the baby down and tried to help her up, but she shook her head. "So hard to breathe," she mumbled. "How far is the road?"

He peered ahead, trying to see through the trees, but there was no sign of it. "Not far, I think." Over to the right he caught a glimpse of . . . something. Not a road. Part of a roof, and a chimney. His hopes rose. "There's a cabin over there. Maybe there's a car, or at least a phone. Can you make it that far?"

She nodded weakly. He pulled her up with his good arm, then picked up the baby.

The cabin was tiny, its old logs weathered dark with age. A hunting cabin, not a summer home. There was no car outside, no electric or phone lines leading to it. His hopes fell.

He eased her down on the porch step and put the baby on the floor a few feet away. They needed shelter—they couldn't go any farther. He'd leave them here and go get help. He tried the door, but it was locked.

A stack of firewood filled one end of the porch. He took a log from it and threw it through the window, then reached in and unfastened the hook and crawled through.

Inside he found two metal bunks with bare mattresses, a wood-stove, a pine table and two chairs, and homemade cupboards. He opened the cabin door, brought in the baby, and put him on one of the bunks. Darby was barely conscious. He picked her up and carried her inside and laid her, coughing blood, on the other mattress.

In one of the cupboards he found an old can of stew, two cans of Pet milk, and a first aid kit. He opened it. Bandages and tape; nothing that would help her. There was no water and no pump. He hurried down to the stream with a mason jar, rinsed and filled it, and brought it back to Darby.

He raised her head. "Can you drink this?"

She opened her eyes and glanced at it, nodded feebly. He held the water to her lips, and she sipped a little, then fell back.

"I'm dying," she said. It wasn't a question. There was no doubt in her voice.

"You're just tired. Rest here while I go get help."

"Matt . . . Michael. Before you go, let's get something clear, all right?"

"Yeah, what?" The road couldn't be far away, he thought. With luck, there might be a car along soon, he could catch a ride into Sweetwater, call the hospital in Bozeman, and . . . and they couldn't do a damn thing. Even if they did have a cure, by the time she got there it would be too late.

"Whoever you are," she murmured, her voice so soft that the words got into him almost without him knowing it, "I love you."

Tears stung his eyes. He couldn't speak.

"Is there anything here for the baby to eat?" she said. "Feed him, will you, before you leave? And if you can, change his diaper. Then take him with you."

She closed her eyes and he hurried to the cupboard, his left arm on fire. He found the can of milk, the label a blur through his tears, and punched a hole in it with an opener from a drawer.

He tasted it. It seemed all right. The baby drank it eagerly, wrapping his sleeper-covered hands around Michael's, smacking, dribbling as much onto the robe as he got into his mouth. Michael wiped the baby's face, then, keeping an eye on Darby, changed his diaper as well as he could with one hand, using a mouse-chewed dish towel.

When he was finished he went over to her and bent down to listen. She was still breathing, but it was shallow and labored, a liquid-filled rattle.

Time to go. He straightened, staggered under a wave of dizziness and nausea, and made it as far as the table, where he sank onto the chair, thinking, *Just sit here a minute, let your head clear, then pick up the baby and walk down the road.*

He put his head in his hands and didn't remember anything more.

Until he woke to find James standing over him.

36

James said, "You're an idiot, Michael. You're the only person I know who'd try to escape through a rattlesnake den." He was standing five feet away in a dirty scarlet sweat suit, holding a Wilson's Stealth .45, his arm at his side. "What were you thinking?"

"It worked, didn't it?"

"Did it? I found you." James rubbed his face. "I hate caves."

"Was that you, following us?"

"No, it was Mother Goose. Who do you think?"

Michael looked at the gun, wondering if he could move fast enough to reach it before he was shot, wondering if he had the strength to take it away if he could. He tried lifting his arm, but he could only move it a few inches. Fire ran all the way through his shoulder.

"Don't do it," James said. "Even you aren't that stupid."

Michael glanced over at Darby. She was lying on the bunk, still, her eyes closed. On the other bunk the baby had fallen asleep. "The feds are on their way," he said.

James smiled. "No, they're not. Satan's forces are being taken care of at Heaven's Door."

Michael stared at him in shock, registering for the first time the scarlet color of the sweat suit. "You're one of them? You're a Ringer?"

"I belong to the Church of True Atonement, yes."

"I thought you worked for a government agency."

"Did you think I was going to tell you the truth?" He pulled the other chair out, turned it around, and sat across the table from Michael, his arms crossed over the back of the chair. "Holy Mother has honored me with leadership of the church's secular arm. I won't let her down."

"What secular arm?"

"The Arm, Michael. You had a chance to be a part of it. Gutless Michael. I should have left you in prison."

"The Arm is part of the Ringers?"

"The secular arm is separate from the church. The church doesn't take lives, except in self-defense. But when you operate in the Satanic world, sometimes survival requires harsh measures. In a sacred cause, the ends justify the means. So Holy Mother established the Arm."

"What do you want?"

"The Holy Child, of course. You took what doesn't belong to you. Holy Mother sent me to get him." He glanced with reverence at the baby. "So that's what he looks like. I wish she'd told me about him before today."

"He's your own sister's baby, James," Michael said. "Ursula gave birth to him. Your so-called Holy Mother had her shot. Your sister! How can you live with that? Or did you do it yourself? Did you shoot her?"

"No. But I would have if I had to. All Satanic blood ties are broken by the holy bonds of brotherhood in the church. And call me Raguel, please."

"I need to get Darby to the hospital. Please let us go."

"It's God's will that she die. And you, too. You defied him by opposing Mother Mary." He smiled. Then he coughed.

Michael raised his head.

James coughed again. His expression turned from one of smugness to one of concern. He doubled over, his body wracked with spasms.

Michael tried to get to his feet, willed his legs to move, but James straightened and lifted the gun. "Don't!" Blood trickled down his chin.

"You've got the virus," Michael said. He was too drained to feel glad about it, to feel anything but numb. "You're dying."

James shook his head. "God is giving me a chance to suffer." He got to his feet and walked over to the bunk where the baby slept. "But he's given me the Holy Child to heal me." He bent over him.

"Leave him alone," Michael said. "You'll infect him, too." He tried to get out of the chair.

James turned and shot him.

The bullet slammed into his left shoulder and through it, splintering the chair and blowing him backward. He looked down in shock as blood bloomed through his sweatshirt. Then the pain hit, hard, as if a spike had been driven through him, driving him live and burning into some dark place.

Through the haze he thought he heard Darby gasp.

"Quit interfering, Michael," James said. "It's time you were taught a lesson. And as soon as I'm healed you will be." He fumbled at the baby's sleeper with his free hand, pulling the mittens away. The baby woke and began to cry.

James picked him up and pressed his face to the tiny cheek. He laid the gun on the bunk and took the baby's hand and pressed it to his own mouth. The baby shrieked.

Michael willed himself to stand, to move toward the gun, but he couldn't. He tried not to watch the stain spreading across his sweatshirt, not to feel the blood running down his thigh. He moved his foot and felt slickness, blood pooling on the floor. He felt dizzy now, light-headed, and leaned sideways into the table, hoping it would prop him upright in the chair.

James was watching him, a fixed grin on his face, his breathing a labored rasp as he rubbed the child's hands over his face. "Poor unbelieving Michael. I'm being healed while you die. You're not in the Book of Life, but I am."

"You're not in any Book of Life."

"Why? Because I've killed people? The ends justify the means, Michael."

"No, they don't," he gasped. "In the end, there's only the evil you've done."

His brother was receding, the whole cabin moving farther away. He heard buzzing in his ears. Had to watch for snakes. No, this was different, a ringing. Needed to lie down. Only the table held him up now. He felt like he was disappearing, almost transparent. He tried to keep his body rigid, but he felt formless, nothing left but air.

James coughed and kept on coughing. He doubled over, clutching the baby to him. Michael managed to get out of the chair and crawl toward his brother. James staggered toward the gun, hemorrhaging from his nose and mouth. He picked it up and turned toward Michael.

As James raised the pistol, his expression changed to one of surprise and fear. Then he crumpled to the floor, the shrieking baby still gripped in one arm. The gun clattered out of his hand.

Michael stared at his brother. He was so far away. He expected him to get up, but he didn't; he lay motionless.

Had to do something, get the baby away from him. Infection. Michael tried to crawl toward him.

The floor came up and struck him.

In his orange Racal biological suit, Special Agent in Charge Willard Perkins stood near the smoldering ruins of the mansion and surveyed the wreckage. The Holy Guards were dedicated; he had to give that to them. And loyal. But all religious fanatics were. He'd given them three chances to surrender. They'd refused all of them, keeping up a rain of fire at his men, even as they died of the virus.

In the end, the survivors had burned the mansion down from inside.

Mother Mary's steel-doored shelter was another matter. Short of a Stinger missile, he doubted they could have gotten her out if a call for help hadn't come from inside, from Mother Mary herself. Now the shining metal door stood open, the shelter deserted.

Willard glanced at the hillside. Half the mountain had come down, it looked like, from an errant rocket. Fortunately, they'd been able to take the LAW out before it did more damage to his men.

He sighed and strode over to the barracks that had been turned into a hospital, if *hospital* was the right word—there wasn't much anyone could do for those who'd been infected. Fifty-three Ringers were dead of the virus and seven of his own agents whose suits had been compromised. But there were signs of hope. An eighth, Joe Grimes, was clinging gamely to life. His vital signs had stabilized, the doctors had told Willard, and it looked like he might actually survive the infection.

Willard stepped inside and watched silently as two orange-suited attendants zipped the corpse of a tiny man into a body bag. His last words had been ravings about the Great Babylon, New York. Willard shook his head. If the virus had escaped the compound, they never would have stopped it in time.

Two cots away, other attendants were lifting the body of Mother Mary, her purple robe stained with blood, into another rubber sack. The cot on which she'd died was covered in blood, as were many of the others. When they were finished with it, the whole building would have to be burned.

He turned and went outside, having seen enough blood for a lifetime.

A man whose Racal suit could barely contain his stomach hailed him and came over. "Looks like her shelter didn't protect her from the virus too well," Nestor Pruitt said into his radio.

He lifted his own radio to his face mask. He didn't approve of bureaucrats on battlefields. "We think she was infected before she went in."

Nestor nodded. "CDC boys tell me the virus dies real quick, too, after it does its dirty work. Area should be clean within a few days."

He nodded again, too weary to keep up a conversation.

"Everyone accounted for?" Nester said.

"Yes," he said. He thought for a moment of Mother Mary's dying words, something about the Second Coming and the baby Jesus being here in her compound. He shook his head. So much craziness, so much waste.

So much evil.

"Well, just wanted to tell you, good job." Nestor started to slap Willard on the back, remembered the suit, and let his arm fall. Instead, he smiled and nodded again and walked off.

Good job, he thought. *Twenty-three agents killed, in all. Nearly a hundred cult members. Millions of dollars in damage to equipment and property. Good job, all right.*

His radio crackled. "Attorney general on the phone, Mr. Perkins."

"Copy," Willard said. He gave a final look around, then sighed and went to talk to headquarters.

37

There was light.

And pain.

And a baby crying.

Michael opened his eyes, squinting at the brightness. Something hard was beneath him and he realized he was lying on the floor. He turned his head. His brother lay in the position in which he'd fallen.

Michael didn't try to move. He wondered if he was dead; he hoped not—if he was, then being dead hurt. He took stock of his body. His shoulder was so sore it made his eyes water, and he couldn't move his swollen arm, but he didn't feel dizzy or transparent. Maybe he could even sit up.

Amazed at being alive, he managed to do it. Whoa, now he was dizzy. He put his head between his knees until it passed; then he looked around for Darby. She was still lying on the bed.

The crying began again. He turned his head. The baby was lying on the other bed, kicking his feet and waving his arms. How had he gotten there? The last thing Michael remembered, the little guy was on the floor in James's arms.

Michael tried to stand and made it. The sick feeling was less and the bleeding seemed to have stopped. It was only then that he realized his shoulder had been bandaged and his arm was in a dish towel sling.

He mumbled, "What's going on here, little guy?"

He weaved over to James and felt the side of his neck for a pulse. He was dead.

Michael went to Darby and bent over her, steeled for what he would find. To his astonishment he found a pulse, a strong one.

At his touch she opened her eyes. Her hand reached up for his and squeezed it weakly.

"You're alive?" he said, stupid with relief and joy.

"As far as I know," she murmured.

"How do you feel?"

She was silent, assessing. "I feel like you look. And I'm very weak. But better than I was."

"What happened?" he said. "What's going on? You were dying. I thought I was dying."

She looked confused. "I'm not sure. I blacked out, then woke up about the time your brother fell over and wouldn't let go of the baby. I was afraid he'd infect him. Then you passed out. I didn't want to touch the baby, I was afraid I'd give him the virus, too, but I was the only one left, so I managed to crawl over to him and . . ." She shook her head. "I got him onto the other bed. After I put him down I began to feel a little better." She looked over at the baby. "And he was crying and I didn't want to leave him, so I . . . I carried him over to you and put him on your stomach while I bandaged you."

"You put him on my stomach?" He turned and stared at the kid, who had started to cry again. Then he looked down at his arm.

They looked at each other.

"Don't jump to conclusions," he said. "Most people don't die of snakebite. And the bullet passed through my shoulder." He tried to move it. "It still hurts like hell, and my arm's still swollen. It was your bandage that stopped the bleeding."

"I had the virus, Michael."

"No virus is a hundred percent fatal. You must be one of the lucky ones. Anyway, you carried the baby and still got sick, remember?"

She eased herself off the bed, put her hand on the headboard to steady herself, then made her way over to the baby. Sagging onto the bed beside him, she took his hand in hers. "Believe what you want."

"Why didn't James make it, then?"

"I don't know." She glanced at his brother's body. "Maybe he wasn't in the Book of Life."

●●●

Wednesday, January 31, 3:27 P.M.

In Atlanta, Annie Soares pulled open her desk drawer for a final check. It was empty. She glanced at her watch. Her cab should be here by now; she just had time to make it to the airport.

As she reached for her purse, Nestor Pruitt stuck his head around the corner of the door. "I wish you'd change your mind, honey."

"Thanks for the offer, Mr. Pruitt, but no thanks."

He stood in the doorway, a rueful look on his face. "You saved my bacon, Annie. Since I'm permanent director now, I'll make you my deputy. Pay you more than the Florida Department of Natural Resources."

She slung her purse over her shoulder. "I'm quitting there, too."

"The heck. How come?"

"My sons. I've decided to set up my own consulting firm. I can work out of my house. But my family has first priority."

Nestor brightened. "Hey, all right. I'm your first client, then."

She smiled. "Give me a call. We might be able to work something out."

He nodded, then grew serious again. "Say, Annie, I been thinking."

"About what?"

"Well, this Revelation business, for one thing. All that pestilence, all those disasters the Bible says'll happen. Even without these diseases that the Ringers caused, look what's goin' on in the world. There's plenty of new viruses and scary bacteria. You got your Ebola and your Marburg and that Bolivian hemorrhagic fever—there's more new diseases every year. The oceans are dying from pollution. Water's unfit to drink in a lot of places. We're destroying the ozone layer. World's going to pieces, don't you think?"

"We seem to be doing a good job of killing the planet, all right," she said.

He looked thoughtful. "So who's to say this isn't what the Bible was talking about? In the last days, I mean. Maybe it *is* a sign of the Second Coming."

She picked up her computer case from the desk. "I'm not a religious person, Mr. Pruitt. But in a figurative sense, I suppose you could say we're bringing nature's judgment on ourselves." She offered her hand. "Sorry to run, but I've got a plane to catch."

"Oh, yeah. Well, don't let me keep you." He shook her hand. "I'll call you."

"Do that." She walked down the hall toward the stairs. By the time she got home, she thought, Raymond Miles from New Mexico should be there to meet her. He'd promised to take her and the boys fishing. She smiled. She was looking forward to it. She liked him. A lot.

•••

Friday, February 2, 1:20 P.M.

On Interstate 80 between Winnemucca and Reno, Nevada, Michael gazed out at the blackened, charred land around him. The forest fires were out, but it would be years before the vegetation recovered. He glanced down at the baby, strapped into his safety seat backward between Michael and Darby. "How's he doing?"

"He's fine," she said. "A little diarrhea still; I think it's from the canned milk. But not bad."

The baby was ignoring the plastic rings she'd bought him and staring at Michael, two fingers in his mouth.

CBS News broke into the cowboy music on the radio with word that a Senate hearing had been called to investigate the shoot-out at the Church of True Atonement. According to the announcer's recap of the incident, twenty-three FBI and ATF agents and perhaps a hundred cult members had been killed, although the exact count would not be known for some time because several buildings had been set afire, it was thought by cult members, and many bodies had been burned. The disease caused by the strange new virus had only been contained, according to scientists, because the virus had mutated to a nonlethal form. Several people who contracted the disease at the compound had survived. The cowboy music resumed.

"OK, so you were right," Darby said. "I was one of the lucky ones."

"Of course I was right."

"But you have to admit that this little guy could just possibly be . . . you know who."

"I don't think so, but at least he's not a Ringer any more; that's what counts." He looked at her. "Thanks for coming with me. Ursula needs you."

"Are you sure we won't be in her way?"

"She insisted," he said. Once she'd regained consciousness, his sister had been moved out of the ICU into a private room. He'd finally been allowed to talk to her. She sounded weak and her speech was a bit slurred, but she told him the doctors had been encouraging. Her brain functions were normal, she said, although her motor coordination had been affected. She'd have trouble walking for a while. But the doctors were optimistic that in time she'd recover fully. He didn't tell her the details of the kidnapping, but his news that her baby was safe made her burst into tears of joy.

"Maybe I'll name him for you, after all," Ursula said.

He felt himself flush. "Don't do that. You'll think of something better."

"Michael, even after I leave the hospital," she said, "it'll be a couple of months before I can take care of the baby by myself. Will you come and stay with me and help take care of him?"

He felt honored but reluctant to leave Darby. He told Ursula about her.

"Wonderful," she said. "Bring her along, if she'll come. There's plenty of room in my house. Two women around you can only help."

Now he glanced over to see Darby studying him. "What?" he said.

"I don't know if I can get used to the name Michael Walker," she said.

He swallowed. It was now or never. "Do you think you could get used to the name Darby Walker?"

"Is that a proposal?" She raised her eyebrows.

"Yeah, and it's a bad one. If you're smart you'll turn me down. James is dead and so are his bosses in the cult, but there could be some Arm members alive yet. And I'm still wanted for killing that man in Denver. I'm a lousy prospect. You'd be marrying a fugitive."

She grew sober. "All I care about is whether I'd be marrying a good man." She watched him, her look so penetrating he had the feeling she could see his thoughts. Finally, she nodded. "Maybe. I think I'll give it a few months to see if you have any other secrets I should know about."

"Does wearing women's clothes count?"

She swatted him.

"Seriously, you know the worst," he said, "but it's obvious I'm no Saint Joseph. I'm not worthy to help raise this kid."

"I thought you didn't believe he was real."

"I don't. He's just a kid. What I mean is, I'm a lousy caregiver. I don't even know how to change diapers right."

A smile touched the corners of her mouth and spread slowly. "Well . . . you might want to start learning."

About the Author

Robert Rice lives with his family in southern Montana. He's also the author of the critically acclaimed novel, *The Last Pendragon*, and of short stories and poetry.